John Galt was born in 1779 in the town of Irvine on the Ayrshire coast where his father was a shipowner and sea captain trading with the West Indies. The family moved to Greenock when Galt was 10, and much of his later writing came from this corner of the West of Scotland. Leaving his job as a junior clerk in Greenock, Galt set out for London at the age of 25. When his business plans did not work out he went on a tour of the Mediterranean and the near east. It was during this time that he met and befriended Byron.

Having published a *Life of Cardinal Wolsey* and a volume of tragedies in 1812, Galt turned to writing full-time after his marriage in 1813. He proposed *Annals of the Parish* but Constable rejected the concept as too local. A second novel, *The Majolo* (1816) was published but met with little success. Galt found his metier with *The Ayrshire Legatees* (1820), purporting to be letters home from a family of Scots visiting London. Appearing anonymously in monthly instalments in *Blackwoods Magazine*, this work led directly to the publication of *Annals of the Parish* (1821), now properly recognised as a gently ironic masterpiece. This was followed in the same vein by *The Provost* (1822), while *The Entail* and *Sir Andrew Wylie* (both 1822) had similar strengths, although structured as more conventional novels. These and other 'Tales of the West' made Galt's reputation as a writer of humour and subtle social observation, but *Ringan Gilhaize* (1823) took a darker turn in a unique psychological and historical study of Covenanting fervour and the 'killing times' in the 17th century.

Becoming involved with the development of Canada, he became a supervisor for the Canada Company. Galt helped to settle Ontario and founded the town of Guelph. He was badly treated by the Directors, however, and after four years abroad his health failed and he returned to London to face bankruptcy and a spell in a debtors' prison. His *Life of Lord Byron* (1830), was a controversial success and the novels *The Member* and *The Radical* (both 1832) took a searching look at his country's political life. After suffering a disabling series of strokes he worked on his *Autobiography* (1833) followed by *Literary Life and Miscellanies* (1834). He returned to Greenock in 1834 and died there five years later.

JOHN GALT

THE MEMBER:
An Autobiography

AND

THE RADICAL:
An Autobiography

———

Introduced by
PAUL H. SCOTT

CANONGATE
CLASSICS
71

This edition first published as a Canongate Classic in 1996
by Canongate Books Limited
14 High Street
Edinburgh EH1 1TE

Notes to *The Member* © 1975 Ian A. Gordon
Introductions and Notes to *The Radical* © 1996 Paul H. Scott

British Library Cataloguing in Publication Data
A Catalogue record is available on request

ISBN 086241 642 6

The publishers gratefully acknowledge
general subsidy from the Scottish Arts Council
towards the Canongate Classics series
and a specific grant towards the
publication of this title.

Set in 10 pt Plantin
by Hewer Text Composition Services, Edinburgh
Printed and bound in Finland by WSOY

Contents

ACKNOWLEDGEMENTS

Cannogate wish to acknowledge the kind assistance of the Association of Scottish Literary Studies for granting permission to reproduce the text of their edition of *The Member*.

Canongate also wish to thank professor Ian A. Gordon for his editorial work on *The Member* and for giving permission to include his notes to the A.S.L.S. edition in the present volume.

Introduction

One of the first reviewers of *The Member*, when it was published in 1832, said that he wished that 'Mr. Galt would do nothing but write imaginary autobiographies'. He was thinking not only of *The Member* itself, described on its title page as 'An Autobiography', but also of Galt's earlier works, *Annals of the Parish* (1821) and *The Provost* (1822). As a novelist Galt was innovative and diverse in subject matter and technique and this particular kind of fictional autobiography was one of his happiest inventions.

There was, of course, nothing new in novels which told the life story, or part of it, of an imaginary character in the first person. Daniel Defoe did that in *Robinson Crusoe* and Tobias Smollett in *Roderick Random* and there are innumerable other examples. Galt's originality lay in some special characteristics of his own, apart from his concentration and brevity. One of these qualities was noticed by Samuel Coleridge in *The Provost*, but it applies to the others as well. He called it an 'irony of self-delusion'. The imaginary autobiographer gives away his weaknesses at every turn, evidently without the slightest suspicion that he is doing so. He continues, Coleridge says, in 'a happy state of self-applause'. Galt gives each of his subjects a personality entirely appropriate to his circumstances, with a style and habit of speech to match, sustained throughout without a single false note.

Another of Galt's strengths is the smeddum and force of the Scots of Irvine and Greenock where he spent the first twenty-five years and the last five of his life. In a prefatory note to one of his last short stories Galt spoke of 'the fortunate circumstances of the Scotch possessing the whole range of the English language, as well as their own, by which they enjoy an unusually rich vocabulary'. This richness is less apparent in *The Member* than in the earlier novels, but again this is appropriate. The imaginary writer, Archibald Jobbry, has spent most of his life in India and can be expected to have lost much of his Scots.

In his *Autobiography* Galt said that he was convinced 'that not in character only, but in all things, an author should have natural models before him'. *The Member* was no exception. Galt says of it:

> The gentleman I had in view as the model, was immediately discovered in the House of Commons, and I suspect he is possessed of too much shrewd humour to be offended with the liberty I have taken. I have represented him as neither saying or doing aught, that, I think, as the world wags, he may not unblushingly have done, nor which, in my heart, I do not approve.

Parliament and Whitehall were familiar territory to Galt. He had acted for years as a lobbyist on behalf of the Union Canal between Edinburgh and Glasgow. In 1820 he was appointed to act as the agent for a group of claimants who had suffered loss when the United States invaded Canada in 1812. This involved him both in taking charge of the settlement of part of Ontario and in protracted negotiations with the government.

Galt insisted that his books like the *Annals* were not novels, but something quite different. They had no plot, and, he wrote, 'the only link of cohesion, which joins the incidents together, is the mere remembrance of the supposed author. It is, in consequence, as widely different from a novel, as a novel can be from any other species of narration'. He used various phrases to describe them: 'a kind of treatise on the history of society', 'theoretical histories', or 'philosophical sketches'. He even went so far as to deny that he hoped to entertain the reader:

> I only desire it to be remembered by my readers that,
> I had an object in view beyond what was apparent.
> I considered the novel as a vehicle of instruction, or
> philosophy teaching by examples, parables, in which
> the moral was more valuable than the incidents were
> impressive. Indeed it is not in this age that a man of
> ordinary common sense would enter into competition
> in recreative stories, with a great genius who possessed
> the attention of all. I mean Sir Walter Scott.

In his irony, humour and richness of character Galt is
one of the most entertaining of novelists. His denial that
he had any such intention is therefore curious. Perhaps he
was betraying a twinge of Presbyterian conscience over the
frivolity of writing novels intended only to entertain. His
sympathies with Presbyterianism, indeed with the spirit of
the Covenanters, are clear from his great historical novel,
Ringan Gilhaize.

At all events, *The Member* and *The Radical* are the most
obviously 'philosophical', or at least political, of his novels.
They were both published in 1832 shortly before the passage
of the Reform Act which began the process of extending the
right to vote in British parliamentary elections to a larger
part of the population. Controversy over this measure,
which was promoted by the Whigs and opposed by the
Tories, was then at its height. The two novels were clearly
intended as contributions to the debate. This was another
of Galt's innovations. *The Provost* was a novel of political
satire on the local level. *Sir Andrew Wylie* (1822) had
introduced episodes of political intrigue. *The Member* and
The Radical were the first novels in our literature centered
on parliamentary politics.

Archibald Jobbry, the narrator of *The Member*, is that
familiar figure in nineteenth-century literature, the Scot
who has made a fortune in India and returns to buy an estate
in his own country. He finds that the peaceful enjoyment
of his retirement is disturbed by the demands of his kith
and kin, 'all gaping like voracious larks for a pick'. His
solution is to buy himself a seat in Parliament, under the old

corrupt system before the Reform Act, to get his hands on some government patronage to satisfy them. Having twice survived what he calls ironically his 'popular election', he settles down to draw what advantage he can from his support of the government. He finds this easy for 'a conscientious man', because he sees little distinction between Whig and Tory. He begins to take a 'sort of attachment to the House' (still a not unusual phenomenon) and develops some quite enlightened ideas. Mr Jobbry is no die-hard Tory, but he is inevitably opposed to parliamentary reform, or in his words, 'giving the unenlightened many, an increase of dominion over the enlightened few'. He sees that his day is over as the Reform Act looms and his seat loses all marketable value. So he retires to his Scottish estate.

The obvious reading of *The Member* is that it is a satire aimed at the corruption of the pre-Reform parliament, a contribution to the case for reform, and therefore support for the Whigs and an attack on the Tories. If we can believe what he says himself in his *Autobiography*, this was not Galt's intention:

> In the Member, I tried to embody all that could, in my opinion, be urged against the tories of my own way of thinking, and I was not aware that it could be deemed very bad, till I saw my friend, Dr. Bowring's account of it, in the Westminster Review, in which he considered it as a reluctant concession to the spirit of the times. I am sure, however, that Mr. Jobbry is not made to make any acknowledgement unbecoming an honest man of the world, nor such as a fair partizan may not avow. [Then follows the passage, which I quoted above, about the 'model' for the character.]

Galt, as here, often describes himself as a Tory, but this is difficult to reconcile with the attitudes which appear throughout his writings. He is no respecter of inherited privilege from the monarch downwards and he is particularly contemptuous of landowners. His sympathies lie with the poor and oppressed and it is not only in *The Member* that he describes the Tories as corrupt. In the *Last of the Lairds*, for example, a character says of ducks in the rain that they are 'as garrulous with enjoyment, as Tories in the pools of corruption'. A man of Galt's sharp intelligence was unlikely to be unaware of this paradox; but I do not know of any attempt that he made to explain it.

The William Holmes MP, to whom the book was dedicated, was a real person, described in the *Dictionary of National Biography* as 'the adroit and dexterous whip of the tory party . . . a most skilful dispenser of patronage'. Galt tells us that the dedication was written by J.G. Lockhart, the son-in-law and biographer of Sir Walter Scott, who, like Galt, was associated with the Edinburgh publisher, William Blackwood. Galt says of the dedication that it was a clever *jeu d'esprit*, and so admirably in keeping with the character of Jobbry that he was proud to have it ascribed to him.

The Member was described on the title page as 'By the author of The Ayrshire Legatees etc. etc.'. Even without this, it is clearly from the same pen as the best of Galt, shrewd, ironic, humane and enriched by Scots vocabulary and turn of phrase. This time, the irony is directed more against the institution than the individual. *The Radical*, in contrast, is so different in atmosphere and style that it would be impossible on internal evidence to conclude that it had been written by the same man. Once again the style is appropriate to the narrator; but, unlike any of the others, it is dry and abstract with a strong flavour of self-obsessed fanaticism. This time Galt presumably had no model, for the book is not in his usual style of social realism. It is not so much a novel with satirical overtones as a satire disguised as a novel. It is entirely in English, although a schoolmaster is given the name Mr Skelper.

The narrator, Nathan Butt (which has a significance to an ear tuned to Scots) is more of an anarchist than a radical. From his schooldays onwards he is opposed to all authority. His goal is 'nothing less than [naethin but] the emancipation of the human race from the trammels and bondage of the social law'. He wants to abolish property, religion, law, marriage and all 'coercive expedients in the management of mankind'; but he still marries and expects absolute obedience from his wife. Like Mr Jobbry, he is no democrat because 'the wise are few, and the foolish numerous'. He is prepared to pose as a Whig and support parliamentary reform as a means to his own 'high and great purposes'. Although elected as a Whig, his election is declared invalid. He will not be in the House to vote for the Reform Bill, which was in fact passed in June 1832, only a few weeks after the publication of the book.

Although the approach of these two books to parliamentary reform is apparently so different, there is perhaps a common idea behind them, which may also be a clue to Galt's idiosyncratic Toryism. It was a commonplace of Scottish Enlightenment thought, expressed for instance by Adam Ferguson, that society was so complex a mechanism that any attempt to change it was liable to have unforeseen and possibly disastrous consequences. Change should therefore be undertaken only when clearly necessary and after very careful consideration. Galt in his youth had steeped himself in the Greenock Subscription Library in the works of Robertson, Hume, Smith, Ferguson and the rest. Like Walter Scott, he accepted the doctrine of the need for political caution. What he is probably saying in *The Member* is: 'All right. The House of Commons is unrepresentative and corrupt, but it does not do much harm. It is probably better to leave it alone.' *The Radical* makes the point that an apparently moderate and desirable reform may open the way to extremists bent on the destruction of all law and social order.

In his *Autobiography* Galt said that *The Radical* was more philosophical in its satire than *The Member*. His object was 'to show that many of these institutes, which are regarded as essentials in society, owe their origin to the sacrifice required to be made by man, to partake of its securities'. He did not think that he had failed in writing it, but he had to admit that it had not sold well. He thought that this might be because it had dealt in truths that were unpalatable at the time. In his *Literary Life* Galt said that the sales of both books had been unsatisfactory; 'although on the Continent, they have attracted more attention than any other product of my pen, they have almost been still-born here'.

The Member was published in January 1832 and *The Radical* in May. The unsold sheets of both were issued as a single volume, *The Reform*, in November. While Blackwood's held the copyright of Galt's best-known novels and kept most of them almost continuously in print for more than 100 years, they were not involved with the two political novels. *The Member* was not reprinted until Ian A. Gordon edited an edition for the Scottish Academic Press in 1973, which was reissued as a paperback in 1985. This text of *The Member* and its notes is used with the kind permission of Professor Gordon. *The Radical* is reprinted here for the first time since its original appearance.

Paul H. Scott

JOHN GALT

THE MEMBER:
An Autobiography

EDITED WITH NOTES BY
IAN A. GORDON

DEDICATION

To

WILLIAM HOLMES, Esq. M.P.

The Girlands, Jan. 1, 1832.

MY DEAR SIR,

I beg leave to inscribe to you this brief Memoir of my parliamentary services, and I do so on the same principle that our acquaintance, Colonel Napier, refers to as his motive in dedicating that interesting work, the *History of the Peninsular War,* to the Duke of Wellington. It was chiefly under your kind superintendence that I had the satisfaction of exerting myself as an independent member, really and cordially devoted to the public good, during many anxious campaigns; and now, retired for ever from the busy scene, it is natural that I should feel a certain satisfaction in associating your respected name with this humble record.

If the Reform Bill passes, which an offended Providence seems, I fear, but too likely to permit, your own far more brilliant and distinguished career as a patriotic senator is, probably, also drawing to a conclusion; and withdrawn, like me, to a rural retreat, in the calm repose of an evening hour, no longer liable to sudden interruption, it may serve to amuse your leisure to cast an eye over the unpretending narrative of scenes and events so intimately connected in my mind with the recollection of your talents, zeal, and genius, in what, though not generally so considered by the unthinking mass, I have long esteemed nearly the most important situation which any British subject can fill; but which, alas! is perhaps destined to pass away and be forgotten, amidst this general convulsion so fatal to the established institutions of a once happy and contented country. If, indeed, my dear and worthy friend, the present horrid measure be carried into full effect, it is but too plain that the axe will have been laid to the root of the British Oak. The upsetting, short-sighted conceit of new-fangled theorems will not long endure either the aristocratic or the monarchic branches; and your old office, so useful and necessary even, under a well-regulated social system, will fall with the rest; for the sharp, dogged persons likely to be returned under the schedules, will need no remembrancer to call them to their congenial daily and nightly task of retrenchment and demolition.

A melancholy vista discloses itself to all rational understandings; – a church in tatters; a peerage humbled and degraded – no doubt, soon to be entirely got rid of; that poor, deluded man, the well-meaning William IV, probably packed off to Hanover; the three per cents down to two, at the very best of it; a graduated property tax sapping the vitals of order in all quarters; and, no question, parliamentary grants and pensions of every description no longer held sacred!

May you be strengthened to endure with firmness the evil day; and if the neighbourhood of London should become so disturbed as to render Fulham no more that sweet snug retirement I always considered it, sure am I, that by making my little sequestered place here your temporary abode during the raging of the storm, you would confer much real pleasure and honour on myself and family. We have capital fishing, both trout and salmon, close at hand; and the moors are well enough all about us, – what with blackcock, grouse, ptarmigan, and occasionally roes, of which the duke's woods near harbour many. Here we might watch afar off the rolling of the popular billows, and the howlings of the wind of change and perturbation, and bide our time.

Once more, dear Mr. Holmes, accept the sincere tribute of esteem and regard from your old friend and pupil, and humble servant at command,

ARCHIBALD JOBBRY

———

P.S. Herewith you will receive 4 brace moorfowl, 2 ditto B. cocks, item 3 hares, one side of a roe, and one gallon whisky (*véritable antique*); which liberty please pardon.

Jan. 2. – I am credibly informed that the weavers of

Guttershiels, over their cups on hogmanae and yesterday, were openly discussing the division of landed properties in this district! What have not these demented ministers to answer for?

When a man comes home from India with a decent competency, he is obliged to endure many afflictions, not the least of which are nestsful of cousins' children, in every corner of the kingdom, all gaping like voracious larks for a pick. This it behoves him to consider; for his bit gathering would be short in the outcoming, were he to help them from that fund: he is therefore under the necessity of reflecting how a modicum of his means can be laid out to the best advantage, not only for the benefit of his relations, but to spare a residue to himself, and to procure for him a suitable station in the world – the end of all creditable industry.

For a time, after I set my foot on my native land, I was troubled in mind with these considerations; for when I left Bengal, it was with an intent to buy a moderate estate, and to live at my ease, having every thing comfortable about me.

Of course, I had no insurmountable difficulty in meeting with a commodious purchase, though maybe I paid the price; for I had to bid against both a paper-money banker and a purse-proud fozy cotton manufacturer. I did not, however, grudge it; for I had the wherewithal, and I had seen enough of the world, in the intelligent circles of Calcutta, to convince me that rural felicity had, like many other things, risen in value.

But no sooner was I enfeoft in my property, than my kith and kin began to bestir themselves, and to plague me for my patronage; pleading, in a very wearisome manner, that blood was thicker than water. Partly to get quit of their importunities, and to get also the means to help them, I began to take shares in divers public concerns, and to busy myself in the management thereof, slipping in a young friend now and then as a clerk. I will not, however, say, that in this I was altogether actuated by affection; for public spirit had quite as much to say with me as a regard for my kindred: indeed, it is a thing expected of every man, when he retires from business, that he will do his endeavour to serve his country, and make himself a name in the community.

These doings, however, I soon saw were not enough to satisfy the demands upon me; finding, therefore, as I read the newspapers, that I had made myself very passably acquainted, while in India, with the politics of Europe, and especially with the arcana of government and the principles of legislation in England, I began to clok on the idea of getting myself made a Member of Parliament. At first I cannot say that I was strongly thereunto inclined – it was only a hankering; but the more I reflected anent the same, I grew the more courageous, especially when I read the speeches of those that had but speech-making to recommend them. To be sure, there were in my neighbourhood several old lairds, that counted their descent from Adam's elder brother, who, when they heard that I was minded to go into Parliament, snorted east and west, and thought it a most upsetting audacity. But I had not been risking my health for five-and-twenty years in the climate of Bengal to pleasure them; so when I heard how they looked, and what they said concerning me, I became the more obstinate in my intention. But it was not so easily accomplished as thought; for as we in Scotland are not so clever in the way of getting into Parliament, without family connexions, as they are in England, I considered with myself that it would be expedient to take a run up to London when Parliament was sitting, and have some conversation there with a few of my old Indian cronies who were already members.

I could not, however, just go off at once, without giving some reason; for it was then only a five-year old Parliament, and it would not have been prudent to have been thought guilty of looking so long before me as two years, unless there was some prospect of a change in the administration. But it happened that, from the first time I looked at my estate, I saw that the mansion-house stood in need of divers repairs; and accordingly I, in a quiet way, set about getting plans and estimates of the alterations. When I had procured and considered of the same, I instructed a carpenter thereon; and I took the opportunity, when the house was in the cholera morbus of reparation, to set out for London, giving it out that I had old Indian affairs to wind up, and heavy accounts to settle.

It may be thought that I was a little overly artificial in this matter; but I had learned in my experience that no business of this world is without its craft, more especially undertakings of a political nature.

Thus it came to pass that I arrived in the dead of winter in London, and was not long of making my arrival known among my acquaintance, and particularly those who had gotten themselves seats. I likewise peutered, in a far-off manner, among the Indian directors, and those that make speeches at their public meetings when the fault-finders give them trouble; still keeping my eye on the main chance.

The first of my old acquaintance whom I fell in with was Mr. Curry. He had been home from India three years before me, and was in all things a most orderly man. We were right glad, as you may well think, to see one another; and yet there was between us a cool distinction. His business in Calcutta was not just of such a genteel order as mine, but it was a shade more profitable; and hence, though he was a year behind me in the outgoing, he was full three years before me in the home-coming, which shews the difference that was between our respective ways of business; for, in comparing one thing with another, I found that our fortunes were counted just about equal, – which is a proof of the correctness of what I say.

He had heard of my coming home, and likewise how I had made myself a public, patriotic character, which he never thought could happen; and, from less to more, I said to him that I was glad of an employment, for the time hung heavy upon my hands, and 'that if I did not take a share in projects for the good of the nation, I would be indeed a waif hand.'

He remarked to me, that what I said was very true, and consistent with his own experience; 'But I would advise you,' said he, 'to do as I have done; get yourself elected into Parliament – it will not cost you a deadly sum; and then you'll have full occupation.'

'Mr. Curry,' quo' I, 'it's not every one, like you, that has a talent; for although I would not grudge to pay for the admission-ticket, between ourselves, I really don't know how to set about applying for one; for you know that in our county in Scotland, the pedigree-family "bear the bell" in all electioneerings; for my Lord Entail, their cousin, has

made as many freeholders on the list as the valuation of
his estate allows, and three of the district-boroughs are
under his thumb; so by that means they have all the rule
and power of the shire. But, Mr. Curry, if you could tell
me of a sober, canny way of creeping into the House of
Commons unobserved, I'll no say that just for a diversion
I would not like to sit there for a session or two; by that
time I would have made myself joke-fellow like with some
of the big-wigs, the which would help to make this country
not so disagreeable after the sprees and merry-go-rounds
of "auld lang syne" in India.'

'I discern,' said Mr. Curry, 'that ye're in the same state
of sin and misery that I suffered myself when I came home;
and therefore I say unto you, speaking from the knowledge
of my own insight, get into Parliament: at the very utmost,
Mr. Jobbry,' said he, 'a few thousand pounds at a general
election should do the business; or, if you would sooner
take your seat, I should think that from twelve hundred to
fifteen hundred pounds per session would be reasonable
terms; for I would not advise you to be overly greedy of
a bargain, nor overly logive at the outset.'

I agreed with him that his remark was very judicious,
but that really I had no confidential acquaintance in the
line; and that it was not to be expected I could, going out
to India a bare lad, with scarcely shoon upon my cloots,
be in a condition to set myself forward.

'Oh,' says he, 'nothing is more easy; ye have just to give
an inkling that if a convenient borough was to be had, ye
would not mind about going into Parliament. Speeches of
that sort are very efficacious; and it's not to be told how it
will circulate that you would give a handsome price for an
easy seat in the House of Commons. Keep your thumb on
the price, and just let out that you have no relish for the
clanjamfrey of a popular election, but would rather deal
with an old sneck-drawer in the trade than plague yourself
with canvassing: depend upon it ye'll soon hear of some
needful lord that will find you out, and a way of treating
with you.'

There was certainly sterling admonition in this; and I
said to him, over our wine, for we were then sitting

together after dinner, in Ibbotson's Hotel, 'that I was not particular in wishing to conceal my hankering for a seat in Parliament.'

'Do you really say so?' said he.

I then assured him that I was not vehemently against it; and so, from less to more, he inquired of what party I would be; and I told him with the government party, to be sure.

'I'll no just say,' quo' he, 'that you are far wrong in your determination, because the Tories have the ball at their foot, and are likely to rule the roast for some years.'

'I daresay they are,' said I; 'but between Whigs and Tories I can make no distinction, – a Tory is but a Whig in office, and a Whig but a Tory in opposition, which makes it not difficult for a conscientious man to support the government.'

'Really, Mr. Jobbry,' said Mr. Curry, 'ye were always thought a farsighted man, that could see as well through a nether millstone as another man through a stone wall; and, without complimenting you, I must say that you entertain very creditable notions of government, not to be yet a member. But, Mr. Jobbry, we are talking in confidence, and what we say to one another is not to be repeated.'

I assured Mr. Curry, with the greatest sincerity, that what he told me anent the diplomaticals should never go farther; then, said Mr. Curry, in a sedate, sober manner,

'I know a solicitor that has a borough that wants a member, the politics of which are of a delicate tint, you understand; now, I could wise him to you, and you might consult him, – or rather, would it not be better that ye would appoint some friend to confabble with the man?'

'Would not you do that for me?' said I.

'No, no,' said he, 'I'm a member myself, and that would not be playing the game according to Hoyle.'

'Very well,' said I; 'but as I have a great inclination on all occasions to be my own executioner, ye might pass me off with the man as the friend of a gentleman that's wishing to get into Parliament.'

'That's a capital device,' said he; 'and if you draw well

together, the cost of an agent and the hazard of a witness may be saved.'

So, thereupon, it was agreed between us that he should speak on the subject to Mr. Probe the solicitor, and that I should enact towards that gentleman the representative of my friend, that was to be nameless until the bargain was concluded.

Next morning I had occasion to be forth at an early hour, to see some of my old friends at the Jerusalem, concerning a ballot that was that day to take place at the India House; and thus it came to pass, that before I got back to the hotel, a gentleman had called upon me, and not finding me at home, left his card, which was that of Mr. Probe the solicitor. I at first did not recollect the name, for it had been only once mentioned; but the waiter told me he would call again in the evening, having some particular private business to transact.

This intimation put me upon my guard, and then recollecting his name, I guessed the errand he had come upon, and told the waiter to prepare for us a private parlour; but in the meantime I would take my dinner in the public coffee-room.

The waiter, being an expert young man, ordered all things in a very perfect manner; and I had just finished my dinner when in came Mr. Probe; a smaller sort of man, with a costive and crimson countenance, sharp eyes, and cheeks smooth and well-stuffed: but one thing I remarked about him which I did not greatly admire, and yet could not say wherefore, namely, he had a black fore-tooth, as if addicted to the tobacco-pipe; and, moreover, although it could not be said that he was a corpulent man, he certainly was in a degree one of the fatties; but he was very polite and introductory, told me his name, how Mr. Curry had requested him to call, and was, in every respect, as couthy and pleasant as an evil spirit.

I desired the waiter to shew us up into the private room that was ordered, and bade him bring a bottle of Carbonnel's claret – all which he soon did; and when

Mr. Probe and I were comfortably seated, he opened the business.

'Mr. Jobbry,' said he, 'our mutual friend, and my client, has told me that you might have some business in my way.'

'My client!' quo' I to myself, – 'mum,' and then I continued – 'He is an old friend of mine, and I was telling him that the time hung heavy upon my hands in the country——Oh! but that is not what I wished to speak to you about. I have a particular friend lately come from India, who is in the same condition: it's far from my fortune, Mr. Probe, to think of going into Parliament; but my friend, who has a turn for public speaking, requested me, as I was coming to London, to see if a seat could be obtained on reasonable terms; and speaking on this subject to our mutual friend, Mr. Curry (I took care to say nothing of his client), he told me that you had a seat to dispose of, and that he would send you to me.'

'Very correct,' replied Mr. Probe; 'but he made a little mistake – I have not a seat to dispose of; but a particular friend told me that he knew of one; and now I recollect of having once mentioned the subject to Mr. Curry.'

'It's very right to be guarded Mr. Probe,' said I, 'especially since the sales of seats in Parliament are as plain as the sun at noon-day, and would make the bones of our ancestors rattle in their coffins to hear of it: but although a seat may be come at by good handling, what would you, just in common parlance, think a fair——

'Oh, Mr. Jobbry, we need not condescend on particulars; but my friend has certainly a capital sporting manor, and will either let it on lease for the remainder of his term, or for an annual rent.'

I patted the side of my nose with my forefinger, and said, in the jocular words of Burns,

'But Tam kent what was what fu' brauly;'

and added, 'Very well, Mr. Probe, that's a very judicious alternative; but what's——I'll not say what. Would it be expected that my friend would have to sit on the right or left hand of a man in a wig; or, in other words, to come to the point, would he have to be a sheep or a goat, for at present he's an innocent lambkin, and unless there be a reason for it, he would naturally be a sheep. I'll no say that he'll ever be a battering-ram; but you understand, Mr. Probe?'

'Your candour,' was the reply, 'is exceedingly satisfactory; but have you any notion of what your friend would give for the manor?'

'I doubt,' said I, 'if he will come up to what our friend Curry said was the price.'

'What did he say?' inquired Mr. Probe.

'Really I can't tell, – I don't recollect exactly, whether it was three or four thousand pounds.'

'Not possible,' exclaimed the solicitor, falling back in his chair with astonishment.

'Oh,' replied I, 'it is very probable that I am in the wrong, now when I recollect that Parliament has only two sessions to run: you are very right, he could never have said so much as three or four thousand pounds – he must have been speaking of the price of a whole Parliament.'

'Excuse me, Mr. Jobbry, you misunderstood him, – either three or four thousand pounds was quite ridiculous to mention in the same breath with a whole Parliament: no, sir, the price that I am instructed to arrange is for the two remaining sessions.'

'Pray, Mr. Probe, is the gentleman in the House?'

'He is, but he does not find it suit; and, between ourselves, although money is no object to him, he somehow has not felt himself at home, and so he has a mind to retire.'

'Ay, he has, eh? did he ever say why, because that is a subject that my friend should consider?'

'No, not particularly; but every man who thinks himself qualified does not find himself so, I imagine, when he once gets in.'

'Then, if I understand you, Mr. Probe, your client——'

'Not my client!'

'Well, well; he wants, as I understand you, to dispose of the shooting for two years at an annual rent.'

'Just so.'

'And what may he expect, to make few words about it?'

'A couple of thousand.'

'What! for two years?'

'No, not so: two thousand for the first year, and two thousand for the next, – four thousand in all, if the humbug lasts so long.'

'Is that the name of the manor, Mr. Probe?'

'Ah! you're a wag, Mr. Jobbry.'

'But one serious word, Mr. Probe: I am sure my friend will give no such price as two thousand pounds per session, – he only wants the seat for recreation: some people like horses, some hounds, some carriages, some one thing, and some another; and my friend's taste is a seat in the senate; but he is a prudent man – he looks to both sides of the shilling before he spends it.'

'I don't know, Mr. Jobbry; but seats in the House of Commons are seats now: – I mean, the stalls in Smithfield are every year more valuable.'

'Well, Mr. Probe, I can make you an offer for my friend, taking the risk of pleasing him upon myself: I can give, I mean for him, a thousand pounds; hear what your client says, and let me know the result: I would say guineas – for I really count on guineas; I wish, however, to have the fifty pounds for a margin – you understand.'

Such was the first consultation, and, considering that I was but a greenhorn in parliamenting, I certainly made an impression.

When Mr. Probe had departed, I had a rumination with myself on what had passed, and I could not but think of his expression, 'my client'. It was very clear to me that Mr. Curry was the gentleman himself, and therefore I resolved to be on my guard towards him, and to take care not to let him know my suspicion: I also thought, it was very probable, if he were the client spoken of, that he would let his man of business know that I was the true Simon Pure; all which put me on my mettle; and thus it happened, that when he called in the morning, I was prepared; indeed, his calling was to me as a proof from Holy Writ that he was the man himself, for he had no particular occasion to call, nor were we on a footing of such intimacy as to make the civility at all necessary.

But Mr. Curry was a pawkie man, and had a reason ready; for he said,

'I just met in the street, as I was coming along, with Mr. Probe, and he told me that he had been with you last night.'

'He was,' replied I, 'and seems to be a civil and purpose-like character; but I doubt, Mr. Curry, if his client and my friend, you understand, will be able to close.'

'Indeed! why so?'

'Because he expects a greater price than I have made up my mind to give.'

'Oh, there may be some modification. He told me that you had offered only a thousand pounds per session: now, Mr. Jobbry, that is rather too little; but you will hear from him what his client says.'

I saw by this that there was a desire on the part of Mr. Curry to let me have the seat for what he called a fair price; but having some knowledge of his repute as a man of business, I said briskly, 'I believe, Mr. Curry, after all, that this is a very foolish notion of mine. What have I to do with Parliament? it's just an idle longing – the green sickness of idleness. Really, my conversation with Mr. Probe has changed my mind in a material degree. What am I to get for a thousand pounds, but two or three franks for letters, and be under an obligation to hear as much nonsense talked across a drinkless table, in the small hours of the night, as ever honest man heard over a jolly bowl? Besides, Mr. Curry, if I am to pay money, I have got an inkling that a much better bargain may be had elsewhere.'

I saw that Mr. Curry was inoculated with the apprehensions when I said this, for he looked bamboozled; so I followed up the blow with another masterly stroke, adding: 'Indeed, Mr. Curry, it would be very foolish extravagance for me to give any such sum as a thousand pounds per session for the vain bauble of a seat; and when ye consider that a whole Parliament can be got, as ye said yourself, for about five thousand pounds, divide that by seven sessions, and ye'll then come nearer what the mark should be.'

'There may be some truth in that, Mr. Jobbry,' was the reply; 'but I understood from Mr. Probe that you had offered a thousand pounds.'

'Oh! that was in words of course.'

'In parliamentary affairs,' said he, very seriously, 'the strictest honour is to be observed.'

'No doubt; but an agent, you know, cannot pledge himself for his principal, – all is subject to approbation.'

'Yes; but, Mr. Jobbry, you are yourself the principal.'

'In a sense, I'll never deny that to you; but Mr. Probe only knows me as the friend of a gentleman who has a turn for public speaking, which I have not, and who may turn a penny out of his talent: in short, Mr. Curry, something between five hundred and seven hundred is more like a rational price, – I'll give no more.'

'But you have made an offer, sir.'

'Oh! that was in a preliminary way.'

'Mr. Probe, however, may insist upon the offer being fulfilled.'

'You must not speak that way to me, or maybe I may, by petition, accuse him to the Honourable House of trafficking in seats, and call you by name as a witness. What would either he or his client say to that?'

I saw that he changed colour, and that his nether lip quivered; so I said to him,

'Between ourselves, Mr. Curry, I cannot see the use of shilly-shallying about this, – I'll only give five hundred guineas per session, which, you will allow, is very liberal for a man of honour, who has it in his power, if not well used, to make his complaint to the House.'

'I can only say, Mr. Jobbry, that from all I know of the subject, Mr. Probe's client will never accept your offer.'

'Very well, that's in his option; but I have an option likewise.'

'What is that?'

'Didn't I hint about petitioning?'

'Mr. Jobbry, such a proceeding would be most unpar-liamentary.'

'No, no, my friend, – don't let us put our heads in the grass, like the foolish ostriches, and think, because we do so, that our hinder ends are not seen: the mat-ter in hand is contrary to law, and therefore we must not apply the rules of law to any thing so nefarious; howsomever, I'll give the five hundred guineas, as I have said.'

'You will never get the seat for that.'

'That may be true; but the Honourable House, like a Spartan judge, is desperate in punishing a detected delinquent: in short, Mr. Curry, if ye have anything to say anent this negotiation, ye'll advise a compliance with my proposition.'

I could discern that Mr. Curry was in a frying condition; but he was a man of experience, and it was not in my power to draw out of him that he was at all art or part in the business; so, not to waste time with more talk, I passed into the news of the day, and Mr. Curry presently took his leave; while I very much wondered at my own instinct in acquiring the art of parliamenting so readily; and I had soon good cause, as I shall presently shew, for the address with which I was on that occasion gifted.

———

There was something which struck me in that conversation with Mr. Curry not altogether conciliatory; and after pondering over it for some time, I came to a conclusion that presently Mr. Probe would come to me with a new offer. I thereupon resolved to bide in the coffee-house all day, that I might not be wanting in the needful season. The day, no doubt, was no temptation, inasmuch as it was rainy, and the streets in a very slobbery condition, and I had no particular business to call me abroad. Accordingly, it fell out just as I expected. About the heel of the evening, the waiter came to see what I would have for dinner, and said to me, in a kind of parenthesis, as I was looking over the bill of fare, that he supposed I should not want the private room that evening.

'My lad,' quo' I, 'that's very correct of you, for I had forgot that maybe the same gentleman who was with me yesterday may call again; I therefore think it will be just as commodious to have my dinner laid in the parlour as in this, the coffee-room; so you'll just attend to that.'

'Very well,' said he, and did as I desired; and well it was for me that he had been so considerate, for, before the dinner was ready, who should come in but Mr. Probe; and after various hithers and yons, I invited him to dine with me, the night being very wet; to the which, after some entreaty, he was consenting, and thereupon we went up into the private room, and had a couple of candles and our dinner duly served.

For some time, and especially while we were eating, I thought that it was judicious to say nothing to him concerning the manor of Humbug; but when we were satisfied, the cloth withdrawn, and Carbonell again upon the table, we opened the debate.

'Mr. Probe,' said I, 'since I had the felicity of conversing with you concerning that weak plan of my friend's about going into Parliament, – for weak I say it is, as I see no whereby he can make profit of his outlay, – I have thought I cannot better do a friend's part than advise him to have nothing to do with such an inconvenience.'

'My good Mr. Jobbry,' said he, 'no one can dispute your prudence in that matter; for no man in his senses, I mean in his sober senses, would ever think of spending his nights in hearing young men, of a very moderate capacity, talking by the hour; but that is not our present purpose: my business is, as they say in the House, to report progress; and what I have to mention is, that I have seen my client and communicated your offer.'

'My offer, Mr. Probe? what do you mean? surely you could never consider our few preliminary words as a serious overture?'

'Mr. Jobbry,' replied the ruddy little man, 'did not you tell me that you would give a thousand pounds per session for I'll not say what?'

'Most certainly I did, Mr. Probe; most certainly I gave it as my opinion that a thousand pounds was quite enough; but there is a wide difference between giving an opinion on the value of a thing, and buying that thing. Now, I was clearly made up in my mind that a thousand pounds was the full value of your client's sitting part; but the worth to my friend was another question.'

'Mr. Jobbry, I considered we had done some business together; you made an offer – I reported that offer – and you have your answer.'

'Very right, Mr. Probe, you speak like a man of business; I like to deal with off-hand people – there is nothing like frankness; but if you thought that I made a definitive offer, you were never more mistaken in your life.'

'You don't say so? – this is very awkward.'

'Oh, not at all, not at all; we were only talking upon the general question; and I think, Mr. Probe, considering it as an opening conversation, we advanced pretty well to the point: but you must know, sir, that I could not bind my principal without his own consent.'

At these words, I observed Mr. Probe looking at me with a kind of left-handed peering, which left no doubt in my mind that Mr. Curry had reported progress too, and asked leave to sit again; but I was on my guard.

'I shall not controvert that, Mr. Jobbry,' said Mr. Probe, 'but the mistake has been committed, certainly.'

'If you think so, Mr. Probe, I shall very much regret it on your account; but with me, in my usual way, all was plain sailing, – and if you will ask our mutual friend, Mr. Curry, who was here with me in the morning, he will tell you that I told him five hundred guineas was the full and adequate price of the article.'

'This is surprising! To what purpose did we speak, if you did not authorise me to offer a thousand pounds?'

'Mr. Probe, I am a greenhorn, and not versed in the diplomaticals; but it was not reasonable to come upon me in that way, without even knowing the name of the borough, and who were to be my constituents. That simple fact, Mr. Probe, shews you have been greatly mistaken in supposing my words of course contained a specific offer.'

'Well, let that pass; all I had to say was, that my client was not indisposed to listen to your offer.'

'Now, Mr. Probe,' said I, 'don't your own words confirm what I was saying? If I had made an offer, would not your client have given an answer either in the affirmative or in the negative? And yet you say that he was only not indisposed to listen to my proposal.'

'Well, well,' said Mr Probe, 'you attach a little more importance to the accidental word "indisposed" than I intended; and therefore you will excuse me if I request you to say in few words what you will give, that there may be no mistake this time.'

'My principal,' said I, 'is a prudent man.'

'So I perceive,' said Mr. Probe.

And I added that, 'I had told Mr. Curry I thought, and did think, five hundred guineas a liberal price.'

'I shall report that,' said Mr. Probe; 'but it is too little.'

'Then, if you think so, let the business end. I am very indifferent about the subject; and, besides, I have good reason to think that, under particular circumstances, seats can be had cheaper, Mr. Probe.'

'My object, Mr. Jobbry, in being with you is to do business: it is nothing to me what you know or what you offer; I am but an agent.'

'I see that,' replied I; 'you are the go-between.'

'Well, well, that office must be done by somebody; let us make a minute of agreement for seven hundred pounds.'

'No, no; five hundred guineas is the ultimate.'

'You are a strange gentleman,' said he. 'Make it six hundred guineas, to end the matter.'

'No,' said I; 'no guineas above the five hundred: but I'll make it pounds, which you will agree is very extravagant.'

Thus, from less to more, we came to an agreement, and signed mutual missives to that effect; and a pawkie laugh we had together, as well as a fresh bottle of Carbonell's, when it came out that Mr. Curry was 'my client', as I had jaloused; and that I was to succeed him as the honourable member for Frailtown, when he had taken the Chiltern Hundreds.

Having thus explained my popular election for the well-known ancient borough of Frailtown, as the member for which I made my appearance among the knights and burgesses in Parliament assembled, I will now proceed to relate what next came to pass.

It will be seen that I took my seat in the middle of the session, which many of my Indian friends thought was a souple trick, because the event at the time made no noise; whereas, if I had waited for the general election, that ill-tongued tinkler, the daily press, would have been pouking at my tail maybe, as I was going in, duly elected, among the rest of the clanjamfrey.

No sooner had I, as it was stated in the newspapers, taken the oaths and my seat, than I lifted my eyes and looked about me; and the first and foremost resolution that I came to, was, not to take a part at first in the debates. I was above the vain pretension of making speeches; I knew that a wholesome member of Parliament was not talkative, but attended to solid business; I was also convinced, that unless I put a good price on my commodity, there would be no disposition to deal fairly by me. Accordingly, I resolved for the first week not to take my seat in any particular part of the House, but to shift from side to side with the speakers on the question, as if to hear them better; and this I managed in so discreet a manner, that I observed by the Friday night, when there was a great splore, that the ministers, from the treasury bench, pursued me with their eyes to fascinate me, wondering, no doubt, with what side I would vote, – but I voted with neither. That same evening, more than two of my friends inquired of me what I thought of the question. By this I could guess that my conduct was a matter of speculation;

so I said to them that, 'really, much was to be said on both sides; but I had made up my mind not to vote the one way or the other until I got a convincing reason.'

This was thought a good joke, and so it was circulated through the House, inasmuch as that, when we broke up at seven o'clock on the Saturday morning, one of the ministers, a young soft-headed lad, took hold of me by the arm, in the lobby, and inquired, in a jocund manner, if I had got a convincing reason. I gave him thereupon a nod and a wink, and said, 'Not yet; but I expected one soon, when I would do myself the honour of calling upon him'; which he was very well pleased to hear, and shook me by the hand with a cordiality by common when he wished me good night, – 'trusting,' as he said, 'that we should soon be better acquainted.' 'It will not be my fault,' quo' I, 'if we are not.'

With that we parted; and I could see by the eye in my neck that he thought, with the light head of youth, that he had made a capital conquest, by his condescension.

Now, this small matter requires an explanation, for the benefit of other new members. If a man has all his eyes about him, he will soon discern that a ministry, if it has three or four decent, auld-farrent men, is for the most part composed of juveniles – state 'prentices – the sprouts and offshoots of the powerful families. With them lies the means of conciliating members; for the weightier metal of the ministers is employed in public affairs, and to the younkers is confided the distribution of the patronage, – for a good reason, it enables them to make friends and a party by the time that they come, in the course of nature, to inherit the upper offices.

I had not been long in the House till I noticed this; and as my object in being at the expense of going thereinto was to make power for myself, I was not displeased at the scion of nobility making up to me; and I have uniformly since found, that the true way of having a becoming influence with government, is slily to get the upper hand of the state fry.

But, on this occasion, there was a personal reason for my so cleverly saying I would call on him for a convincing reason. My second cousin, James Gled, when he saw my election in the newspapers, wrote to me for my interest, knowing that I would naturally be on the side of Government, and stating that the office of distributor of stamps in our county was soon to be vacant. So it just came into my head in the nick of time to make a pleasant rejoinder to my lord; and accordingly I was as good as my word; and to make the matter as easy as possible, I told him, in my jocular manner, when I called, that I was come for the convincing reason.

I could see that he was a little more starched in his office than in the lobby; but I was determined to be troubled with no diffidence, and said, 'My lord, you'll find me a man open to conviction – a very small reason will satisfy me at this time; but, to be plain with your lordship, I must have a reason, – not that I say the Government is far wrong, but I have an inclination to think that the Opposition is almost in the right.' And then I stated to his lordship, in a genteel manner, what James Gled had said to me, adding, 'It's but a small place, and maybe your lordship would think me more discreet if I would lie by for something better; but I wish to convince his Majesty's Government that I'm a moderate man, of a loyal inclination.'

His lordship replied, 'That he had every inclination to serve an independent member, but the King's government could not be carried on without patronage; he was, however, well disposed to oblige me.'

'My lord,' said I, 'if I was seeking a favour for myself, I would not ask for such a paltry place as this; but I'm a man that wants nothing: only it would be a sort of satisfaction to oblige this very meritorious man, Mr. Gled.'

We had then some further talk; and he gave me a promise, that if the place was not given away, my friend should have it.

'I'm very much obliged to you, my lord, for this earnest of your good-will to me; and really, my lord, had I thought you were so well inclined, I would have looked for a more convincing reason': at which he laughed, and so we parted. But, two days after, when the vacancy was declared, he said to me, with a sly go, 'That I was a man very hard to be convinced, and required a powerful argument.'

'My lord,' quo' I, 'I did not hope to be taunted in this manner for applying to your lordship to serve an honest man with such a bit trifling post.'

'Trifling?' he exclaimed; 'it is a thousand a-year at least!'

'Well, my lord, if it be, Mr. Gled is as well worthy of it as another; I want nothing myself; but if your lordship thinks that the Government is to be served by over-valuing small favours, my course in Parliament is very clear.'

His lordship upon this was of a lowlier nature than I could have expected, and therefore I reined myself in to moderation; for I saw I had gotten an advantage, and in more ways than one. This was the case; for in my Indian ignorance I thought a distributor of stamps was some beggarly concern of a hundred a-year, but a thousand was really past hope; it was, however, not judicious to think so before my lord.

When I came to consider that the place I had gotten for my relation James Gled was so very lucrative, I really felt as if I had committed a mistake, and was very angry with myself; but in reflecting a little more upon the subject, I saw that it might be turned to great public good: for inasmuch as the places and posts of Government belong to those members and others that get nothing else for their services in support of Government, a judicious man will husband his share of them, so as to make the distribution go as far as possible. Accordingly, as I well knew that two hundred and fifty pounds a-year would have been a most liberal godsend to James, I thought that if it were three it would be a great thing, and that there would be seven hundred over, to apply to other public purposes. I thereupon wrote to him, and said that I had got the place for him, but that his salary was to be three hundred a-year, the remainder being subject to another disposal.

In due course of post I received a most thankful letter for my beneficence, agreeing most willingly to be content with his share of the allowed emoluments. When I got this letter, and got James established in his place, I then bethought me of the most judicious appropriation that could be made of the surplus; and there anent I called to mind a son that I had in the natural way, who was in the army. To him I portioned out three hundred pounds per annum, for he had been a very heavy cess on me, notwithstanding he was serving his king and country; and this, it will be allowed, was as correct a doing as any arrangement of the kind; far more so than that of those who have large pensions themselves, from which they make allowances to their sons, although these sons be of the patriots that make speeches to mobs and multitudes, declaring themselves as pure men, unsullied by any ailment drawn from the people; which is, in a sense, no doubt, the fact, for their allowances are from their fathers.

Having given the three hundred to Captain Jobbry, I then thought of old Mrs. Hayning, my aunt, who was the widow of the minister of Dargorble, and had nothing but her widow's fund to live upon. So I gave her one hundred pounds, which, it will be allowed, was to her a great thing, and it was a very just thing; for as the clergy have no right to make money of their stipends, if they keep up their station and act charitably, the nation should provide for their widows. The remaining three hundred I stipulated with James Gled should be laid aside in the bank, year by year, to be a fund from which I should, from time to time, contribute to public subscriptions; and few things in my life have I been more satisfied with: for so long as James Gled lived, it will be seen by the newspapers what a liberal subscriber I was thereby enabled to be to public charities, by which I acquired great rule and power in them; and many a poor man's child, and orphan likewise, have I been the means of getting well educated. Indeed, I take some blame to myself that I did not more rigidly enforce the same principle of distribution in the salaries of all the posts that I got, at different times, for my kindred and constituents.

There is, however, no condition of life without a drawback on its satisfactions; and of this truth I had soon due experience. From time to time it had been a custom with the member for Frailtown, when he happened to be of ministerial principles, to give a bit small postie to some well-recommended inhabitant of the borough; and accordingly, some anxiety was always taken to ascertain that their new member was a man of the convenient sort. Thus it came to pass, that I had not well warmed my seat when Mr. Spicer, a shopkeeper, and a member of the corporation, called on me one morning and introduced himself; for, as I had never been at Frailtown, I was, of course, in dead ignorance of all my constituents; but when he had made himself known, I received him in a very civilised manner, and inquired in what way I could serve the borough.

Thereupon we had a conversation concerning a canal that was to pass at some short distance from Frailtown; and Mr. Spicer shewed me a very great advantage that it would be of, could ways and means be raised, to make a cut into the town; plainly, as I could see, thinking that, if I did not do it at my own cost, I might, by a liberal contribution, be helping thereunto.

This I thought, at the time, in my own heart, was a very barefaced hope of the corporation to entertain; for I had paid the full price of my seat. But as I had ends to serve with the borough, as well as the corporation thought it had ends to serve with me, I replied to Mr. Spicer, in a very debonair manner:

'Mr. Spicer,' quo' I, 'it really gives me great pleasure to hear that you, in that part of England, are in such a very thriving condition; by the by, in what county is Frailtown?'

When he had made answer that it was in Vamptonshire, I said, 'That I had no notion it was such a prospering district; and that surely I would do all in my power, as a Member of Parliament, to further any bill for the benefit of a community with which I was so nearly and dearly connected': adding, 'It was, however, with me a rule never to contribute to the improvement of any other property than my own, especially as I was at that time laying out a great sum in repairs upon my house, in addition to the improvements on my estate. But,' continued I, 'you are free to use my name as patronising the undertaking.'

'Well,' said he, 'that's, no doubt, something; but though it may not be commodious to you to advance money, I have thought – considering your great influence with the Government – that some time or another you may have it in your power to befriend an honest man.'

'Nothing,' said I, 'would give me greater pleasure: what sort of a post are you looking to?' I added, laughing: 'something, no doubt, more lucrative than the gallows?'

'Oh, me! I am looking for none, thank Heaven; I am content with my own business for the present; but I have a daughter married to a most deserving young man, who would be right glad to be made post-master in the village of Physickspring, which is within two miles of our town, and which gets its letters by an old man from our office.'

'I should think, Mr. Spicer, such a place would not be worth the asking for.'

'Nor would it,' said he, 'but Physickspring is growing a watering-place, and it is for futurity that he will accept it.'

'But does your son-in-law live there, that he would take such a place?'

'Not yet, Mr. Jobbry; but he intends to take up a shop of perfumes and nick-knackeries, jewellery, and other gaieties; and he thinks it would help to bring custom to his shop, if he could conjoin the business thereunto of post-master.'

This seemed a very rational proposition; though I could not help laughing in my sleeve to hear that the honest man believed, in seeking to help a friend, I did not see he was really helping himself; – but we are short-sighted creatures, and such self-delusion is not uncommon.

However, to oblige Mr. Spicer, I promised to exert my best capability to serve his friend; and as the thing was but a trifle, I soon secured it for him; although I learned with surprise that there were no less than five other applicants.

'Oh, ho!' thought I, when I heard this, 'it cannot be such a trifling place.' However, as little was known concerning it, I said nothing, but got the appointment for Mr. Spicer's son-in-law. The five applications, however, stuck in my throat; and before communicating to him the appointment, I thought it was a duty incumbent to make some inquiry; and accordingly I did so, as I shall shew forth in the next chapter.

I found, on inquiry, that Frailtown was, a decayed place, and that Physickspring was fast flourishing in repute – that in a few years it had outnumbered Frailtown by a great deal – and that from the time the Duchess of Driveabout had made it her place of resort, the visitors were most genteel and select; insomuch, that for one letter that went to Frailtown, a score at least went to Physickspring. This assured me that the separate post-office that was to be established would beat the old one all to shivers. I likewise learned, that the post-office in Frailtown had been long kept by the widow of a former mayor, who had brought up a decent family of daughters in the church of England and the Christian religion; and that since the increase of Physickspring they were well to do in the world, being milliners. It was therefore very plain to me, that the new establishment would not only be a great drawback on them, but a total loss to old Edward Dawner, the man that distributed the letters in Physickspring.

This, it will be seen, was a case that required prudent handling; and I resolved to weigh the whole circumstances thereof in a judicious balance. At first, my natural inclination was to advise the milliners to move their business to Physickspring, and to keep old Edward Dawner as the postman to go with the letters to Frailtown; in fact, just to reverse the practice. I heard, however, that the Misses Stiches had the whole business of Frailtown, which they would lose if they removed to Physickspring, where they had no chance of success, as a fashionable nymph of the gumflowers, from London, had forestalled the trade. Indeed, I saw that when a man obtains a share in the distributions of the good things of Government, it behoves him not to allow himself to be overly yielding to his natural tender feelings; and thus I was constrained, by a public duty, to make the best arrangement I could in the difficulties of the case; and what I did, got me great respect over all that country side. I got an inkling from the post-office concerning the value of the postmastership of Frailtown, the which I saw was very handsome in moderation. I therefore wrote to Mr. Spicer, that I had got a conditional grant of the office for his son-in-law, but which I was afraid made it so little worth, that he would not think of accepting the same – that the conditions were to the effect that one Edward Dawner was to be indemnified by an annual sum of money, whenever the postmaster's allowance exceeded thirty pounds a-year – I had ascertained that it was well on to four times that amount; and that Mrs. Stiches was likewise to have an indemnity, and should be paid, whenever the emoluments exceeded fifty pounds a-year clear, all surplus till she had five-and-twenty pounds a-year.

After stating these particulars to Mr. Spicer, I said to him, in my letter, that he would tell his son-in-law what I would do for him, provided that the place, with such burdens, was an object.

As I expected, back in course of post came a letter accepting the offer, but in a cool way. The arrangement, however, was greatly applauded by the inhabitants of the borough, as well as by the gentry at Physickspring, and every one there said it consisted with reason that there should be a post-office at such a growing place; and that it shewed I was a man of reflection and observation to put such a judicious idea into the head of Government. In short, I was a very popular member; and I must say, though I say it myself, deservedly so. 'Deal small, and serve all,' was an ancient proverb that I gave great heed to; and the first session of my parliamentary career shews that I understood its application.

So much anent the second administration of my influence in my first session, when I was in a manner innocent of the ways and means of dealing with patronage. As I became better acquainted with the usages of Parliament, no doubt I grew more dexterous; but on no future occasion did I ever make such a sensible appropriation as on those just mentioned, which I partly attribute to my being a fresh hand in the business – 'new brooms', as the saying is, 'sweep clean'; and I was then spank new in ministerious trafficking: indeed, I had then more leisure, and had time to consider what I was about; but afterwards, as will be shewn by and by, when I came to have my hands full of committee-work, private bills, and local affairs, I could afford less time to attend to the distribution of the salaries in the manner I have described; and here it becomes me to make a very cogent remark.

In those days there had been none of that heresy about savings, which has been such a plague both to ministers and members of late years. We then all sat each under his vine and fig-tree; and there was then really some enjoyment in making the people happy, especially those who had for friends members that were of the salutary way of thinking. I am, however, anticipating much of what I have to relate, and the sore changes that have come to pass among us since that fatal night when a late member betrayed us, by calling our right to share in the patronage by the ignominious epithet of candle-ends and cheese-parings; for, ever since, it has been thought that we have been wanting to our own wisdom in being so inveterate to retain the distribution of places and pensions – the natural perquisites of Members of Parliament.

My first session in Parliament was a time of bustle; as much, however, owing to my being still a novice in the business, as to the concerns in which I took an interest: but I gradually quieted down into more method; and, as practice makes perfect, before the session was concluded, I began to know, in a measure, what I was about, and could see that some change of a molesting kind was impending over us.

The French revolution had done a deal of damage to all those establishments which time and law had taken so much pains to construct; but nothing which it caused was so detrimental to the stability of things, as the introduction of that evil notion among mankind, that the people were the judges of the posts and perquisites about Government; for although it is very true that the means of paying for these things is drawn from the nation at large, it is not very clear that there is any class of the people competent to judge of the whole subject. It is surely consistent with nature that governments should be made out of the first people for rank, talent, and property, in the kingdom, and that they should have allowances and privileges, under regulation, suitable to their high stations. Now, how can the lower orders and the commonalty be judges of what is a fit recompense for persons of the degree alluded to? Operatives would think a very small salary a great deal, as compared with their earnings; and, no doubt, the higher orders are equally unjust when they attempt to value the remuneration of labour. The democratical, for example, think state salaries always exorbitant, and the aristocratical never think wages low enough: out of this controversy between them has arisen many of those troubles which eyes that are not yet opened will be closed by old age and death before they are ended; for it is now no longer possible to prevent the world from conceiving itself qualified to judge of what a nation should pay to its servants. Every man, now-a-days, thinks he has a right to tell what the nation shall pay, and yet conceits that no one has a right to interfere with him. Surely it is not consistent with common sense, that the nobility, who talk so much about the corruption of places and pensions, should be the judges of the recompense that is due for the services of men of high degree; and yet it is this which is the cause of our vexations. No doubt, it is very wrong that any class, faction, or party, in the state, should monopolise the patronage of the whole state: but there is a wide difference between *that*, which some say renders reform needful, and that pretence to regulate the emoluments and salaries of the state by the public voice. Salaries are great or small relative to their duties and stations. The chiefs of the state must keep up an equality of station with those of the highest rank in the kingdom; and those of every degree under them must maintain a like equality with the class of persons that their public duties require them to act and associate with: it is therefore, in my opinion, a most heterodox way of thinking, to imagine that the private property of individuals of high rank is to remain untouched, and yet that the officers of state, who must necessarily be their associates and companions, shall be reduced to comparative poverty. I am the more particular in explaining my view on this subject, because, in common with other honourable members, I have felt, as will be in due time shewn, very serious annoyance from the new-fangled doctrines of the Utilitarians. And here, before I proceed with my narrative, I may as well observe, that there is, in my opinion, a great fallacy about this new-light doctrine of utility, as something distinct from happiness. I consider, and it has been so considered from the beginning of the world, that the object of all utility is happiness; but every man's happiness does not lie in the same circumstances, and therefore there can be no universal method of producing happiness by utility. No doubt it is useful to get public affairs administered as cheaply as possible; but if the chiefs of the state must be the companions of the high and rich, you will never get men of talent to fill these offices, without exposing them to the hazard of committing high crimes and misdemeanours, to procure indirectly the wherewithal to keep up their equality.

Having thus stated my ideas upon the rightfulness of regulating salaries of public officers by the way of living among those with whom their public duties require them to associate, it will be seen that I have, in always voting with the ministers against the reduction of salaries, only acted on the soundest principles; for even in the matter of sinecures, I have adhered with constancy to my principles. Sinecures ought not to be considered as salaries for doing nothing, but as salaries set apart nominally for the use of those dependants of influential people whom it is necessary to conciliate to the Government. All governments must have various means of conciliating various men: there must be titles and degrees for those whom such baubles please; there must be enterprises and commands for those who delight in adventures; and there must be sinecures and pensions for the sordid. It is as much to be lamented that such humours are entailed upon our common nature, as it is to be mourned that it is liable to so many various diseases; but it is an ignorant mistake of the nature of man to think the world is to be ruled by one class of motives.

Such were the reflections which occupied my mind during the recess of Parliament after my first session. I was thankful that my fortune enabled me to be independent, and that I had no natural turn for the diplomatics of politics; but I learned, from conversing with politicians, something of the state at which society was arrived, and saw the necessity of having clear ideas regarding those matters in which I was most interested; for my object in going into Parliament was to help my kith and kin by a judicious assistance to Government, and it was of great importance that the assistance should be given on a conscientious principle. Accordingly, by these reflections I was persuaded, that, from the state of the times and public opinion, no member of the House should, without the clearest views as well as convincing reasons, consent to the creation of new places, nor, be it observed also, to the abolition of old places; and this led me to a very manifest conclusion.

It appeared, when I came to think of it, that the great cause which stirred men to be in opposition to Government was to provide for their friends and dependants, and that that was the secret reason why the Opposition found such fault with existing institutions and places, and why they put forth new plans of national improvement, which they pledged themselves, if ever they got into office, to carry into effect. Time has verified this notion. Under the pretext of instituting better official and judicature arrangements, new ones have been introduced by the Opposition when they came into power, which enabled them to provide for their friends and dependants; but they were obliged to indemnify those who enjoyed the old offices. Whether the change was an improvement or not, I would not undertake to maintain; but the alteration was very conducive to the acquisition of a new stock of patronage. With very little individual suffering, the change necessarily superseded and set aside those who did the work under the old system; but as there would have been gross injustice in turning adrift the old servants, they were provided for by an indemnification, and the new servants had all the new places to themselves over and above: in time, as the old servants died off, the evil was remedied.

When my second session was about to commence, I went to London several days before the opening of Parliament. In this I was incited by a very laudable desire; for the more I reflected on the nature of my public trusts, the plainer I saw that the obligations on a member were more and more manifold; so I resolved to occupy the few preliminary days in going about among the friends and acquaintances that I had made in the former session, and to consult with them concerning the state of things in general: thus it happened that I was very particular in conferring with old Sir John Bulky.

The baronet was a member for a borough in his own county, and had been so for six successive Parliaments; being a good neighbour, a very equitable magistrate, and in all respects a most worthy country gentleman, upholding the laws and the power of Government around him with courageous resolution in the worst of times. But he was grown old and afflicted with the gout, suffering indeed so often from it, that his attendance in the House was frequently interrupted. I had seen his superior sagacity the preceding year, and sometimes we took tea upstairs together when there was a heavy debate, out of which grew between us a very confidential friendship.

Sir John and I very cordially met. He had during the recess been not quite so well in his health as usual, but he had been free of the gout; and it had happened that his eldest son, who had been abroad to see the world, had come home, and that, in consequence, his house had been filled with company for the summer. Many of the guests were also travelled men; and he had opportunities of hearing from them more concerning the state of the continent, as well as respecting society at home, than usual. We had therefore, at our first meeting, a very solid conversation on public affairs, and were quite in unison in our notion that, although the French revolution had gone past the boiling, it was yet in a state to keep the world long in hot water.

'Depend on it, Mr. Jobbry,' said the worthy baronet, 'it will be long before the ruins of the earthquake settle into solid ground; and although Buonaparte and his abettors must be put down for our own sakes, it cannot be denied that the French are well content with him; yet when they are put down, it will be only another revolution. The first came out of themselves upon their neighbours – the next will come from their neighbours upon them; so between the two, at the end of the second revolution I should not wonder if the world were to be found in looser disorder than at the first, which will make the part of Britain the more difficult; for, of all nations in Europe, we are the most apt, by our freedom, to catch the infection of opinions.'

'That's strange, Sir John,' quo' I; 'for inasmuch as we are in a state of advance to the nations of the continent, it's wonderful that we should think their crude dreams and theories objects of imitation for us to follow, which indeed we cannot do unless we go backward.'

'It is, Mr. Jobbry, however, the case. I have lived long enough in public to observe that every season has its own peculiar malady both moral and physical, and that it rarely happens that men continue in the same mind on public questions for two years together; in short, that the art of keeping the world steady, and which is the art of government, is to find the ways and means to amuse mankind. It is, no doubt, true that the disease of every year is not attended with such high delirium as we have seen of late; but still there is always that morbid disposition about nations that requires great delicacy in the management; and experience has taught me to have a great distrust of general reformations; indeed, it seems to be the course of Providence to make the most fatal things ever appear the fairest; and I never hear of the alluring plausibilities of changes in the state of the world, without having an apprehension that these changes, which promise so much good, are the means by which Providence is working an overthrow.'

When we had discoursed in this manner for some time, he then told me that he had heard it said the Government was going to reduce all things that could be well spared.

'In a sense, Sir John,' said I, 'nothing can be more plausible; but they cannot reduce the establishments without making so many people poorer and obliging them to reduce their establishments, thereby spreading distress and privation wider. It is not a time to reduce public appointments when there is national distress; the proper season is when all is green and flourishing.'

'Very true,' replied Sir John; 'it would seem that the best time of providing for those who must be discharged when governments reduce their appointments, is when new employments are easy to be had; but things at present look not very comfortable in that way, and therefore I am grieved to hear that the distemper of making saving to the general state at the expense of casting individuals into poverty, has infected the Government. In truth, Mr. Jobbry, this intelligence has distressed me quite as much as a change of administration would; for a change of administration does not make actual distress, inasmuch as the new ministers always create, in redeeming their pledges, a certain number of new places, and commonly indemnify for those they abolish; but a mere system of economising – of lessening expenditure during a period of general hardship – is paving the way to revolution; and accordingly, as I am too old now to take a part in so busy a scene, I intend to retire at the close of the present Parliament.'

'And,' quo' I, 'have you arranged yet for your successor in Easyborough?'

'Not yet,' said he; 'for, to tell you the truth, that's the chief object that has brought me to town. I have sat for six Parliaments for the borough, and it has never cost me any thing; and I know that whoever I recommend will be received with a strong feeling of good-will, which makes me a little chary on the subject; for I would not like to recommend to them a man that was not deserving of their confidence.'

'That's very creditable to you, Sir John; but I should think that they would be right willing to accept your son.'

'True, Mr. Jobbry, I have no doubt they would accept very willingly my son; but I am not sure that he is just the man fit for them; for though he is a young man of good parts, he has got too many philosophical crotchets about the rules and principles of government, to be what in my old-fashioned notions I think a useful English legislator. He's honest and he's firm, but honesty and firmness are not enough; there is a kind of consideration that folly is entitled to, that honesty and firmness will not grant. I don't know, Mr. Jobbry, if I make you understand me; but as the object of all political power is to make people happy, the right sort of member for Easyborough is a person well advanced in life, and of more good-nature in his humours than rigid righteousness in his principles. My son would do better, and would be a good member for a patriotic community; but the orderly and sober-minded inhabitants of Easyborough require a man of a different character.'

'And have you found nobody yet, Sir John, that you would recommend?'

'No,' says he, 'no.'

'I wish,' quo' I, 'that you would think well of me; for I would fain make an exchange for Frailtown; could not you let your son and me make an arrangement for an exchange?'

'No,' said Sir John; 'because I could not recommend you to Easyborough.'

I felt the blood rush into my face at this very plain dealing; and, just to be as plain, said,

'What's your objection, Sir John?'

'Nothing to you as a man, Mr. Jobbry, for I think you both shrewd and clever; but because you have not yet got right notions of what belongs to the public; you take too close and personal an interest for your own sake in your borough. Now that does not consort with my notions – my constituents have never cost me a guinea, and they have never asked me for a favour – a constituency of that kind would not suit you, Mr. Jobbry.'

Soon after this point of conversation, I bade him good

morning, and came away; but what he said made a deep impression, and I was really displeased at his opinion of me, which led me to adopt the resolutions and line of conduct that will be described in the next chapter. But the House of Commons, it is well known, is a school of ill manners; and a long sederunt as a member does not tend to mitigate plain speaking.

A man who observes sharply, as I have been in the practice of doing all my reasonable life, will not be long in Parliament till he has full occupation for his faculties. It is a place not just like the world, but is, in fact, a community made up of a peculiar people, and the members are more unlike to one another than the generality of mankind, and have upon them, besides, a stamp and impress of character that makes them as visibly a distinct race in the world, as the marking of sheep distinguishes one flock from another at tryst or market.

This diversity, in my opinion, proceeds from two causes; the one is, that every thing a member says in the House is received as truth; and thus it happens when an orator is under an obligation, either from friendship or party spirit, to blink the veracity of his subject, he is put to a necessity of using roundabout words, that feed the ear and yet cheat the mind in the sense; and this begets a formality of language that really makes some Members of Parliament very quiscus and unsatisfactory to have business to do with. The other cause comes from the reverse of this, inasmuch as there is no restraint but a man's own discretion, in what he states; and as all men are not alike gifted with that blessing, a Parliament fool is far more remarkable than a weak man out of doors; and thus it is, that honourable members have, in addition to their worldly character, a parliamentary character; but some put on the parliamentary character, not having those habits by which it is induced; and these, to any observant man are really very amusing and ridiculous: they are, for the most part, the silent voters on both sides of the House; chiefly, however, of the Government thick-and-thinners.

When I had, to my perfect satisfaction, ascertained the accuracy of this opinion, I came to a resolution that begat me in time a very sedate and respectable reputation. Several times, during my first session, I had a mind to speak; and, really, there were speeches spoken which were most instigating to me to hear, and provoking me to reply; but, somehow, my heart failed, and the session passed over without my getting up. This at the time was not very satisfactory to myself, and I daresay if the session had continued a little longer, I might have been so bold as to utter a few words: but during the recess I had a consultation with myself relative to my habits and abilities; and I came in consequence to a resolution, that, as I was not sure of possessing the talent of eloquence, never having tried it, I should not, without a necessity, make the endeavour, – a resolution which I have had great reason to rejoice in, because, in the second session, various questions were debated, that, if I had possessed a disposition to speak, I would have expressed myself in a manner that might not have been applauded by the public. My silence, therefore, enabled me to escape animadversion; and I was protected also from acquiring any of that parliamentary character, as to the choice of terms, to which I have been alluding. Thank Heaven! I have had gumption enough left to avoid assuming it; for verily it is a droll thing to hear men that are everlasting silent ciphers in the House, speaking (when you meet with them at dinner) across the table as if they were the very ora rotundas of the Treasury bench.

I had another advantage in resolving to be only a vote – and that was, it committed me upon but few questions; by which I was left free to do as I pleased with ministers, in case a change should take place between the two sides of the House. In all the regular business of Government, my loyalty and principles led me to uphold the public service; but on those occasions when the outs and ins amused themselves with a field-day, or a benefit-night rather, I very often did not vote at all, – for I never considered pairing off before the division as fully of the nature of a vote; and several times, when the minister who had the management of the House spoke to me for going away before the debate was done, I explained to him why I did so, by saying that I always went off when I saw that the Government party had the best of the argument, and thought that maybe if I had staid till the back of the bow-wows against them were up, I might be seduced from my allegiance, and constrained by their speeches to give a vote according to my conscience, as it might be moulded by their oratory.

I will not say, in a very positive manner, that all the members who pair off during the middle of a debate are actuated by the principle of fairness that I was; but some, no doubt, are; for it's really a hard thing for a man to be convinced by a speech from the Opposition, and yet be obliged, by the principle that attaches him to the Government, to give a vote against his conscience. In short, by the time that the second session was half over, I had managed myself with such a canny sobriety, that my conduct was regarded with very considerable deference. I was a most attentive member, whether in my attendance on committees or in the House; and I carried my particularity to so exact a degree, that even in the number of my daily franks I allowed myself to incur not the loss of one; and I was so severe in the administration of even this small privilege, that I never borrowed a frank from a friend.

It may seem that my correctness in this matter of the franks was a trifle not worth mentioning; but I had my own ends for it. It was the last session of a Parliament; and it is very curious what an insight it afforded me of the puetering that some men that had boroughs to contest carried on; for whenever I saw a friend writing often, and needing many franks to the same borough, I concluded that he had an election purpose to accomplish.

Towards the end of the session, I observed that a young man, Mr. Gabblon, was very industrious, almost every day getting franks; and although I was regular in the smoking-room, he never once applied to me. One day, when I was sitting there by myself, and he came in to get a cover additional to his own, – seeing me alone, he went immediately out, without asking my assistance. This I thought very comical; and it immediately flashed like lightning on my mind, that, surely, he could not be undermining my interest in Frailtown?

It is wonderful to think what queer and ingenious thoughts will come into people's heads. No sooner did the surmise rise in my mind, than I was moved by an inordinate impulse to learn if there was anything in his correspondence to justify the suspicion, and I was not long left in doubt; for soon after came in another member, with whom I was on the best of footings; and he had a blank cover in his hand, which he addressed at the table and gave out to Mr. Gabblon, who was standing in the lobby. When my friend had done so, I said,

'That young lad, Mr. Gabblon, has a wonderful large correspondence. What can he be about? for these several days he has been always in want of franks; and yet he is not a man of commerce, but a squire.'

My friend, Mr. Henwick, looked to me very slily, and said, 'Did I really not know what Mr. Gabblon was about?'

'No; I don't trouble myself with other people's affairs: but it is surprising how men that have no business should have such a correspondence.'

'Well,' said Mr. Henwick, 'what you say is extraordinary. Have you not heard that Mr. Gabblon intends to succeed you in Frailtown; and his correspondence is with the influential people of your own borough?'

'No possible!' said I.

'But it is true,' said he with a smile; 'and some of us, seeing you were taking no step, concluded that you intended to retire from Parliament.'

'This is news, Mr. Henwick,' replied I, 'and it behoves me to look after it. I wonder, indeed, what could make him think of cutting me out.'

'Why,' said Mr. Henwick, 'it is reported that Mr. Spicer, who is of great influence with the corporation, is not content with the way in which you are said to have used him.'

'He's a d——d ungrateful vagabond. Didn't I get his son-in-law made the postmaster at Physickspring? I must look to this immediately.'

And with that I rose, and took a hackney coach in Palace-yard, and drove straight to the counting-house of Mr. Probe, the solicitor, determined to sift this abominable parliamenting to the bottom.

Hot as I was at the House of Commons, I yet had time to cool in some degree between it and Lincoln's Inn Fields, where Mr. Probe had his writing rooms – but not quite to an indifference; so when I reached the place, and went in, I found himself there alone, for it was then past four o'clock; and I said to him as soon as I entered,

'Mr. Probe,' quo' I, 'what is the meaning of this?'

'I don't know,' replied he; 'what is it that you mean?'

'It is just as well, Mr. Probe, to be candid with me,' said I, 'and therefore I request to know the cause of Mr. Gabblon having a nefarious correspondence with that unprincipled miscreant, Mr. Spicer.'

'Has he?' said Mr. Probe.

'That he has, and I want to know all the particulars.'

'Surely you cannot think that I am privy to all Mr. Gabblon's correspondence?'

'Do you know, Mr. Probe,' exclaimed I, waxing warm, 'that to me it is most unaccountable that he should have this great letter-writing to my borough of Frailtown.'

'I cannot help it,' said Mr. Probe; 'the borough is open to any candidate.'

'Do you say so, sir? have not I paid for my seat?'

'Well, sir, if you have, haven't you your seat?'

'But, sir, have not I a right of pre-emption for the next Parliament?'

'I don't recollect that, sir; nothing was said on that head, and of course I could not but do the best for the corporation, with my Lord's permission.'

'And why did you not come to me, sir, before you went to this Mr. Gabblon? – I see very well that I have been cheated of my money.'

Upon my saying which he bounced up like a pea in a frying-pan, and said, with a loud voice and a red face, that he didn't know what I meant.

'I thought, Mr. Probe,' replied I, with a calm sough, 'that you were a man of more sagacity; but not to waste words, I would just ask if Mr. Gabblon is the new candidate?'

'He is,' said Mr. Probe calmly; 'and as I am engaged for his interest, you must excuse me for not answering more questions.'

I was dumfoundered to hear a man thus openly proclaim his malefactions, and I turned on my heel and came out of the writing-rooms, a most angry man; and so, instead of returning to the House of Commons, I went straight to the neighbouring chambers of Mr. Tough, a solicitor, whom I had observed in a committee as a most pugnacious man, and of whom I said to myself that if ever the time came that I stood in need of an efficacious instrument in a contest, he was the man for my money. Most felicitously, Mr. Tough was within, and also alone; and I said to him with a civil smile, 'that I thought it would not be long before I would need his helping hand. You see, Mr. Tough,' said I, 'that not being entirely well acquainted with the usages of Parliament, I had not thought proper to make a stipulation with the agent of my borough to give me the first offer at the next election; and, in consequence, he became susceptible – you understand – and has gone over to the side of another candidate: now I want you to be my adviser on the occasion.'

Mr. Tough said he was much obliged to me, and that I would not in him put faith in a broken reed. 'But on what ground do you intend to canvass the borough, for much of your chance of success will depend on that?'

'Mr. Tough, I am but a 'prentice in the craft of Parliament, and cannot advise a man of your experience; but last year I had gotten a good repute there for a piece of honest business that I did concerning the post-office, by which I made an arrangement most satisfactory to the public, and far better than was expected for the behoof of those more immediately concerned.'

'Oh, I heard something of that, and that Mr. Spicer had

vowed revenge for the way you had caused a short coming to his son-in-law.'

'Yes, Mr. Tough, I understand that for the pains I took to get his gude son that office, which he represented to me was worth nothing, he has rebelled against me; now, as in that affair ye will allow I acted a very public-spirited part, it is not to be supposed that all the corporation will be of his way of thinking.'

'You have, Mr. Jobbry, come to me in the proper time; a few days later and all had been lost. But we must bestir ourselves. If you are intent to gain the borough again, you must make a stir this very night; though it is to me a great inconvenience, we must set off together for Frailtown, and pay our respects to the leading members of the corporation; and, to shew our independence, let me suggest to you that our backs must be turned on this Mr. Spicer, who certainly has merited the greatest contempt for his conduct.'

The corruption of my nature being up, this advice was very congenial; and I told him to get a chaise, and to come to me at my lodgings by nine o'clock that night, and in the course of the journey we would have time to lay our heads together, and concert in what manner it would be best to proceed.

Accordingly, as there is nothing like despatch and secrecy in getting the weather-gauge of your opponent in an election, I went from Mr. Tough's office to the House of Commons, and was there before five o'clock, by which expedition no one suspected where I could have been; and I remained in the House, taking my chop upstairs, and shewing myself well to every one about, so that none could think I was meditating an evasion. I saw Mr. Gabblon sitting, well pleased, on the Opposition side; poor, infatuated young man, little suspecting the sword that was hanging by a single hair over his devoted head. Others of my friends saw something of a change about me, and came asking what stroke of good fortune had come to pass that I was looking so blithe and bright? and my answer to them was most discreet, knowing that it was commonly thought I intended to retire from Parliament when the session was over. I said to them that I was only glad to see our weary labours and drowsy night-work drawing to a close; and that Parliament, which I had chosen, in a great mistake, as a place of recreation, had proved far otherwise. Thus it came to pass, that after 'biding in this ostentatious manner in the House till past eight o'clock, I slipped quietly out, and hastening home to my lodgings in Manchester Buildings, had just time to get my *valise* made ready, when Mr. Tough, in the post-chaise, came to the door, and sent up his name. Down I went to him with the *valise* in my hand – in I jumped beside him – and away we went. But clever and alert as I was, when the chaise was driving out of Cannon Street, a fire-engine, with watermen and torches thereon, stopped us a little while; and, as it was passing, the flare of the torches cast a wild light in upon us, and, to my consternation, there, in the crowd, did I see the red face and the gleg eyes of Mr. Probe, who was standing on the pavement and looking me full in the face, with Mr. Tough beside me. This was, to be sure, an astounding thing, and I told Mr. Tough of the same; but he made no remark further than saying to the post-boy, in a voice loud enough for Mr. Probe to hear, 'Drive straight to the Elephant and Castle.' This was a souple trick of Mr. Tough, for it was quite in an opposite direction to where we intended to go; and, as we drove along, when we came to the obelisk in St. George's Fields, he again directed the post-boy to make all the haste he could over Blackfriar's Bridge, and get to the north road with the utmost expedition.

In the course of the journey to Frailtown, we arranged together a very expedient system; and, as Mr. Tough said, 'we could not but succeed'. He was really a very clever and dexterous man, and I was so content with what he advised, that, being somewhat fatigued on the second night, I proposed that we should sleep at Beverington, which is a stage short of Frailtown, and which, being a considerable manufacturing town, has a much more commodious inn. To be sure, we might have gone to the hotel at Physickspring, a most capital house; but I had understood that the sedate inhabitants of the borough had no very affectionate consideration for that hotel; and therefore, as it was my business not to give offence to them, I thought it would be just as well to sleep at Beverington, and go on betimes in the morning to the borough.

Accordingly we did so; and in the morning we resumed the remainder of the road, and were not a little surprised, when we were crossing the bridge of Frailtown, to hear vast shouts and huzzas rising from the heart of the town, and to see all hands, young and old, clodpoles and waggoners, all descriptions of persons, wearing purple and orange cockades, and bellowing, like idiots, 'Gabblon for ever!'

My heart was daunted by the din, and Mr. Tough was just a provocation by his laughter; especially when, before we got to the Royal Oak Inn, in the market-place, we met a great swarm of the ragamuffins drawing Mr. Gabblon and that ne'er-do-weel Probe, in their postchaise, in triumph, without the horses. The latter, limb of Satan, as he was, had suspected our journey, and had gone immediately to his client; off at once they came from London, and while we, like the foolish virgins, were slumbering and sleeping at

52

Beverington, they had passed on to Frailtown, and created all this anarchy and confusion.

But the mischief did not end with that. The ettercap Probe, on seeing us, shouted in derision, and the whole mob immediately began to halloo and yell at us in such a manner, flinging dirt and unsavoury missiles at us, that we were obliged to pull up the blinds, and drive to the inn in a state of humiliation and darkness. To speak with decorum of this clever stratagem of the enemy, we were, in fact, greatly down in the mouth; and for some time after we got safe into the inns, we wist not well what to do. Gabblon and Probe were masters of the field, and Mr. Spicer was their herald every where. At last, Mr. Tough bethought him of an excellent device to cut them out; and accordingly he sent for the landlord, and spoke to him if there was nobody in the town who had a grudge at Mr. Spicer, and would, for a consideration, befriend us in our need.

There was, to be sure, some hazard in this, as Mr. Gabblon and his familiar were likewise inmates of the same inn, and the landlord was, or pretended to be, reluctant to side with either of the candidates. But Mr. Tough persuaded him to send for a man whom he said he knew, who bore a deadly hatred to Mr. Spicer, and was, moreover, a relation of the Misses Stiches, for whom I had done so much. This man was accordingly brought forward. His name was Isaac Gleaning, an elderly person, and slow of speech, but a dungeon of wit. We received him with familiar kindness; and told him of the misfortune that had overtaken us, by our fatigue constraining us to sleep at Beverington.

'It has,' said Isaac, 'been a great misfortune, for your adversaries have got the ears of the mob, and the whole town is in such an uproar that you must not venture to shew your horns in the street.'

'What then,' said I, 'is to be done?'

'Well,' replied Isaac, 'I have been thinking of that; the players are just now at Physickspring, and they have a very funny fellow among them: could not you send for the manager and the clown, and pay them well to be a mountebank and merry-andrew this evening in the market-place; and get them to throw funny squibs and jibes to the mob, against Mr. Gabblon and his compeers?'

Mr. Tough rubbed his hands with glee at this suggestion, and no time was lost in sending for the manager: over he came, and we soon privately made a paction with him; whereupon due notice was sent by the bellman through the town, that a great physician from the Athens of the north, with his servant, a learned professor, was to exhibit his skill and lofty tumblings in the market-place.

By the time that the bellman had proclaimed these extra-ordinary tidings, all the players, tag, rag, and bob-tail, came over from Physickspring, and set about erecting a stage for their master and the clown in the market-place. They had brought their play-actoring dresses; and they mingled in the crowd with Mr. Gabblon's clanjamfrey, insomuch that Macbeth king of Scotland, Hamlet the Dane, and Julius Caesar, were visible in the streets.

Mr. Tough, who was in his way a wag, undertook to instruct Dr. Muckledose and his merry-andrew in what they should do; and the whole town was on such tiptoe of expectation, that Mr. Gabblon and his friends were in a manner deserted – and the multitude gathered in swarms and clusters round the stage, to secure good places to see the performance. In so far the device was successful beyond expectation, for Mr. Gabblon and his coadjutors found themselves obliged to return desjasket to the inn, so much superior were the attractions of the other mountebank.

It was not, however, in this only that the counselling of old Isaac Gleaning was serviceable; he went about among the friends of Mrs. Stiches and her late husband, and gathered together about twenty of the topping inhabitants, whom I invited to dinner; and Mr. Gabblon and the bodie Probe having engaged themselves to dine with their patron, Mr. Spicer, we had a most jovial party.

In the meantime it began to spunk out what a liberal man I was; and the whole mob were as pleased when they heard of the great dinner, as if every one had been an invited guest. Besides, when it was known that the players were hired by me to come over to entertain the town after dark, they in a great body came to the fore part of the inn, and gave me their thanks in three most consolatory cheers. There was, however, a small popular error among them, for I had not bargained for more of the players than the manager and the clown; but Mr. Tough, who was a knowing hand, told me not to make two bites of the cherry, but to hire the Mason Lodge, and make the players a compliment for a gratis entertainment of songs and scenes for the edification of the people. This I agreed to do; so that long before the dinner was ready, the wind had changed, and Mr. Tough told me to be of good cheer, for we were sailing before it with a steady breeze.

Frailtown is situated in the centre of Lord Dilldam's estate, and his lordship is in a manner considered the patron of the borough – at least he was so when I got my seat from Mr. Curry. It cannot, however, be said that his lordship meddles much in the matter, for he is an easy, plain man; and if the candidates be of good Government principles, he never interferes, but leaves the management of the borough, as a perquisite, to the members of the corporation. In this case between me and Mr. Gabblon, he was neutral; for the Whiggery of Mr. Gabblon was neither of a deep nor an engrained die, but ready to change as soon as the friends he acted with could get themselves in office, and him a post.

There was a curious thing in the constitution of the borough which well deserves to be mentioned here. By an ancient charter, the corporation consisted of six burgesses of repute, with the mayor at their head; but if, on any occasion of an election of a Member for Parliament, only five councillors happened to be present, and votes were even, the mayor had not a casting vote. To remedy this inconvenience, however, it was ordained, that the mayor should go to the market-place and summon, at the height of his voice, five burgesses by name, who were of a capacity competent to reckon five score and a half of hobnails; and these five burgesses he was to take with him to the town-hall, and they were then and there to give their opinion collectively and individually as to the candidate that should be preferred.

This, it will be seen, was an arrangement fraught with inconvenience, especially in a contest where the candidates had about equal chances; and accordingly,

on some occasions it had been the practice at controverted elections to abstract one of the council, and
thereby oblige the mayor to put in force the ancient
alternative.

Before my visit to Frailtown I had not heard of this
abstruse charter, nor had Mr. Tough; but when we did
hear of it, we were put a good deal to the stress of our
ability to determine, when the election would come on,
what should be done, especially as there was some risk
that the ungrateful Mr. Spicer would be the new mayor
before the day of election.

'There is no doubt,' said Mr. Tough, 'that if he is
mayor, the Gabblon party will abstract a councillor, to
give Mr. Spicer the power of going to the market-cross
and summoning five of his own friends whom he will have
in readiness there, and thereby secure the election to your
adversary; how are we to counteract this?'

'It is perplexing, Mr. Tough; for no doubt that regulation
in the charter is to secure to the mayor's party always
the power of returning the member. But do ye think,
Mr. Tough, and it's a device that they have never had
recourse to, if we also abstract a councillor, the mayor
will not have to go to the market-place?'

'That would do,' said Mr. Tough, 'that would do; but if
we did so, there would then be but five votes; and suppose
the council divided, the mayor would make three to our
two: it's a very difficult case.'

'Nevertheless, Mr. Tough, we'll work on that scant-
ling.'

And accordingly we did so: we did our best to secure as
many as we could of the council; and when we had three,
our course was plain sailing. But we were more successful
– we got four; and yet every one considered our chance of
success rendered very doubtful, because it was foreseen that
the mayor would have recourse to the ancient usage. But we
kept our intention secret, only assuring the people, before
we left the town, that on the day of election I would be at
my post.

As we had foreseen, Mr. Spicer was chosen mayor, and
the day of election was appointed in the week following.

Mr. Tough and I went down the day before, and had a consultation with old Isaac Gleaning, who was quite down-hearted; for he considered that Mr. Spicer, by the mayor's privilege, would carry the day, notwithstanding our majority in the council. But when he was informed of our intention to keep back one of our council likewise, a new light broke in upon him.

'To make assurance certain, I would advise you,' said he, 'to try and get one of the Gabblon councillors taken off, and keep your own four on the spot.'

This was not, however, easy to be done; for as the attempt, not the deed, would confound us, it was hazardous to offer a consideration. He, however, undertook to negotiate the business, saying, that he was well acquainted with one of them, a James Curl, who was a hair-dresser. Still, this was a very difficult thing, and greatly tried our wits; but while we were in the perplexity, a young smart man, a friend of the Misses Stiches, came to the town, and presently old Isaac, as we called him, threw out a clever suggestion.

'I'll go,' said he, 'and bring young Tom Brag to you; and as Tom is in his way a blood, give him a sum of money, say five hundred pounds, and bid him go slily to James Curl, and say to James that he has a great bet, in connexion with others, about cutting a particular man's hair in Beverington during the hours of the election; and I suspect, as James is not likely to make so much by the Gabblon job, that he'll take the money.'

Five hundred pounds went to my heart like the sting of an adder; but it could not be helped, and I consented. But, to our great consternation, James Curl would have nothing to do with Tom's wager.* James was an upright patriot, and, as he said himself, in a general election, England expected every man to do his duty, and he was determined to do his. In short, the plan would not take, and we were driven to our wit's end; for, saving James Curl, Tom Brag had no influence nor acquaintance. Late in the evening we were very dull on the subject; at last said Mr. Tough:

---

* A true bill – the facts of the case are even much more honourable than this to a barber and his conscientious old wife.

'We must keep back one of our own men, or find out where their man is to be concealed, for concealed he will be, and constrain him to the town-hall.'

Now, as James Curl was above purchase, it was clear that Aaron Worsted the woolcomber, would be the abstracted; and accordingly it was determined to watch him. Luckily this was resolved upon in good time; for, just as we were speaking, a man came into the room where we were sitting, and brought out of an inner apartment a large bass-viol in a case, which he carried away. The thing attracted no attention at the time; but, very much to our surprise, soon after another man came back with the naked bass-viol, and put it back into the room.

'Ha, ha!' said Mr. Tough, 'what tune are they playing, to keep the case and send back the fiddle?'

Old Isaac clapped his hands, and, with a sniggering laugh, said, 'I have caught them. Aaron Worsted is a very small man – he could very easily be stowed in the case; and I'll wager my ears and my eyes that it's for his use that the case has been borrowed.'

And with that he rose; and among some of the servants down stairs he did learn that the case was taken to the house of the mayor, which left no doubt on the subject, but assured us that Aaron Worsted was to be hidden therein. Now, the next thing to be done was to get him, in the case, transported to the town-hall, to be ready in the hour of need to be brought forth; and this was not very easily managed. But just, however, when the council was assembling, and the mayor was in the town-hall by a device of Mr. Tough, a countryman, taken from the market-place, went with his cart to Mr. Spicer's house, along with a groom of my lord's, a cunning chap, whom, for a guinea and the pleasure of the spree, Mr. Tough sent to the mayor's wife, to say that he was come for the bass fiddle that ought to have been sent to the castle that morning. Poor Mrs. Spicer, like an innocent daffodil, knowing his lordship's livery, never doubted the message, and consented that the bass-viol should be delivered to him, which was done. But instead of taking his way to the castle, he conducted the cart, with it, to the town-hall, and, with the help of the countryman and others, brought up the case and all its contents into the room where we were all assembled, and laid it down on the floor as a musical instrument. But, by some accident, the lid was laid downmost, at which the poor Mr. Worste within was almost suffocated, and began to heave and endeavour to roll about. In short, he was relieved from durance vile, and the election, with a full board, proceeded; so that Mr. Spicer, for all his stratagems, was obliged to return me duly elected.

Being much fatigued with the day of election, I was little inclined to make a speech from the window, as the use and wont was; but Mr. Gabblon, though he was a mortified man, had still pluck enough to resolve to do so; and accordingly, when the election was declared, he went to one of the windows of the hall, and paternostered to the crowd in a most seditious way, as was to be expected. But they lent a deaf ear to all he said, and he did not make his case a jot the better by it.

For some time while he was speaking, I thought but little of what he said – it was just a bum that went in at the one ear and out at the other; but towards the end I was a little fashed to hear him listened to with sobriety – for he was not without a gift of the gab – and I saw it would be necessary for me to say a few words in return, in the way of offering thanks to the crowd for my election, who, by the way, had as little to say in it as the wild Scot of Galloway.

When the honourable gentleman had finished his oration, I went to the window, very little inclined to be elocutionary; for, as the election cost me a power of money, I could not see wherefore it was to be expected that I should be at any great outlay of words. However, at the incitement of Mr. Tough, I went to the window, and there I beheld, when I looked out, a mob of human cattle, such as may be seen at a fair, the major part of whom were plainly not of the town; so I said with great honesty.

'Gentlemen! I'm much obliged to you all for your assistance this day, and more especially for the votes by which you have returned me the representative in Parliament of this borough of Frailtown, and vindicated your privileges. Not one of you but may lay his hand on his heart and declare that you have given a conscientious vote. I therefore most cordially thank you for maintaining the freedom of election and supporting the independence of your member. But, gentlemen, I am not a man of many words; I am a plain man like one of yourselves; the height of my ambition is to resemble my friends. I can say, therefore, no more to convince you of what I feel on this occasion, than that I thank every one of you from the bottom of my soul for the everlasting obligations you have laid me under.'

I then bowed three times, east, and west, and south; and retired from the window amidst a hurricane of applause, the eldest inhabitant of the borough never having heard a speech so much to the purpose.

In so far I was certainly the hero of the day; but the crowning peace of all was shewn to Mr. Gabblon. I said to him, in the presence of all who were in the hall, that the contest being now over, we should shake hands as friends; and I held out mine, which he had the good sense to take; and thereupon I invited him and his friends to be of our dinner party, and it is not to be described what an hilarious evening we spent together.

Next morning, when all was quiet, Lord Dilldam, with several of his guests that were at the Castle, came over to the borough, and was prodigiously glad that I was chosen, and invited me and my friends to dine with him. Mr. Tough, who was then at my elbow, whispered, 'Decline, decline!' but as I was in a good-humoured vogie mood, I did not perceive the reason of this, and accordingly accepted the invitation; thinking that he would ask Mr. Gabblon likewise, and that all would go off in a most agreeable manner.

But when his lordship took his leave and went away, Mr. Tough said to me, that he was in doubt if I did right, as the new member, in accepting the invitation; 'for,' said he, 'Lord Dilldam is known, at the Treasury and elsewhere, as the supposed patron of the borough; but you owe him no favour, and therefore you should have been upon your guard; for I would be none surprised if from this scene, it were said that you were my lord's member, and counted by the Treasury as such, more especially as his lordship paid no attention to Mr. Gabblon and his friends.'

'We shall see about that,' quo' I; 'his lordship has been very civil in asking me after the fray to come to his house, which I am not loth to do, for I do not think that independence is inconsistent with civility; and therefore, till he makes me a proposition grounded on a sense of obligation, I can see no reason why I should deny myself the gratification of partaking of his hospitality.'

'Well,' said Mr. Tough, 'your sentiment is a very good one if you can adhere to it, but we shall see the result by and by: his lordship is a good country gentleman, one of the king's friends; but we'll see what's thought of you and your independence hereafter by the Treasury. You have, however, Mr. Jobbry, lost an opportunity of standing forth as an independent man, that days and years may wear away before you again recover the 'vantage ground'.

This remark of Mr. Tough disconcerted me at the time, for although he instilled a suspicion into my mind, my easy nature did not allow me to see it was so fraught with danger; but to make a long tale short, we certainly spent a very pleasant day at the Castle. Then I went to Scotland, and put things to right among my affairs there. By that time, the day fixed for the meeting of the new Parliament was drawing near, and I made my arrangements to go to London, to be there at the very opening.

But, guess my astonishment, when by the post before I was ready to set off, down came a letter from the Treasury to me, requesting that I would be present at the meeting of Parliament, as it was understood there was to be a division on the King's speech.

'Oh, ho!' said I, 'the fears of Mr. Tough are about to be verified. Of a certainty I will go, and before the meeting I will give a morning call at the Treasury, to ascertain how it is that I am summoned by their circular, being as independent a man as any other in Parliament, and not reverencing the scowl of a minister of state more than my own shadow in the sunshine.'

It would be wrong to say that I was irreconcilably angry with the understrappers at the Treasury, to dare to consider me as one of the bondmen of the Ministers, but I was not well pleased: so the very same day, on my arrival in London, which was the day before the Parliament met, I happened, Heaven knows how it came to pass, to be daunering past the Horse Guards; and I thought to myself I would just step into the Treasury, and ask what particular business was coming on. I did so, and was received in the politest manner possible; which caused me to remark that I had got their circular, a mark of attention I never expected.

'Oh,' said the secretary, 'we are always very particular to the friends of Lord Dilldam; and when his lordship considered you as one of his members, we could do no less than invite the early attendance of one so distinguished for loyalty and undependence.'

'I am greatly obliged to you,' said I; 'but I did not know before that I was under a particular obligation to his lordship; however, I will attend the address on the King's speech, and no doubt his Majesty's Ministers will make it a net to catch as many fish as they can; and certainly if, with a safe conscience, I can, I will give it my support; but mind, it's not to pleasure Lord Dilldam, but only my own religious conscience.'

It is surely a very extraordinary thing to observe at the meeting of every new Parliament how it is composed; but nothing is so much so as the fact that there is a continual increase of Scotchmen, which is most consolatory to all good subjects. Both England and Ireland have many boroughs represented by Scotchmen, but never yet has it been necessary for Scotland to bring a member out of either of these two nations. This, no doubt, is a cause of her prosperity, quite as much as the Union, of which so much is said, and proves the great utility of her excellent system of parish schools.

The remark occurred to me on the night of the first debate, when I looked round the House and saw of whom it consisted; and I said to a friend near me, before the address was moved, that it was a satisfactory sight to see so many very decent men assembled for the good of the nation; and it was an earnest to me that we would have on that night a more judicious division than for many years past. And, accordingly, it was so, for the King's Ministers had cooked their dish with great skill: no ingredient was in that could well be objected to, and it passed unanimously; so that my principles were put to no strain in doing as the other members did. The next important debate was concerning a matter in which some underling of office took upon him to meddle with an election; and, as I don't much approve of such doings, I resolved, though it was a Government question, to vote against Ministers, and to shew, on the first occasion, that I was independent of Lord Dilldam.

The question itself was of no great consequence, nor a single vote either way of much value; but it was an opportunity to place myself on a right footing with

Ministers: indeed, after the cost that I had been at for my election, it was not pleasant to think that Lord Dilldam was to get all the credit of sending me into Parliament, and my share of the public patronage likewise. Accordingly, to the very visible consternation of the Secretary of State for the Home Department, the Chancellor of the Exchequer, and two young Lords of the Treasury, who were in a great passion, being rash youths, I was found in the patriotic band of the minority. To be sure they said nothing direct to me, but I could discern that they spoke with their eyes; nevertheless, I was none afraid, and resolved to wait the upshot, which I had not long to do; for, in the course of two days, I received a letter begging my interest for Tom Brag, of Frailtown, who had applied to Lord Dilldam for a particular place, but whom his lordship had declined to assist, having promised to give his patronage to another. As Tom had been useful to me in the election, I was, of course, disposed to serve him; and, moreover, I was glad of such an early opportunity to convince Lord Dilldam that I was not to be counted one of his neck-and-heelers. So I went straight to the Secretary of State for the Home Department, and requested that he would let Tom Brag have the place, which he said he would be very happy to do; but he was greatly surprised at the way in which I had voted the other night, Lord Dilldam's members being always considered as among the firmest supporters of Government.

'That,' quo' I, 'may be very true; I am not, however, one of his, but standing on my own pockneuk: the rule does not apply to me. There is no doubt that I am naturally well-disposed towards his Majesty's ministers, but I must have a freedom of conscience in giving my votes. If you will give the lad Tom Brag this bit postie, I will not forget the favour, – giff for gaff is fair play, and you will find I observe it.'

The Minister looked at me with a queer, comical, piercing eye, and smiled; whereupon I inquired if my young man would have the post.

'It will be proper,' replied the Secretary, 'before I give you a definitive answer, that I should have time to investigate the matter.'

'No doubt,' said I; 'but if the place is not promised away, will my friend get it?'

'That's a very home question, Mr. Jobbry.'

'It's my plain way, Mr. Secretary; and as the place is but a small matter, surely you might give me the promise without much hesitation.'

'Yes, Mr. Jobbry, that is easily done; but do you know if it would please Lord Dilldam that we gave it to you.'

'I'll be very evendown with you: as an honest man, Mr. Secretary, I cannot take it on me to say that the appointment of Tom Brag would give heartfelt satisfaction to his lordship; but I have set my mind on getting the place for Tom; and really, Mr. Secretary, you must permit me to think that it's not just proper that an independent member should be refused a civil answer until my lord this or that has been consulted.'

'I beg your pardon, Mr. Jobbry. I hope that you have no cause to think I have been uncivil: a system of conciliation and firmness belongs to Ministers on all occasions.'

'True, true,' said I: 'so Lord Sidmouth said would be the conduct of his ministry towards France, and then he went to war with them. But even, Mr. Secretary, although you may go to war with me in your conciliation and firmness, as I consider a refusal in this matter would be, it will make no difference in the ordinary questions in Parliament; but you know that, from time to time, the Opposition make harassing motions, in which the good of the nation has no concern, though the felicity of Ministers may. You understand.'

'Really,' replied the Secretary of State, laughing, 'you are a very extraordinary man, Mr. Jobbry.'

'I am an honest member of Parliament.'

'I see you are,' was the reply.

'Then if you do, Mr. Secretary, you will promise me the place.'

In short, from less to more, I did not leave him till I got the promise; and from that time I heard no more of my Lord Dilldam.

I have been the more particular in this recital, as it was the first occasion on which I had to vindicate my independence; and it was well for me that I did it in a manner so very complete, for soon after there was a change of administration; and had I not done as I did, I must have gone to the right about, and lost every benefit and advantage that induced me to leave my pleasant country improvements in Scotland, to stew myself at the midnight hour with the cantrips of the House of Commons.

But, though this affair was not without the solace of a satisfaction, it was rather an inroad on my system; for, as my object in procuring a seat was to benefit my kith and kin, and to stick a harmless feather in my own cap, I was not quite content to give my patronage to a stranger. Thomas Brag had, no doubt, a claim upon me, and I very readily acknowledged it, especially as it helped to shew me in my true colours; but it would have been far more congenial to my principles had I got the post for a son of my own cousin, whom it would have fitted to a hair. But men in public life, and trafficking with affairs of state, must not expect every thing their own way; so I said nothing, but pocketed the loss, and pruned my wing for another flight, like the hawk in his jesses.

There is not a more confounding thing in the whole art and system of the British Government than the accident of a change of ministry. To those who are heartily bound, either by principle, ignorance, or selfishness, to the men that have been in power, it is most calamitous;- for those of principle are naturally grieved to see themselves cut off from further ameliorations; the ignorant, not knowing what to do, are as helpless as the innocent babes in the wood; and the selfish are the worst off of all, not being sure if they shall be able to get themselves enlisted by the new set. None are safe on such an occasion but the independent members. Thank Heaven! I was of that corps, and sat still in my place when the change happened. It is very true, that the gentleman who was the Secretary of State when I spoke my mind so freely anent Tom Brag, said to me, on the first night after the change, in a satirical manner, 'that I seemed to find my old seat very comfortable'.

I replied, with a dry dignity, 'that I had a deaf ear, and could only properly understand what was said on the ministerial side of the House'; and I looked very grave as I said this, which caused him to look so likewise, and to redden as if he could have felt in his heart to be angry; whereupon I nothing daunted, added: 'You know, Mr. Secretary that was, that I am an independent member, and that it is only the weathercocks that veer about with every wind of doctrine. Depend upon it, Mr. Secretary that was, that I am as steady to the point from which the right wind blows as the cock on Kitrone steeple, that the plumber so fastened that it should ever point to the warm and comfortable south.'

'You are a strange man,' said he.

'And you,' said I, 'intend to account me a stranger!'

He was still more confounded; and seeing myself in possession of the advantage, I continued, for it was very impudent of him to notice to me on what side of the House I sat. Wasn't I free to choose?

'And so, Mr. Secretary that was'; and I gave him a cajoling wink to mitigate the sarcasm, 'if an impeachment be likely to take place, I will be found at my post and doing my duty.'

This sent him off with his tail between his legs; for there is a great difference visible in the courage of a minister in or out of place and the termagant fellows that rule the roast.

This brief conversation took place in the House, and I saw the eyes of all parties fixed on me; but I was true blue. At the same time I could not but have a sympathy and a sore heart for the humbled and dejected creatures that I saw filling the benches over against me, – so I said to Mr. Shiftly, one of those that had come over to our side, that it was a very distressing thing to see men who had been so proud and bold, carrying every thing with a high hand and such lofty heads, not able to get a vote for love nor money, – love, of course, they had none, and as for their money, poor men! notwithstanding their sinecures they were objects of condign pity.

But, besides the claims which the occurrence of a change of ministry has on the tender generosity and compassion of independent members, it is most delightful to observe how the new ministers comport themselves. Being unacquainted with business, they are of course naturally very much averse to receive hints and suggestions; but then they are also wonderfully complaisant; and, as Mr. Shiftly, when we were talking on the subject, said to me on this head, 'that all Arabia breathed from the Government offices'.

It might be so; and I will not deny that I had a blandishment of the universal dalliance; but as they became better settled in their seats they grew less and less courteous, and at last hardened down into as cold a marble as their predecessors. Many that had come over to them spoke to me of this official petrifaction; and, to tell the truth, I was not myself without a grudge at the grandeur they began to assume; but as I had an object of my own to serve, I thought it as well to see no more than was just prudent; by which discretion I was soon on as satisfactory a footing with them as I had been with the foregoing set: in sooth, I was rather better; for Lord Dilldam and his own members stuck to the heels of the outs like loch leeches to the old women's legs that wade for them; and it was a marvel among the best informed how I could be so venturesome as to keep my seat, and still sit on the same side of the house. For this I was called Abdiel.

The most grievous thing of all, however, which happens in a change of administration, arises from the complaints that come in from all the airts of the wind against the old ministry, and which are chiefly directed to those members who remain stanch in their independent support of Government. I had my own share of this trouble; and how to manage it in between what was due in justice to the complainants, and what was called for by expediency to my old friends, was most perplexing. At first, I received several petitions and applications with every disposition to look into their merits; but the more I received, and the more I was willing to listen to them, the number increased, till I saw there was no end to it but to shut the doors of impartiality on them all.

For the most part this was a judicious resolution; for, attached to every case was a long story, and if I had not come speedily to the resolution which I did, the whole of my precious time would have been taken up in hearing nothing all the morning but 'wally, wally up yon bank'; and the o'ercome of the same song at night – 'wally, wally down yon brae'.

But let it not be supposed that I was altogether iron-hearted, and would admit no petition, for I had my exceptions to the rule, or rather, I was constrained to have them by my friends, who knew my perseverance when I had a turn in hand, urging me to interest myself, sometimes when the case was very imminent; but, for the most part, really, it seemed to me that men who have causes of complaint are often as unreasonable as those of whom they complain; and it was in consequence of being persuaded of this truth that I resolved to be abstemious in undertaking the redress of grievances and the righting of wrongs. Still, as I say, it behoved me to make, now and then, an exception; but in this I drew a line of distinction, saying to myself, 'It's not possible for a member, be he ever so honest and independent, to take up all cases for the aggrieved; and therefore a discreet man will first make a distinction as to the general class of grievances that he will patronise, and then select particular cases deserving his patronage.' It thus came to pass that I made my selection upon the following principle: First and foremost, I resolved to confine myself to the line of widows and orphans; and accordingly, unless the matter referred to a widow with children, or orphans without parents, it was out of my way. This limited my trouble to a comparatively moderate class, and of that class I limited myself to cases of singular hardship and great distress. It nevertheless happened, now and then, that an importunate petitioner would force me to break through this rule; and, by dint of argument, or the power of persuasion, seduce me to take his part. Instances of this were, however, rare; but the new Ministry had not been many weeks in the saddle, and were going at an easy canter – a Canterbury trot, as easy as Chaucer's pilgrims from the Borough along the Kent road – when a sedate man called on me to advocate his suit. But as it is a story of some length, I must make it the substance of another chapter.

Mr. Selby was a private gentleman, who had lived in one of the colonies, and who had suffered a great deal in his property by an invasion of the enemy, in consequence of which he was greatly reduced; but his conduct under his distressing circumstances was so exemplary, that the governor, in the king's name, promised that he would be repaid. But many years passed before any thing was done, during which every expedient was put in force to get rid of the obligation to pay him. At last, however, the stubborn truths of the case could no longer be withstood; and a bankrupt dividend was advanced to him, with promises.

The poor man seeing himself so treated, but having still a great affection for Government, bethought him if he could point out a way, and with their consent, by which the requisite fund could be raised, he would be remunerated. This he did, and a very large amount, which did not cost the Government a shilling, was obtained; but, lo and behold, when he applied for the payment of his debt, he was told that the money was appropriated to other purposes!

'Very well,' says he, 'if that be the case, pay me for my trouble in being the means of doing so much public good by getting to you so large a sum of money.'

This was his case; and on my advice he wrote to the minister in whose department the affair lay; but, instead of getting any redress, he got a point-blank refusal, without a word being assigned of any reason for such contemptuous treatment. Thus the man was ruined and driven to beggary, for nothing more was afterwards paid him of his great losses; and he was, in consequence, obliged to become a clerk to a merchant; and what added anguish to his misfortune, he was told that the situation, which had as little to do with

Government as the man in the moon, not so much maybe, was ample compensation.

To take up a case of this kind after all had been done that was possible, and to reason in the public offices, and bring it before Parliament by one that was no speaker, required consideration. I was in my humanity well disposed to do what I could for the poor man, and I told him that it would greatly strengthen his cause if he got the opinion of divers other members and acute men to say what they thought of his claim. This, it will be allowed, was judicious advice on my part, inasmuch as I could not see very clearly that it was a matter of law, though it was plainly one of right and justice.

He did so accordingly; and every one who examined his case was of my opinion, and bore the strongest testimony to the fairness of his demand, and the equity of making him a compensation for his trouble: they only differed about what the amount should be. Fortified with these opinions, I then advised him to petition the Honourable House; but at that crisis the change of administration took place, and I thought that as there might be a more lenient spirit in the new Government than had been among those with whom he had formerly to deal, I said to him, we would stop going forward with his petition, and apply to the new ministers.

Thus it came to pass that I was myself, in the end, rendered accessary to a very cruel transaction. The poor man's means had been in a great measure exhausted by his losses; but, still flattered by hope of ultimate redress, he kept on his way in an even tenor, until all the relics of what he had were nearly exhausted, and his time spent thriftlessly. In these circumstances I went to the new minister and stated his situation, but days and weeks passed without an answer; and at last, when one was given, it was to the same effect as the former; and Mr. Selby, with his family, were in consequence utterly undone. I did not, however, think so, or rather, I wished to think otherwise, and advised him still to go to Parliament; but he remarked, 'that although moderate disappointment is sometimes a spur to endeavour, continual disappointment never fails to break the heart. I have not the means left of going to Parliament, for justice has its money-price in England; nor can I afford the time: my case, I apprehend, is not uncommon, but it is not the less hard to me.'

I was very sorry to hear him say this, and comforted him, as well as I could, with hopes that I well knew were as empty as blown soap-bells and bubbles; and it cut my tender feelings very much when he said: 'Mr. Jobbry, I am greatly obliged to you for your friendliness in this matter; but adversity is an eye-salve; and when distress comes, good subjects grow scarce.'

I inquired what he meant, and he replied, 'I think, sir, if you look at my case, both first and last, you will see that I have cause to say, that there is no sedition in being of opinion that a reform is wanted in the British Government.'

'Wheesht! Mr. Selby, – wheesht! you must not allow yourself to hint of such a thing.'

'I cannot help it, Mr. Jobbry; I am only sorry to see that the roaring multitude make a sad mistake in the question, crying out for reformation in Parliament, when the whole ail and sore is in the withers and loins of the executive government.'

'What do you mean, Mr. Selby?'

'Only this, – the business of all governments is to enforce the law, but their own practice is to regard its principles as little as possible; and thus all reforms are but changing words, until governments are as much bound towards their subjects by principles as one individual is to another. It cannot, however, be long endured, that governments may continue to do only their own will, and have no respect for justice unless it happens to be supported by parliamentary influence. A man of a just and high mind, who will trust to his rights, and not to the interference of his friends, has no chance, under the existing system, of getting even a moiety of justice.'

'Hoot, toot, toot! Mr. Selby, ye must not speak in that manner.'

'I have reason, Mr. Jobbry. To be sure, the atom which an individual is in a great state may seem an insignificant thing in the view of those that sit in high places; but the poor beetle that we tread upon feels as much in its anguish as the giant. Till Governments, and Houses of Commons, and those institutions which the sinful condition of man renders necessary, are made responsible to a tribunal of appeal, whose decisions shall control them, there can be no effectual reform. The first step is to take away all will of its own from Government – for statesmen are but mere men, rarely in talent above the average of their species, from what I have seen – and oblige it to consider itself no better than an individual, even with respect to its own individual subjects. Let the law in all things be paramount, and it will little matter whether the lords or the vagabonds send members to Parliament; at least, it is my opinion that it will not be easy to find five or six hundred gentlemen much better than the present members of Parliament.'

'That's a very sensible remark, Mr. Selby.'

'Nor,' continued he, 'is it likely that half a million of electors will make a better choice than a smaller number. In fact, the wider the basis of representation is spread, the greater will be the quantity of folly that it will embrace: and we have only to look at the kind of persons whom the multitude send to Parliament, to anticipate what will be the character of a reformed house. Look at the moiety of Westminster, for example.'

'All that may be very true, Mr. Selby; and I am glad to hear that ye're not a reformer.'

'I beg your pardon; I am a very firm one, but not of the parliamentary sort. I desire to see the law purified and exalted, that mankind may enjoy the true uses of government – protection. But it was a wish and an aim – it is so no longer.'

With these words he went away; but there was a tone of sorrow and anger in my remembrance of them, like the scent of sour in a vessel that has been used for holding sweet ingredients; and I was for some time very uneasy. Soon after, I met him in the street a very altered man. I stopped, and kindly inquired how he was.

'As well as can be expected,' said he.

'You don't look so.'

'No,' said he; 'because the disappointment is working

to its effect. At my time of life it is not easy to learn a new way of living to what I have been accustomed to – new friends, new habits – all the world a-new – especially when to privation is added a galling sense of wrong – contumely in return for good.'

'Oh! you must not let yourself think that way; it will only make your distress greater.'

'I intend it should do so,' said he, sternly: 'I only wish it would do it a little more quickly.'

He then went away, and I never again saw aught of him; but in due time I shall recite the sequel.

The concern of Mr. Selby troubled me a great deal; for although I could see that he was fully entitled to a handsome recompense, there was yet evidently a rule applied against him of an unsatisfactory kind. For the man himself I was sincerely grieved, because, as he had rendered a service which could not be denied, it seemed to me that something must be rotten in the state of Denmark which allowed the time and ingenuity of any man to be taken from him without a compensation, especially as John Bull is a free payer of all that do him any good. From the impression that Mr. Selby had made upon me, I began to turn my mind more on the frame and nature of our Government; for although I went into Parliament with the full intention of administering my share of the Government patronage with judgement and sensibility, and to keep aloof as much as possible from political matters, particularly of those that related to France and foreign countries, I yet saw that there was some jarring and jangling in the working of the State, that was not just agreeable. Thus it happens that knowledge grows upon us; but when I came to reflect that the choice of the limbs and members of Government is naturally limited to a very few, who, from their station in society, have not the best opportunities of acquiring a right knowledge of the world, my opinions underwent a change; and I soon perceived a wide difference between reverence for the Government, and attachment to the men of whom it is composed.

'Every government,' said I to myself, one night when I came home early from a drowsy wrangle of a committee on the estimates – 'Every government is a sort of machine, that is naturally formed out of the habits, morals, and manners of its respective people. We in this country are fond of monarchy: in no country do people know their respective situations with regard to one another so well as in this. Indeed, I have heard most intelligent men in India say, that the order of castes, though of a different kind, prevailed as strikingly in England as among the Hindoos; and certainly the sense of subordination in the different degrees of life is here very perfect: even Nature seems herself to minister to this; for just look at the stout, short, civil, spirited little men that she breeds for grooms and servants, and compare them with the tall, lank, genteel aristocracy of their masters. To follow out the comparison to the different orders of society would not be consistent with my plan: it is only indeed necessary that I should advert to the natural cause that produces the political effect. We are plain and palpably to the sight a nation disposed to a monarchical form of government, and I have no doubt that where other kinds of governments prevail, other sorts of people will be found. This fact granted, as it must be, and the choice of rulers being limited to a small number, it must of course come to pass that talent – which nature does not seem to give out to ranks, like physical peculiarity – will, as it has ever been, be distributed among the community at large. There are not distinct races of genius, which does not procreate, as there are races of horses and dogs; and thus it happens, that from time to time the natural class from which the government is formed is obliged to borrow talent from the inferior classes. It is, however, not a very safe and solid thing: when this is requisite, it either betokens mutations and revolutions, or is an effect of them.'

This very well-considered opinion of mine has grown into an article of faith; and yet it has not made me greatly content with a very common practice among those who, by their station, are entitled to bear the bell in the Government, namely, that of their too frequent custom of sucking the brains of their inferiors, and casting away the rind. But still, though it is a custom that cannot but be condemned, it rises, I fear, out of circumstances that are beyond the control and measures of man. It no doubt breeds discontent: the sappy brains that are sucked without being paid for, grow acrid and sour, and, like rotten oranges in a box, they infect their neighbours; and thus it often is, that those to whom governments are most obliged, become their most dangerous and evil subjects, inasmuch as from them proceed those acrimonious opinions that, sooner or later, corrode the established well-being of the state.

But although it is very fit that I should here describe the course of reflection into which the unjust and ill usage that Mr. Selby suffered led me, his was not the only case of the kind that tended to rivet my opinion: several others soon after occurred; and although none of them could be said, like his, to be a claim for reward in consequence of success, yet all and every one of them were for authorised services of an experimental kind, in which the remuneration was withheld.

To what conclusion this course of thought might have led me, I cannot determine; – certainly never to have sided with those who were diffusing the delusion, that a redress of the causes of discontent was to be effected by giving the unenlightened many, an increase of dominion over the enlightened few. Governments are things of nature, and cannot be changed nor removed but by the progress of seasons and time, except with great confusion. They are like hills——However, my meditations were interrupted rather abruptly; for, not meddling myself overly with even our home politics, I was roused out of what I would call my easy acquiescence with the proceedings of Government, by a sudden dissolution of Parliament. Some difference on a speculative question caused a division in the cabinet, and the new ministry appealed to the people, as it is called: I had therefore to cleek Mr. Tough in my arm and hurry away to Frailtown; where I was told that Lord Dilldam, though an excellent quiet country gentleman, was so offended at my adhering to the opponents of his party, that he was determined to oust me from the borough.

I had an apprehension that my abiding on the Treasury side of the House, at the change of ministry, was not agreeable to Lord Dilldam, and was therefore none surprised when informed of his determination to throw the weight of his influence against me in the election; insomuch that I had begun to have some conversation with Sir Abimelech Burgos, who was proprietor of three boroughs in the West; but the suddenness of the dissolution broke off the negotiation, and, upon the advice of Mr. Tough, a real clever man at an election job, I resolved to try my own luck again at Frailtown.

When we reached the borough – and I took care on this occasion not to slumber nor sleep by the way – we drove at once to the Royal Oak; and Mr. Tough, with most excellent dexterity, agreed with the landlord that we should have the use of the whole house for a certain sum of money.

This was a very capital stroke of policy; for as all the other public houses in the town were of a mean order, he considered that Mr. Gales, my lord's new candidate and kinsman, would make his head-quarters at the grand hotel in Physickspring; because he was a beau that dressed nicely, and was in all things dainty and delicate. But the main reason that Mr. Tough had in driving Mr. Gales to that hotel was, a dislike which the inhabitants of Frailtown bore to the upsetting garish pride of every thing about Physickspring.

'It may seem,' said Mr. Tough, 'that this is a trifling matter, considering the close corporation and singular constitution of the borough; but the generality of mankind, unconsciously to themselves, are governed by public opinion; and we may rest assured, that the populace will not be satisfied with Mr. Gales, and that their dissatisfaction will more or less tell on the town council.'

I thought his remark very shrewd, but we had both great fears of my success; for that inveteracy, Mr. Spicer, was mayor a second time; and old pawky Isaac Gleaning was in an ailing way, and could not give the effectual assistance that I received from him, for a consideration, at the former election: so, after we had paid a few visits together, I came home to the Royal Oak rather in a subsiding mood, and had just said to Mr. Tough, in meditative sobriety, that

> 'The troubles which afflict the just
> In number many be;'

when who should come into the room, to pay me his respect, but that ramplor young fellow, Tom Brag, that I had got the post so cleverly for.

His office was not in Frailtown, but in the neighbouring more considerable place of Beverington: no sooner, however, had the thankful lad heard of my arrival, than he came over in his gratitude to offer me his services. He was a prize; for although he had no great weight with the town council, he had a supple hand at a trick. It was not, however, my business to be seen in any thing of the sort; so I left Mr. Tough and him to concoct their own stratagems; and, in the mean time, being perfectly independent, I did not think it necessary to shew myself under any particular reverence for my Lord Dilldam. Accordingly, just as a matter of course, I threw myself into a post-chaise, and drove over to pay my respects in an ordinary civil manner at the Castle. His lordship, at the sight of me, was in the greatest consternation, especially when I said to him: 'My lord, although me and Mr. Gales are likely to have a rough tussle in the oncoming election, there can be no reason why I should not continue to behave with decorum and respect to your lordship.'

'In truth, Mr. Jobbry,' was his reply, 'I never thought, from the ease with which I allowed you to carry the election last time, that you would have made so light of that favour.'

By this short speech I got some insight into his lordship's

character, and could see that, although he was a most respectable nobleman, consistent in his principles and moderate in his public temper, yet he had not an ill conceit of himself; – so I said, touching my lips as it were with honey, that 'it was a great pity I did not rightly understand the potentiality of his lordship in the borough; and that I was not a politician, but a sober domestic member, attending chiefly to the local improvements of the kingdom, only voting on occasional political questions with ministers; and, really, that I had thought his lordship's great experience of business in Parliament would, without any explanation, have satisfied him that changes in the heads of the Government were but secondary matters with the like of me; my great end and purpose being to get my own obligations to the public righteously performed, which could not be done if I veered about from side to side like a party man.'

On hearing this, his lordship looked most well pleased; and said, 'that my principles did me honour as a man, and that it was to be regretted we did not understand each other better; for,' continued he, 'it was not so much because you gave in your adherence to the new ministers that I objected, as it was because you were supposed to act independent of me.'

'My lord,' said I, feeling the full force of what he said, 'misunderstandings will arise between the best of friends; and I am very sorry to say that, to all appearance, I am likely soon to repent I was not so conjunct with your lordship.'

'Yes, Mr. Jobbry, you may have cause to repent; for now you will feel the force of my influence; and you may be assured that I shall leave no means untried to secure the borough for my young relation, Mr. Gales. At the same time, Mr. Jobbry, I will do you the justice to acknowledge, that had a better understanding existed between us, I would not have allowed Mr. Gales to oppose you; for, although he made some figure at college, – he's an excellent classical scholar, and can compose and deliver speeches of great promise, – he is not exactly the sort of man that I would have chosen; for I want a man of business among those whom I make the depositaries of my influence.'

In short, his lordship and me became very couthy, and he said 'he would return my visit next day; for that in all things he thought we should act as honourable rivals for the love of that fair damsel, the borough of Frailtown, (an unproductive old maid, or rather unmarried lady,) and seek to win her smiles and favour by our chivalry, maintaining a mutal courtesy towards each other.'

So far my visit to the Castle was auspicious; and when I returned to the borough, I told Mr. Tough what had passed; upon which he laughed, and said, – 'In the desperation of our circumstances, you cannot do better than so continue the war in the enemy's territory; for, to tell the truth, your protogee, Tom Brag, is not very sanguine in his opinion of our success; but the fellow has great tact, and he tells me that our only chance lies in annoying Mr. Gales personally, so as to disgust him with the borough; for he is morbidly sensitive, and is easily molested by a small trifle. Now, your tactics are to conciliate my lord, and I have settled with Tom Brag that his are to annoy Mr. Gales, which we are in the better condition to do by having the commonalty on our side, and by taking up our residence in this plain homely manner in the town.'

I agreed that the view which Mr. Tough had taken of the state of my case was very judicious; and accordingly we arranged to act upon what I called the double-dealing principle, – for really it was so, both in its morality and practice. But men have a licence in the time of a general election, and I availed myself of no more than the common privileges of the saturnalia.

I am, of course, having been the candidate, not very well acquainted with the devices which had been concerted between Thomas Brag and Mr. Tough; I heard, however, that, among others, they agreed to keep in their pay a gang of skittle-players, fearless, ne'er-do-weels, who were kept constantly on the ree with ale and strong liquor, and were to hold themselves in readiness for any exploit at a moment's call.

With these, accordingly, when my lord returned his visit next day, in great pomp, with four horses and outriders, and yet without Mr. Gales' cockade, the phenomenon attracted public wonder; and, somehow, Tom Brag's skittle-players got an inkling of the business, and during his lordship's visit they gathered round the inn-door, with all the ragamuffinry of the town, shouting and making a fearful noise. I could see, when my lord heard them, that he was a little disturbed; but I told him how I had quietly allowed it to be known that his lordship's visit to me was entirely of a friendly nature, and therefore I wished that it should not be mixed up with the business of the election.

'That was most considerate of you, Mr. Jobbry,' said his lordship, 'and I might just have expected so from a man of your sagacity; and therefore I hope you will come in a friendly manner and dine with me at the Castle tomorrow.'

'Your lordship has a fine taste,' said I; 'and certainly nothing will give me more pleasure; but since you have condescended to put our intercourse upon that dignified footing, I will only make one condition.'

'Well,' said his lordship, 'it is granted, without knowing what it may be.'

'My Lord Dilldam,' quo' I, 'in doing so, you have only shewn the courtesy of your own nature, and paid me what I feel to be a great compliment. The condition, therefore, that I propound, is one that I humbly hope will be congenial to your lordship's own benign nature: I but request that you will invite Mr. Gales and his friends to be of the party; and that all about it shall be of the same conciliatory and chivalric description.'

'You have plucked the idea from my own head,' said his lordship; 'I was just about to propose the same thing; I only hesitated lest you should think I was taking too great a liberty.'

'My dear lord,' said I, 'liberty! – it is an honour that I was diffident to propose.'

We accordingly shook hands in the most cordial manner. I saw him to the steps of his carriage, assisted him in, and expressed to him, as the door was about to be shut, how deeply I felt the honour of his visit. At these words, Tom Brag, who was in the crowd, gave me a knowing wink, and presently his skittlers and the crowd gave three cheers, and his lordship drove away, as proud as a cock on his own dunghill.

Presently after, Mr. Tough came to me to hear what had passed, and I told him; at which he really chuckled with delight, requesting me to ask no questions; but adding, 'that Tom Brag was, for a trick, the very eldest born of Beelzebub.'

Just while we were speaking, it came to pass that Mr. Gales came riding with great pomp and pageantry; but as the Little-good would have it, Tom Brag's crew – as if to shew a distinction between the scented classical young man and his lordship – gave enfeoffment of the borough, as the Scotch lawyers say, with yird and stane – that is, they pelted him with all manner of abominations from the street, till they made him a perfect object, and sent all his coadjutors after him in whirlwinds of mud, yelling and yelping out of the town.

What was to be done for this uproar? It was clear that his lordship, in his visit to me, had been received with every demonstration of the greatest respect; but the treatment of his candidate was a proof, beyond all doubt, that it was not his lordship, but the candidate, that was unpopular.

'You must,' said Mr. Tough to me, with as grave a face as he could possibly put on, 'reprimand Tom Brag for not checking this ebullition of popular fury, and send at once to his lordship to express your regret at this untoward action.'

'I will leave the matter,' said I, shaking my head, (whether I smiled or frowned, the reader may guess) 'entirely to you, Mr. Tough; but be sure and make it plain to his lordship's understanding how displeased I am that my party should have manifested such a spirit against his lordship's candidate, while they treated himself with so much respect.'

This was no sooner said than done. Tom Brag, who was himself the very head and front of the offending, was dressed in his best in a jiffy, mounted on his horse, and away to Dilldam Castle, with my compliments; where he did not remain long, but came back to me before my consternation was half over, and told me the many kind things his lordship had said to him concerning my character, and how he thought that if every contested election in the kingdom was managed in the same spirit of candour and fairness, how very little trouble there would be; that as for what had happened to Mr. Gales, it was a thing to be expected; and that party spirit, he could himself see, ran high in the borough, but it was only among the lower orders; thank God! the candidates, as principals, had no share in the licentiousness of the mob.

An elder of the kirk of Scotland, from behind the plate on the Lord's day, could not have told his tale with more decorum than that unreverent young man, Tom Brag; but it was with a great difficulty that I could reply to him in a becoming manner; so I only shook my head, at the which he ran out of the room as if he would have died of laughter.

'Now,' said Mr. Tough, who was present, after Tom had gone away, 'you have made a good lodgment with my lord, let us not lose the advantage, for it is our only chance. That acrimonious fellow, Mr. Spicer, the mayor, is all alive and awake to the manner in which his power under the charter may be exerted: we shall not be able to counteract him; he has already settled who are to be the five good men and true that he is to summon from the market-place, all firm adherents of his own. At the same time, he calculates that there will be no need to have recourse to that alternative; but I have heard that, since my lord's visit to you, he has been looking a little black. You must therefore, as your only chance of carrying the borough, establish yourself well with his patron, my lord.'

'Never fear,' quo' I, 'a nod and a wink are both alike to a blind horse: but what shall we do, Mr. Tough, even were his lordship brought over to my side, if this ungrateful devil be so against us, either in the council or by the five good men and true?'

'Trust to Providence, and do your best,' cried Mr. Tough.

This shews to what desperation our cause was reduced.

Next day I was ready betimes to go to the Castle, where it was publicly understood that I was to dine; and when I set out I was attended by a great retinue of the commonalty. In going along I saw behind a clump of trees an assemblage of men and boys having Mr. Gales's cockades in their hats: the sight daunted me, but the crowd that was round my carriage gave them three cheers; and as I happened just at the moment to discern among them Tom Brag in a smock-frock, my dismay cleared off like a cloud in a May morning; and I drove on cheerfully to the Castle.

It was well I did so; for soon after, Mr. Gales came in full puff in his barouche; and the crowd, coming from the plantation, received him with shouts, and laughter, and great applause. He seeing that they wore his colours, was greatly delighted; and a proud man was he when he saw them take the horses from his carriage, and bidding the servants get down, dragged him along, like captivity leading captive.

He thought they were drawing him in triumph to Castle Dilldam; but, to his astonishment, they took another road, and drew him into a pool in the river, where, wishing him good day, they left him sitting in his horseless carriage, cooling his heels, till his servants could get him out.

The servants were not, however, long in coming up, and, with the assistance of Tom Brag and his skittlers, they made haste to draw the carriage from the pool; but, by some accident, it so happened that in this business the carriage was overset, and Mr. Gales tumbled headlong into the water, where he would have been drowned but for the presence of mind and ready hand of Tom, who caught him just in time by the cuff of the neck, and dragged him, more dead than alive, to the shore.

Such is the account that I received of the disaster; but what happened at the Castle, and which was within my own knowledge, requires me here to make a more circumstantial recital.

Lord Dilldam was very energetic on points of punctuality connected with his dinner-hour; and accordingly, as he had for the occasion assembled many of his neighbours, he was vexed that Mr. Gales did not come at the time appointed. We sat down to dinner, and still he was not forthcoming. It was not, however, my business, considering the object in view, to take much pains to appease his lordship's displeasure, and therefore I said,

'It was surprising that Mr. Gales, who knew our party was one of reconciliation, should neglect to come.'

I saw that my remark troubled his lordship still more, and it was soon visible to the whole company that he was an angry man.

A short time after dinner Mr. Gales made his appearance, and his reception was not one of the most cordial kind.

He excused himself by stating, rather, I must say, with good humour, in what way he had been deceived by the false colours of Tom Brag and his party.

'Pooh, pooh!' cried Lord Dilldam, 'don't excuse your own heedlessness: you ought not to have been deceived by a mere electioneering trick. What would rescued Europe and the British nation have thought of the sagacity of the Duke of Wellington at the battle of Waterloo, had he been deceived by Napoleon dressing his army in scarlet like the English soldiers?'

Mr. Gales, who was still a little disturbed, replied,

'Upon my honour, my lord, I do not see much fitness in the comparison.'

'I daresay not, and that makes your inattention the more palpable; for the numbers you had to contend with were a mere trifle compared to the thousands on that illustrious day. In fact, Gales, I am not pleased. This was an occasion on which the political tranquillity of the county depended; and if your condition was really such that you were obliged to go back to Physickspring, you might have sent one of your fellows to apprise me of your disaster.'

Here I thought fit to edge in a pacifying word:

'My lord,' said I, 'you must excuse Mr. Gales under such a comical misfortune; for every one would not, in such circumstances, have been able to preserve his self-possession. No doubt, self-possession during a debate in the House is——'

'Yes,' said his lordship, 'I know it; and it is that – the want of self-possession – that makes me the more grieved, sir; it is the first quality in a Member of Parliament – eloquence is but the second; and a man possessed only of eloquence, without self-possession, is very apt to make a fool of himself.'

The rector of the parish, Dr. Bacon, who was there, remarked that his lordship had made a philosophical observation. It was plain, however, that the harmony of the company was broken, and that Lord Dilldam was in no very good humour with his candidate. Indeed, it was quite evident that a very little persuasion would have induced his lordship to cast him off; and it was equally obvious that Mr. Gales himself did not think very complacently of his part in the election drama. Indeed, a hope began to dawn in my bosom that they would quarrel, and that I should only have to walk the course. However, nothing happened that night; and I returned to the borough, after having spent a most agreeable evening; for, although my lord's temper was in a state of erysipelas, I could not, without a breach of truth, say that it did not give me satisfaction. This was increased when, on my return, I saw a great light shining from the market-place, and on approaching the Royal Oak, beheld the front illuminated with letters made of wine-glasses fastened by strings, with small lighted wicks in each, like lamps, displaying the words, in great splendour, 'RECONCILIATION – DILLDAM AND JOBBRY FOREVER,' – and all the town ranting and revelling before the door.

At first I thought this was a little too much; but when Mr. Tough laughingly told me that it was a suggestion of his own, I knew it was not without sagacity.

'In truth,' said he, 'this is not a time for modesty. We

must make the most we can of your visit to my lord: it has already abashed our adversaries. Mr. Gales, it is known, damned the borough when he was pulled out of the water, and threatened to give up the contest. If we are to be defeated, let us not fall without a struggle.'

I then told him what had passed at dinner; upon which he said, 'All works well; and before the mob dispenses, we shall circulate a story about the quarrel of my lord and Mr. Gales: no particulars will be given, but only that there has been a quarrel, – the imagination of the populace will soon supply particulars.'

The young stand by principle, the old by law, the wise by expediency, and the foolish by their own opinion. Much of this truth was visible in the controversies of our election. All the youth of the town were next morning on my side, – the elderly persons did not approve of such a departure from ancient custom, as the countenance which they thought Lord Dilldam gave to me against his own candidate, – and the judicious few were of opinion that one of the candidates should withdraw; it being of little importance which, for any good the borough was to get by either: but the great bulk of the people had declared themselves for me, and were determined to support me through thick and thin.

Such was the report of the state of public opinion I received in the morning. 'But,' said Mr. Tough, when he had made it, 'the aspect of all things is brightening. Your most determined enemy, Mr. Spicer, is indisposed, and confined to bed: his disease, I have no doubt, comes of the reported quarrel between my lord and Mr. Gales; and he is mortified that he may be required by Lord Dilldam to support you. I suspect, from the pride and pertinacity of the man, that he will rather remain at home ill than attend the election. I think we have the ball at our foot. If he absents himself tomorrow, the great day, from the town-hall, then the oldest counsellor must go to the market-cross and summon five good men and true; and if he do not, then the next senior counsellor must go. Now the senior counsellor is a weak, old, infirm man, not at all likely, in the present excited state of the town, to venture to the market-place; and the next counsellor is stanch to our party, and will readily do the duty; I shall, therefore, instruct him on the subject, and he will call by name five who will serve our purpose, and whom I shall have ready on the spot.'

Greatly, however, to our surprise, next morning no new occurrence had taken place. Mr. Spicer was charming well again, and every thing wore a frown to my cause. The multitude from all parts of the country round poured into the town in flocks, to conserve their rights and privileges; but no message nor tidings were heard either from the Castle or Mr. Gales; yet Mr. Spicer was courageous, and went buzzing about as brisk as a bee.

I did not like, nor did Mr. Tough like, the ominous silence of no messenger from the Castle, nor forerunner from Mr. Gales: we were confounded; for this sudden secession of Lord Dilldam was inexplicable, and the conduct of Mr. Gales was irreconcilable with his interests as a candidate; and yet the bravery of Mr. Spicer, the mayor, in this uncertainty, was equally unaccountable.

Mr. Tough and I were thus reflecting together, when suddenly starting up, he exclaimed, 'The day may be our own, but ask no questions.'

Out of the room he instantly ran; and Tom Brag, on horseback, was soon seen galloping on the road to the Castle.

'What is he about?' said I to Mr. Tough; who only replied, 'Ask no questions.'

In a short while after, we went through the shouting multitude to the town-hall together, where we beheld, to our dismay, the mayor and council assembled; and Mr. Gales, who had come in by a back door, fearful of outrage, standing at Mr. Spicer's right hand.

'We are undone,' whispered I to Mr. Tough. 'Not yet,' said he, panting with awe and dread.

Then an officer being about to open the courts to begin the business, a cry got up that an express had come from my lord, with a letter to the mayor. Who brought that letter was never known to me; for the hall being crammed with spectators, and surrounded by the populace, it was handed over head from one to another till it was delivered.

The mayor on receiving it opened it with a trembling hand. It was a note with Lord Dilldam's compliments –

then some unreadable words – then 'hoping' – and then other unreadable words – then 'interested', – and other unreadable words; – concluding with, 'that the election of Mr. Jobbry had taken place'; thereby, as it seemed, intimating that he was interested in me alone.

Mr. Spicer shook like the aspen, for the job was odious to him; and presently he complained of being suddenly taken unwell, cried out for fresh air, and was with difficulty assisted out of the room. Upon this, Mr. Tough, all of a tremble, cried out that the business of the election must proceed according to law, the charter of the town having provided for such accidents.

'In the king's name,' cried he, waxing bolder, 'I demand of you, Mr. Idle, as senior counsellor, to go into the market-place and summon five good men and true, burgesses of this borough, to repair with you to this place, to assist the council in the election of a member.'

'Dear me, dear me!' cried Mr. Idle; 'I am an aged man; I cannot do that: I am in such a flutter that I can scarcely recollect my own name, far less five others.'

'Then,' cried Mr. Tough, 'the senior of the council having refused, on the plea of inability, to perform the duty, it belongs to you, John Gnarl, to perform it, and without delay, for the business of the election has now commenced.'

John Gnarl, with an evident inward laugh, made no bones of the business, but alertly starting up, he went forth from the hall; all the crowd giving passage to him as he passed, amazed at this high solemnity, which had not been performed in the memory of man; and on reaching the cross, he there summoned five burgesses by name and craft, who, greatly to the astonishment of all present, were accidently standing together, dressed in their Sunday clothes; and back John came to the hall with them behind him.

When the names of the two candidates, Mr. Gales' and mine, were read over, the whole five burgesses, without even speaking to one another, unanimously advised the council to elect me – which was a very extraordinary electioneering coincidence.

Mr. Gales looked aghast; but his lawyer, a genteel young man, peremptorily told him it could not be avoided: the charter had established the principle, and Mr. Jobbry was duly elected.

While this little fracas was going on, I saw Mr. Tough quietly lift my lord's note from the table, which the mayor had in his consternation left, and putting it in his pocket, began to chew bits of paper out of the same pocket; but whether they were fragments of the note or not, I could take my Bible oath as to my ignorance of the fact.

Thus was I a second time *elected* the independent representative of Frailtown.

The aspect of a new Parliament after a change of administration is very comical. On the left side there is stern
and vindictive frowns; and on the right, exultation and
complacency, interspersed with young unknown visages,
of a serious senatorial cast, prognosticating oratory. It is
a lucky thing, however, for the country, that the number
of these and other speakers is comparatively very few; for
at the best they are but a necessary evil, and only help the
more sagacious editors of the newspapers to make wiser
reflections. The prudent, those that set a watch on the
door of their lips, never speak at all, or, at the most, only
put a young man right when he happens, in the warmth of
debate, to be caught tripping in a Parliamentary fact. – But
I have less to do with the House than with what happened
to myself in and about it.

Whatever resolution a member may form for the guidance
of his conduct on first entering Parliament, he will see, as he
grows familiar with its usages, that he is constrained by some
inscrutable power to conform very generally in all things to
the conduct of his neighbours.

I have already said, that the House of Commons is a
peculiar community; and every day that I belonged to it,
I was the more and more convinced of this truth. Out
of doors men are regulated by public opinion, in their
thoughts, their actions, and their enterprises; but within
the walls of that House there is a different atmosphere;
members become less and less susceptible of the influence
of public opinion, and more and more to the dogmas of
Parliament, which the populace, with their usual wisdom,
always think are less sound than their own.

I make the remark, because when I took my seat after

the election which has just been described, I felt myself elevated above many persons that I saw around me, whom I had previously considered as in some things my superiors; – if I were to feign candour, I would say in all things; but I adhere to the conclusions of my own understanding.

This consciousness of superiority puzzled me a good deal; but I soon saw that it proceeded from the same sort of thing that gives men an advantage over one another in the world, and which often passes for superior understanding. I had only, by being a member of that peculiar community, learned some of those sleights of art inherent in it, similar to those which give men a power over mankind in the world, and likewise often passes for talent. Although, therefore, it could not be said that I was a distinguished Member of Parliament – my name was never seen in the debates in the newspapers – I yet discovered that I was accounted one of a clever sort, especially among my junior brethren; and thus it came to pass, that I was bit by bit solicited from my own determination, and, without becoming a partyman, to have a leaning towards those who were more inveterately touched with the patriotism of making long speeches.

For the first session, I know not how it happened, probably in consequence of the Parliament being new, and expectants having in the new members more quarry, I was less troubled with applications for patronage than ever before; but I lost something of my relish for regulating the distribution of what posts I did get: in truth, I ought not to take great credit to myself for this, as the Government was quite as much the cause, fancying that if a young man got a post, the emoluments of which he allowed to be taxed with an annuity, – for example, to the widow of his predecessor, – it was opening a door to corruption, by uniting the widow's interests with his. The custom was, therefore, stopped, and the officer received his full emoluments.

I remember very well, that this at the time was thought a notable reform, and it was very acceptable to the people at large: but I had my doubts of its practical wisdom; for if a man could afford to give an annuity out of his emoluments, surely he could have paid as much back to the state, and thereby caused an important item of savings; for, be it to seduce the burgesses; I pricked up my ears at this, and looking from under my brows, and over the table to where the honourable gentleman was sitting, gave him, in spite of myself, a most, as he called it, taunting smile. Now, the truth was, that I only happened to call to mind what Mr. Tough, my solicitor, had done with Doctor Muckledose at the Frailtown election.

The mention of the mountebank did not, however, make a deep impression on the committee; indeed, some of themselves, if all tales be true, were well accustomed to such antics; but an answer to a very small question, which I put to one of the witnesses, threw great light on the subject.

'Friend,' quo' I to him, resting my arms and elbows on the table, and my chin upon the back of my hands, – 'did your mock-doctor vend medicines?'

'Oh, yes!' said the man; 'he had pill-boxes and salves.'

'And nothing else?' said I, seeing him hesitate.

'There was a wrapped-up paper.'

'Ay; and what was in it?'

'It was a printed note, saying that the doctor would be consulted by the freemen and their families gratis, every day till the election was over.'

'This looks serious!' exclaimed my Rhadamanthian friend; and I thereupon said to the witness, – 'And what was the result?'

'All,' quo' he, 'that consulted the doctor, it was said, were inoculated.'

'What do you mean by inoculated?'

'At the election they all voted for Mr. Gabblon.'

'Well, my friend, but what had Mr. Gabblon to do with that?' and, on saying this, I turned round to the chairman and said, 'The doctor and the merry-andrew should be called before us as witnesses.'

Upon which Mr. Gabblon's lawyer objected, saying, 'They could not be legal witnesses, inasmuch as they were rogues and vagabonds by law.'

This was, however, overruled; and I saw Mr. Gabblon turn of a pallid hue when it was determined to bring them before us.

We then adjourned to afford time, and in due season met

observed, by the new arrangement the poor widow was left destitute, and became in so much a cess upon her friends, who of course became discontented. I have often wondered how an auld-headed old friend of mine, that then was in office, should have consented to such a frustration of the widow's hope, without making the public benefit by the alterations, especially as he was a Scotchman.

I have no respect for such nugatory regulations; and I trust my public conduct warrants me to say, that concerning the same, great delusion beguiles the world; for although I have ever been a Government man, I have not always been blind to the tubs that the ostriches in office throw to the whales; and the courteous reader I am sure will think with me, that it was a very doubtful regulation that deprived Custom-house officers and consuls of their fees. Indeed, I have always thought that the latter should have no salaries at all, but be paid by fees from those whose business they do; but let their fees be strictly regulated. It is a very hard thing for an old wife, in the wilds of Inverness-shire, to be paying in the price of her tea for consuls on the back of the world, whose only business is with men and matters that neither directly nor indirectly can she have any thing to do with.

But I am falling into an overly digression on this head; for I only meant to set forth that true national representatives, members such as I was, should in all alterations, even in things deemed corrupt, see in what manner the change has been beneficial to the public. Clear to me it is, that it was not the abolition of fees that was required, but only their regulation; and whoever was the father of that job, though it was one of the artificers of a new ministry, to curry favour with popularity, it was but a weak invention, and shewed no right conception of the business of the commercial world.

But it is time I should resume my narrative; for, although this explanation may in some degree be necessary to explain my conduct, I do not profess here to state my principles in any direct form. My object is to shew by my actions what they were, and it will be seen they continued as pure and independent after I became more of a politician than I was or intended to be in my early career. When I say this, I beg to be understood as in no sense implying that I gave much heed to international affairs; it would have been indeed an extraordinary departure from the consistency of my character, had I done so; for on that subject there are always between both sides of the house something less than a hundred members who are well qualified to keep their friends right. My endeavour, therefore, was not so much to acquire superior knowledge myself, as to acquiesce judiciously in the opinions of those who were best informed. And in this respect I was not singular in those days; for many sound and solid-headed elderly gentlemen, who did not know, when they entered the house, whether Portugal was in the kingdom of Lisbon, or Lisbon in the kingdom of Portugal, did the same thing, and their votes were always highly approved; for it so happened that they pinned their faith, like me, to the opinions of men that the general world out of doors respected for their talents, knowledge, and integrity.

CHAPTER TWENTY-FIVE

Although the first session of my third parliament worke[d] on myself a considerable change, and led me on to be mor[e] of a public and party man than was in exact conformity with my own notions of what a plain member should be, who has the real good of his country at heart, I yet had some small business in my own particular line; the most remarkable piece of which was in being balloted a member of a committee to try the election for the borough of Wordam, in which it was said that some of the most abominable bribery practices had taken place that ever offended the sight of the sun at noon-day. In this affair my old adversary at Frailtown, Mr. Gabblon, was the sitting member; and to be sure the petitioners alleged against him such things as might have made the hair on the Speaker's wig stand on end 'like quills upon the fretful porcupine,' had they not been so well accustomed to accusations of the same kind.

It is true that there are few tribunals more pure and impartial than the election committees of the House of Commons; but incidents will occur in the course of an inquiry that are very apt to make the proceedings seem questionable; and thus it came to pass, that as we reported Mr. Gabblon not duly elected, I suffered in the opinion of his friends, as having been swayed by the recollection of the trouble he had given me at Frailtown. No man, however, could act with stricter justice than I did: one of the committee, indeed, a new young member, fresh from Oxford, and aspiring for renown, said openly, that I had shewn a conduct throughout the investigation worthy of Rhadamanthus; which nickname, by the by, did not stick to me, but to himself.

Among other charges, it was alleged against Mr. Gabblon that he had hired a mountebank doctor and a merry-andrew

again. The doctor and his fool were really very decent, just as respectable to look at as any member of the committee: the merry-andrew was dressed in the tip-top of the fashion, with an eye-glass, hung by a garter-blue riband. But what surprised me most was, that I was some time of discerning in him the same young man that had been so serviceable to Mr. Tough at my own election.

As it was evident to the meanest capacity in the committee, that the inoculation had been performed by matter obtained from Mr. Gabblon, I made a dead set at that point, and said to the clown in a conversible manner:

'And so, my old friend, for I see you are such, we have rather a knotty business in hand: what said the doctor, your master, to you when he mentioned that you were hired to play your pranks for the edification of the good people of Wordam, as you were once hired by a friend of mine to do for me at Frailtown?'

'He said,' replied the young man very becomingly, 'that I should have five guineas.'

'Well, considering your talent, that was moderate; but I don't think you have improved in prudence since we met; for, according to report, you had as much from my friend for one day as for all the seven you performed for Mr. Gabblon.'

'But, sir,' replied the witness, nettled at the idea of his prudence being called in question, 'I had five guineas every day.'

'Oh! I thought you only performed one day.'

'Yes, sir, only one day in public; but the private practice was no easy job.'

'No doubt,' said I; 'but what was this private practice?'

'It was bamboozling the natives before some of them were in a condition to take the doctor's drugs.'

'That was hard work, no doubt; but what was the doctor's medicine that the patients were so loath to take? To be sure drugs are very odious things.'

'I never saw him administer any.'

'You're a clever lad,' said I, 'and you'll just step aside and let the doctor come forward'; which being accordingly done, I continued:

'Doctor,' quo' I, 'I hope you're very well, and have been

this long time; you keep your looks very well: no doubt you take a good deal of the same physic that your young man has been telling us was administered, *pro bono publico* and Mr. Gabblon, at Wordam.'

'Not so much as I could wish,' replied the doctor; 'times are very hard.'

'No doubt they are; but what were the doses that operated so efficaciously at Wordam?'

'The Melham bank,' replied the doctor, 'had stopped payment.'

'Hey!'

Mr. Gabblon gave a deep despairing sigh, and I said,

'Doctor, not to trouble you with these trifling questions, for I am sure your medicine was as precious as gold——'

'It was all sovereigns, for the cause I mentioned.'

Mr. Gabblon gave another sigh, and his lawyer, albeit of a rosy hue, turned for a moment white as his wig, and then laughed.

'Doctor,' was my comment, 'we are very much obliged to you; your answers have been exceedingly satisfactory: but one point; it's of no consequence; you should however have mentioned it; and that is, how you got the sovereigns.'

'Oh! Mr. Gabblon's groom brought them every morning, and staid with me as long as patients came.'

'I daresay, doctor, you had many doubtful cases – what was the prevailing complaint?'

At these words, Mr. Gabblon, not the wisest of mankind, suddenly started up, and called the doctor an ass, not to see how I was making a fool of him.

''Tis you,' said the clown, 'that he's making a fool of'; at the same time winking to the Committee with one of his stage faces, forgetful where he was.

In short, not to lengthen my story into tediousness, bribery and corruption was clearly proven; and Mr. Gabblon, as I have already stated, was set aside; for he was not cunning enough, in a parliamentary sense, to be honest, – a thing which leads me to make an observation here, namely, that it is by no means plain why paying for an individual vote should be so much more heinous than paying for a whole borough.

My third parliament was more remarkable for talk than trade. A great many motions were vehemently discussed, not one of which was of the slightest benefit to the nation. Those in the two early sessions were altogether what my friend Colonel Armor called 'drilling recruits', – that is, affording opportunities for young orators to shew the calibre of their understandings and the weight of their knowledge; and yet the sittings were busy and bustling to public members, and to the newspapers, for they filled their columns. For my part, I was sick of it; and a very little of the drug that the doctor distributed at Wordam would have made me retire to my cool sequestered neuk in Scotland, even though there is something in the air of the Parliament House that does wile a man on, from day to day, to thole with a great deal of clishmaclavars, – at least so it proved with me.

One advantage I derived by giving more ear to politics than in the two former Parliaments, – I was less troubled by applications for places, which are really very vexatious. As an independent member, applicants to me were both Whigs and Tories, – neither, to be sure, of a deep dye, but still party men; but when I began to adhere to the one party, I was none troubled by those of the other, it being an understood thing that I would only attend to applications from my brethren in feeling and principle. This I did not dislike to perceive and to know.

My own nature, and a rightful regard towards the Government, made me of a Toryish inclination, which I soon saw was the prevalent inclination of the House. By far the greatest part of the members were disposed to stand by the Government in all things, though there were schisms of a personal kind that it was fitting John Bull should not discern. These, accordingly, were ascribed to principles; but were, in fact, personalities which governed the selection of men for power and office.

By the best of my calculations the number of real Tories in the House never reached sixty persons; that is to say, sixty who would on no account listen to the slightest proposal for any alteration in the frame of our constitution and the ancient establishments, which they called its bodily organisation: they would have as soon listened to a proposition to change the physical position of the kingdom itself on the globe, as to change the relative position of the orders and institutions which time, and the frame of our government, had established; and which they thought were things that came as much of nature as the oak, or any other indigenous product. These I looked upon as the pillars of the state; but I was not myself one of them: on the contrary, I was more in conformity with the greater number, who thought that if a diseased limb was incurable it ought to be cut off, to preserve the health and strength of the whole body.

With the exception of the sixty unchangeable Tories, there was undoubtedly a disposition in all the rest of the House to encourage Government to persevere in a course of amendment, even to a recasting of the most consecrated usages and establishments of our ancestors. Among these were included, at this time, fully more than sixty Whigs; that is to say, men dissatisfied with the whole frame of existing things, and who thought that the world would be mended were that frame entirely removed, and a new system substituted.

Much did I meditate on the curious fact of the seeming equality in numbers between the inveterates of both sides of the House, or, rather, on the predominance which the Whigs appeared really to possess, without being themselves aware of it, till I began to institute a comparison of their respective individual qualifications; in which comparison the Tories, alike in talent, experience, and practical sense, so bore away the bell, that I soon ceased to wonder at their superiority of influence. Taking the numbers of deadly Whigs and

Tories to be equal, I persuaded myself that, in point of those qualities which rule mankind, one Tory was equal to two Whigs; and that luckily for the nation it was so, otherwise we should have had nothing but changes, until not a stool was left to sit upon. It was merely in practical talent, however, that the Tories had the advantage – certainly not in numbers; for the House, in general, bent toward that course of action which the Whigs recommended. Throughout the whole of that parliament, a practical man among the Whigs was only wanting to have made them the masters.

Among other ineffectual controversies which arose out of the otherwise unproductive results of this debating Parliament, was what may be called the Money Question – a subject on which mercantile opinion is alone deserving of attention, but which has not been attended to throughout. The question concerning it, instead of relating to the thing itself, turned chiefly on the material of which the thing is made, the country gentlemen insisting that the money should be money's worth: thus, that Government should always keep a vast sum, in the value of the material of tokens, circulating from hand to hand throughout the kingdom.

I was grievously puzzled in this matter, for some of those to whose opinions I pinned my faith in abstruse matters of policy, had really what seemed to me very wild notions on this subject. This arose from the theory being so different from the practice, as in many other things of Government; for certainly nothing can be plainer than that a banknote, valid for its value, is as good as gold: and yet, notwithstanding the great cost of gold, the country gentlemen insisted that many millions' worth of it should be kept in circulation, and paper put down. The reason of their opinion, however, never appeared in the debates; they knew that the craft and fraudulency of the world would substitute an unsound paper, and that those who issued it would draw the gold into their own coffers. It was this craft and fraudulency that were dreaded, when the cry was got up that paper should be put down; and thus it happens, that the appearance of gold for bank-notes is a lasting testimony against the integrity of those bankers who then issued notes.

But my ultimate opinion on the subject was, that Government should have taken the matter into their own hands, and never have parted with the privilege of coining; for I could not discover that there was any difference, in the principle of coining, between stamping with a copper-plate on paper and with a die on gold.

As there was a frequent cry of money being scarcer at one time than another, I thought there must be some capricious operation at the ventricle from which it flowed. Accordingly, my conclusion was, that much of our embarrassment in money matters came from the Bank being allowed to vary in the amount of its issues; and it appeared to me, that in permitting this discretion in the Bank, sufficient consideration was never given to the power it had of extending or contracting its issues; or, in other words, of enlarging or diminishing the amount of its discounts.

But while I thought so, I was not so obstinate in my opinion as to be very pugnacious; therefore, in all the arguments concerning the Money Question, I uniformly paired off. I never heard such fulness of wisdom on the one side as to contradict the theories of the other. But in this matter I stood not alone; nor will I allow that it was a question which had any thing to do with the principles of Government, though it has been much made use of as such.

CHAPTER TWENTY-SEVEN

But although in this Parliament I was, as I have stated, spared, in a measure, from the distress of many applications, compared to what I had been previously doomed to endure, yet I was not altogether spared; and one of the few – but these were enough – that gave me trouble, was rather more of a private than of a parliamentary nature.

I have had occasion to mention a Mr. Selby, and how, in my opinion, he was not used well by the administration of the Government towards him. There might be faults on both sides, if things so unequal as a single subject and a Government can be supposed to stand in such relative comparison; but, as it seemed in his case, I must say, as a Government man, the chief fault lay on our side, and I will always think so; for the war was waged between two unequal adversaries – if war it can be called – the attacks of which, on the one side, consisted only of earnest and humble petitions.

One night, after a very jangling debate, of which I could make neither head nor tail, and came away from sheer weariness of spirit before it was ended, as I was leisurely picking my steps along the plain stones up Palace Yard, the Abbey clock boomed twelve. It was a starry night; the sounds and buzz of the far-spreading city around were sunk into a murmur, as soft as the calm flowing tide on the sands of the seashore; – it was a beautiful night, and the moon rode high and clear; not a breath was stirring, and the watchman, with his cry of 'past twelve o'clock', seemed as suitable to the occasion as the drowsy effigy of a dream going towards a weary politician's pillow.

I thought, coming out of the foul air of the close House, that I had never seen such a serene sweet night since I had left the cool and hallowed shores of the Ganges: a new sense, as it were, was opened in my bosom, like the fresh spring which Moses drew from the rock in the desert; and I said to myself, if I am becoming an older man, surely it is also pleasing Heaven to make me a better: and yet I was never much of a saint, though, in a parliamentary sense, I had an inclination for the pastures of these innocent and pawky creatures.

Stepping thus along with easy paces towards my lodgings in Manchester Buildings, as I passed the steps from Cannon Row to the back way that leads to the bridge, I beheld, by the glimpses of the moon, a remarkable young woman sitting there, with several children about her.

At such an hour and time, this was a sight that would have interested any man; and it found me in the season of my softness.

'Young woman,' said I, 'what are you doing at this time of night, with these children, sitting in such a melancholy posture, and in such an out-of-the-way place?'

Her head, at the time, was resting on her knees, and her face was pale and shining, like the moon in the heavens.

'We are,' replied she, 'waiting.'

'This is,' quo' I, 'a strange place to wait. For whom are you waiting?'

She looked up again, and all the children did so likewise, and then she said, 'For death!' and stooped down again, as if she cared not what I thought of her sad answer; but all the children gave a very pitiful wail.

Really, thought I, this is a strange scene to happen to a member coming from a debate for the good of the nation; and I was greatly rebuked and confounded.

'My good young woman,' said I, in amazement, 'what has put it into your head to make me such a reply?'

She looked up suddenly again for a moment, and said, 'Want.'

'Want! my leddy, what do you want?'

'Every thing, – parents, shelter, food, clothing, friends, – every thing that makes the curse or blessing of life.'

This was said as one that was well educated, and it put

me in a most disordered state; I could therefore do no less than exclaim, 'My God! what are you to do?'

At which she started up on her feet and said, with a stern voice, 'To die!'

The other children at this began to cry, and she turned round and chided them, and then said to me,

'Sir, we are a family in utter misery. I have told you our condition – we are starving: can you help us? will you? if not, go away, and disturb us not while we perish.'

I was astonished, for she was but young in her teens, though she spoke as dreadful as a matron in years. What could I do but relieve their immediate grief with what small change I happened to have in my pocket? and I told her to take the children with her to where they had been sheltered the night before, and come to me in the morning and tell me her story. So I gave her my address, and bade her only to make haste to a refuge with her small sisters, and then bade them good night.

I can never think of that mournful adventure without a gruing of grief; for although nocturnal sights of unsheltered folk are not rare in Bengal, there is a mercifulness in the temperate air that mitigates the tooth of misery. Mankind suffer less, although their afflictions be equal, when the climate withholds the anguish of the cold that exasperates disease and starvation.

CHAPTER TWENTY-EIGHT

I did not pass that night with agreeable dreams, and I rose betimes for breakfast, with the discomfort of one that had suffered unrest. I had no relish, in fact, for the meal, and my Findhorn haddock was sent away untasted.

Just as the table was cleared, and my writing-desk placed before me, the young woman was announced; and having desired her to be shewn into the room, I prepared myself to hear a very deplorable story. I had not, however, inquired more than her name, which was Mary Selby, when a deputation from the country, of three gentlemen, was announced, respecting a new canal; I was thereupon obliged to request Mary Selby to retire for a little time, telling her I would see her when the deputation was gone. Accordingly, she rose to go out just as the gentlemen came in, and I observed, as she passed them, that she looked with a very remarkable expression of countenance at one of them, an elderly man with thin haffits and a bald forehead, but said nothing.

This deputation was from a part of the country of which I had no knowledge, and in which neither friend nor acquaintance; but their spokesman said to me, that they were under an obligation to intrude in consequence of the great power that was exerted against them.

I replied, 'that they were very right in the step they had taken; for I could not see that any reason existed why a member should not be canvassed for his vote and interest, in turn, as well as either a potwalloper or freeholder, or any other of the elective gender;' at the same time remarking, however, 'that they ought to have a clear explanation of their case, for ordinarily, on private bills, this was too little attended to, the friends of the parties trusting chiefly to the votes they could muster; and thus it came to pass, from less to more, that we fell into a discourse concerning some of the usages of Parliament, and the inattention of Government to private bills, as if speculations that altered the interests and face of the country were things of no account.'

Some of the remarks made by the gentlemen on this head appeared to me at the time very striking, and have continued to stick by me since, particularly those of the old man, at whom the young woman gazed with surprise and wonder. He was, indeed, a shrewd, solid, observing gentleman; and one of his sayings I shall never forget.

'In truth,' said he, 'it is a great defect in our Government, that the plans of public improvement are left entirely at the discretion of their projectors, who, if they be plausible persons, soon find support enough, by which works are undertaken that supersede others of more utility, and yet afterwards prove great losses. No private bill, for improvements of any sort, should be allowed to go before the House of Commons until the importance of the improvement proposed has been certified by a board or department of Government.'

I said to him 'that he was very right; but it was thought that these things were best left to the freedom and discretion of those who were interested in them.'

'I would, perhaps,' said he, 'leave a good deal to that opinion; but if the business of government be the protection of property, and I can see but little use for it besides, surely it is a blameable negligence to let the nation grow rife with public projects without investigating their utility.'

Soon after, the deputation went away; but, in leaving the room, something appeared to me in the behaviour of the old gentleman that shewed, as I thought, a disposition on his part to hold a private conversation with me. Accordingly, I said that every morning I would be found at home about the same hour, and if any of them had aught to say to me I would be glad to see them.

I then desired the servant to shew in the young woman, for I was fashed about her; but James replied to me that she was a strange behaved girl; 'for,' said he, 'though she is a beggar in rags, she's as proud as Lucifer, and would rather stand in the passage than come down stairs.'

'Very well, James,' quo' I, 'I'll look at that, and ye'll just send her in.'

Accordingly, in she came; but, instead of the sedate sadness of her former demeanour, I was surprised to see her weeping very bitterly, and yet with an air about her by common, insomuch that I was in a manner constrained to say, – 'My good girl, you see, business must be attended to; and it was not for disrespect to you that I gave a preference to the gentlemen.'

'I am well aware of that,' she replied; 'but in one of the gentlemen I discovered an uncle, who could never imagine that I or my mother's family were in such distress. Thank Heaven! I have been endowed with fortitude enough to conceal myself from him in the presence of those he was with.'

This news startled me exceedingly; and her name recalling to my recollection that of the gentleman for whom I had been formerly so interested with Government, I inquired if she knew any thing of him.

'Yes; he was my father,' was the reply. 'He is dead, and my mother is dead, and every thing she left is gone and sold; and last night, had you not pitied us, perhaps we had been this morning all no more: but the sight of my uncle has revived my hope, and the despair that was at my heart begins to relent.'

'Why did you not seek out your uncle?'

'We had not time, distress came upon us so rapidly; nor did we well know where to find him.'

After some further discourse, I agreed to get her uncle's address in town, which was done that same forenoon; and he behaved towards her like a worthy man, taking her and her sisters under his care with a sympathising heart. Two striplings that were younger than her, and older than the little girls, had gone upon the world to provide for themselves, and some days elapsed before they were found. At last they were rescued, and the whole family were removed into the country.

It was in the course of this transaction that he explained

to me what he was moved to say privately to myself on our first interview; and this was to tell me, that he had heard his unfortunate brother mention my name warmly, as one of the very few about the House of Parliament that would listen long enough to understand his grievous and peculiar case.

This I was both proud and sorry to hear, because, to give the devil his due, there is not any wilful shutting of the ear about a member of Parliament on either side; and it only requires a reason and method in applying to them to get their good will, if the matter you trouble them with will bear sifting. So that out of this small adventure, painful as it was, I reaped some good fruit, for, besides the complacency which I enjoyed at hearing how well pleased a most unfortunate man was with me in a very cruel predicament, I had the satisfaction to discern that the course I pursued, of listening with patience even to strangers on private bills, was judicious, and in salutary accordance with what the Government naturally expects from members of the private and domestic kind.

CHAPTER TWENTY-NINE

The do-little Parliament, as I have always considered that third one to have been with respect to the nation, was however of some effect to myself, inasmuch as in the course of it, growing something more of a politician than previously, my attention was directed to divers things of consequence, which at first I did not perceive: as such, not the least of these was our foreign affairs and the Holy Alliance: the latter subject, I never thought was rightly considered among us.

We regarded that conjunction of monarchs in too special a manner, as I thought; for somehow we took it into our heads that it was an alliance of sovereigns against subjects; whereas, if we had regarded it as an alliance for the upholding of governments as they are, with respect to one another, it would have drawn us to a wiser conclusion.

Before it was contrived governments had no tribunal of appeal against the aggressions of each other, but only arms; and this, in the existing state of knowledge, was but a poor and barbarous alternative. There was, however, no reason why the community of governments or of kings should remain in this base condition; and whatever therefore the artifices and craft of diplomaticians may have turned the Alliance to, there was, undoubtedly, something wise and grand in the first conception, of making the nations of the world responsible to an earthly tribunal, like individuals in private life to the courts of law.

No doubt the French revolution had caused the governments of the world to look with apprehension on the internal movements of nations; but there was a wide difference between upholding an established government, and denying to it the power and privilege of conceding the reforms which its people demanded. This distinction, however, I for one thought our politicians never very accurately made; at least, I never could exactly see that the Holy Alliance, which took upon itself only the preservation of peace, presumed to meddle with the internal affairs of nations, until the existing government was in danger of overthrow, and was unable to maintain itself.

This notion of mine was not, however, very general among my friends, but I have ever abided by it; and will to the last of my days remain persuaded, come what may, that it was a great improvement in the international system of the world to make governments responsible to one another. War, as we all have seen and experienced, is a dreadful alternative, and too much of the machinery of nations is contrived to render it at all times easily undertaken; as if the warlike strength of a state constituted its chiefest glory.

But as I am not writing political disquisitions, I may as well no further advert to the subject here, than to observe an effect which the Alliance had among us, leading to considerations that at one time it would have been thought very strange to have entertained.

Without being aware of the tendency of what they said, those politicians who have cried out so lustily against the principle of the Holy Alliance, now see a very bad effect of their conduct fast coming to a head. They have sown distrust between subjects and governments – by their arguments endeavouring to shew that the governors have interests apart from the governed; and this has weakened their reciprocal ties to such a degree, that even the foundations of property, the oldest and most consecrated of temporal things, are now in a state of being moved: the result who can tell? In a word, a wild and growing notion prevails that governments, and all things pertaining to them, are of less use than had been always supposed; a doctrine which, in the struggle of asserting, the most civilised and refined communities will be driven to the wall.

Before the time of this Parliament, according to my reflections, the kingly portion of the state was considered a thing necessary and indestructible, and whose utility it was denying first principles to call in question; but, from some of the discussions alluded to, it has ceased to be an undisputed thing, whether in England there should be a monarchy, or any other principle of government acknowledged than the opinion of the present age. By and by we shall see that this notion has been extending itself, and that, in consequence, many of those things which made the grandeur of England, have been, by the unconscious invidia of those whose lot in life makes them of the lower orders, deteriorated not only in veneration but utility.

However, it is of no consequence now to state my opinion of the Holy Alliance, nor to lament that so little use was made at the time of the magnanimity in which it was conceived. It was received in a mean and distrustful spirit by the radical politicians, and it was no more than natural that the authors should resent to the utmost the ill-humour with which their gracious intentions were even in this country repelled. In the House of Commons, I very well recollect, that not a few decent, gash, and elderly carles laughed, forsooth, at the pious terms in which the objects of the Alliance were expressed, and also a number of the juvenile Machiavelli that infest the benches saw nothing in it but the raw-heads and bloody-bones of bastiles and tyranny. It is no doubt true that the Holy Alliance had not been long promulgated, till several of its members drew back in the performance of promises which they had made in times of peril to their people; but little heed has been given to the cause – the fact only has been recollected. Now, although I am free to confess, as we say in Parliament, that this is a black fact, still I am not so thoroughly versed in continental politics as to be able to give it a downright condemnation, because we soon saw, that what was called the peace of Europe was but as ice upon the surface of a lake, that was liable to be tossed by a storm. In no other respect, but as the outbreakings of a deep and wide-spread disease, have I ever been able to look on those Carbonari, and other discontented eruptions, which, from time to time, took place; and which served to shew that the rightful season for changes in the old establishments of the governments of Europe had not come to pass. There was not that sane and wholesome understanding existing between rulers and people, without which the attempt to improve is always dangerous. And in consequence, for the life of me, as an honest man, I never could see that the kings and princes who promised constitutional governments were to blame for withholding them, merely from feeling their hands strengthened by joining themselves together in an equitable league.

CHAPTER THIRTY

Many things in the midst of the do-little disputations indicated to older members that a change of some kind was coming over the British Government; and it was pointed out to me, by the late Sir Everard Stubble, that there was more passion and less firmness in the tone of public men towards one another than he recollected in better times. He was one of the stanch Tories, and, probably, on that account more sensitive to mutations than me; at least so it happened, that although he felt the chilness of a coming shadow – the shadow of change, and spoke of it as a certainty, he yet could not point out the reasons of his belief.

I saw, however, that men spoke to one another with less severity about reform, and anent Catholic emancipation, than they had done in times bygone; indeed, many of the lighter-minded, who look to a division of the House of Commons as the settling of a question, expressed a wish that the latter business was determined, seeing that sooner or later it must be given up. To say the truth, I was not myself, as an independent member, far from that opinion; for when I considered that a matter was so ripened by many discussions as to carry the minds of the majority out of doors, it was no longer prudent to let it be delayed.

But I cannot say, that in acceding to this notion my judgment just entirely approved the expediency of granting full relief to the Catholics; for I could not shut my eyes to the historical truth, that the church endowments had once been theirs, and that their priesthood had as good a right, from that circumstance, to share, in proportion to their numbers, the loaves and the fishes with our own, both on this side of the water and in Ireland. Thus, though in the subsequent Parliament I did give my vote for the

Catholic Relief Bill, still I have never ceased to fear that I thereby assisted to open a door for the admission of new troubles. But while I say this, I would not retract that vote, unless there was a clear visibility that the human mind was going backward. It was, however, a vote in obedience to the signs of the times; and I have never ceased to lament the night on which public duty, rather than private judgment, compelled me to give it.

Had the great sacrifice which was then made of the constitution of 1688 been followed by the requisite measure of equalising, according to their numbers, the claims of the Catholics and the Protestants on the property of the church, I would have submitted with more contentment, even although in doing so the pretensions of Dissenters to a share of that property had been considered. But when I saw nothing of the kind done, I began to be afraid; for in making Catholics no better than Dissenters, we were stirring up anew an enemy that it had taken both time and trouble to lay; and it only saddens my heart and deepens my sorrow for the vote I gave, seeing that it has been followed by no proposition to redress the grievance which the necessity of giving it implied.

The more I reflect on this measure, wise in its object, but abortive in the hopes it promised, the more am I satisfied, that the great predominant party in the State, which had so long held the reins of government, was at the end of its stage. I could discern that there was not, as formerly, that true stubborn adherence to Government which characterised its old supporters; and that there was, in fact many among them with anchor a-trip, ready to join the other squadron. Altogether, my reflections on the Catholic emancipation gave me no pleasure: not that I find fault with the measure itself, for that was carried in a high and masterly manner; but because, after it was done, nothing else followed, but only those evils which the adversaries of granting the relief predicated – evils which are full rapidly kithing. But to return. Although the issue of the Catholic question was seen to be inevitable, during the Parliament that I will never cease to describe as the do-little, other things that greatly shattered the consistency of the Tories.

From time out of mind there had been certain rules and laws for the regulation of shipping and commerce, which we, of our party, had all along maintained were essential to the support of our national superiority. They were made expressly for that object; and the greatest talents which our statesmen ever displayed, were exerted in vindicating those ancient national measures. It was, therefore, a dreadful shock to our affections when we heard the merits of them condemned. I am really not sure that this did not do more to dissolve the Tory adherency than even that laxity of constitutional principle which afterwards led to the measure of the Catholic Relief Bill.

No doubt, in the abstract, there was much truth in the reasons urged for the alteration, considering the facility which the then state of the world afforded; but the difference of condition between us and foreign countries was not considered with that fulness it ought to have been. Theoretical principle was more consulted than practice, and the result was, at least to many of us, doubtful. I therefore look upon the free-trade doctrine, and the doctrine upon which the Catholic relief was founded, viz. that all mankind had natural rights in society, as truths of the same science, but as such liable to be regulated by expediency.

In all this it was plain to me, as well as to others, that the Whig party was strengthened in the House, by an accession of those who called themselves Liberals going over from our side to them, not in a palpable body; and that the Tories were losing strength and numbers. A third party, mongrel Whigs, was forming.

This state of things was very puzzling to me, especially as the retrenchment, of which old Sir John Bulky had given me notice, was duly lopping off the means that I had looked to for my share of patronage – one of the principal inducements which led me originally to think it advisable to go into Parliament. In short, it seemed to me that Government was unconsciously weakening itself on all hands, and that the lofty pile of our monarchy was sustaining, by our contempt for old experience, and the substitution of new theories for ancient customs, some detriment, that might go hard in time with its very existence.

CHAPTER THIRTY-ONE

The corn-laws, although it cannot be said that any new light has been thrown upon them in the course of my parliamentary life, have yet occupied no small share, during it, both of public and of private attention. Respecting them I never have considered myself as very competent to judge; for when I bought my estate of the Girlands, I knew that I had paid for it what is called a high war-price, and that it was only by future improvements I could ever expect to make it a profitable investment; in so far, therefore, I could take a free and common-sense view of the matter.

The ordinary argument among the country gentlemen, as it struck me, was, that the produce of the soil was as justly entitled to protection as the produce of the loom, or any other manufacture. This seemed a very fair statement; for if we prohibited, in any degree, by duties or regulations, the importation of raiment, and articles of that sort, there could be no injustice in doing as much towards food, which was not more necessary.

The operatives, however, who, without disparagement, may be said to cherish a selfish feeling on every question in which their own interests are concerned, have uniformly taken a very different view of the subject. Nothing would, to them, be more satisfactory than an entire prohibition of all foreign articles similar to those of their own manipulation; yet they cry out, as if they were the victims of gross legislative partiality, at every step which the farmer takes to insure a protecting price for the produce of the soil and his labour.

The question, stated thus, seems reasonable, and ought to lead both parties to a right understanding; but it does not do so, and there does exist, in consequence, a very unfair and unjust opinion among the operatives against the agricultural interest.

How the difference between them is ever to be reconciled, is a knotty point of policy, and much have I reflected upon the subject, evening and morning, and midtime of day – yea, even in the watches of the night. But the o'ercome of my meditations has ever been, that the spirit of the times runs strong and unjustly against the lords and traders whose business is with the soil; and the conclusion to which I have come is now a part of my parliamentary creed, namely, that a judicious legislature should only endeavour to regulate the trade in corn, and that the abolition of the laws against the importation of foreign corn should be according to the traffic which foreign countries hold with us for our manufactures.

A plan of this sort, however, will not satisfy the operatives, who, in their one-eyed view of commerce, imagine that a different law should regulate the trade in earth or grain from that which regulates it in silk or cotton: and upon this subject I have had several solid conversations with friends and neighbours – merchants, manufacturers, and country gentlemen – without acquiring much instruction from them.

It appears to me that there is a disposition of a general kind existing in the public, to regard the produce of the soil as something foreign from other descriptions of produce. The operatives think they have a right to exchange the productions of their art for things which they cannot produce; and that if they can find food cheaper by sending their articles for it abroad, they have a right to do so, and that nothing but a usurpation on the part of the country gentlemen prevents them. This is surely not sound, for the manufacturer – the collective representative of the operatives – cannot do without the merchant; and he it is who regulates the markets, and who considers corn a merchandise as much as any of the other stuffs and manufactures in which he deals.

Though it may serve the merchant's turn, were there no corn laws, to bring at times the cheaper corn of foreign countries into our markets, it behoves the operatives to consider by what means this is to be done. If he can bring, for a given quantity of their productions, a greater quantity of foreign corn than the same things would procure of home growth, then the argument of the operatives would so far be correct; but, if instead of sending our manufactures abroad to obtain corn in return, he is obliged to send money, look at what would be in the end the effect to the operatives? Would not the money thus sent be taken from the capital of the kingdom, and would not that capital so diminished lessen the means of employing the operatives, and thus bring round to them an evil as great as the difference of price between what they pay for corn brought in under regulations, and what they would pay were the trade free in that article.

But I will say no more on this head. All I intended by stating it was, to shew with what views I have been actuated in the different votes which I have given on this abstruse question. I cannot, however, restrain my indignant pen from noticing, with the strongest expressions of reprobation, those bad and ignorant men who go about the country stirring up strife and opposition between the two great interests into which the nation is naturally divided – the landed and manufacturing. It is to men of common understandings so plain that these interests are inseparable, that it seems scarcely inferior to a species of treason to make any sort of distinction between them; and yet how widely and wildly has this been done, and how strenuously have the malignant advocates of a free trade in corn deceived the operatives, and taught them, disastrously, to think, that a great, populous, and enlightened nation can have any reluctance to adapt its code of corn or of commercial law to any but right expedients?

CHAPTER THIRTY-TWO

Whilst this change and enlargement of my mind was going on, his Majesty King George IV, that gorgeous dowager, departed this life; an event of a serious kind to me, and to those with whom I acted; for although our grief on the occasion was not of a very acute and lachrymose description, it was nevertheless heartfelt; for he stood in our opinion as the last of the regal kings, that old renowned race, who ruled with a will of their own, and were surrounded with worshippers.

'Never more,' said I, 'shall we have a monarch that will think his own will equivalent to law. His successors hereafter will only endeavour to think agreeably to their subjects; but the race of independent kings is gone for ever.' In a word, the tidings of his death, though for some time expected, really smote me as a sudden and extraordinary event. Had I heard that the lions had become extinct on the face of the earth, I could not have been more filled, for a season, with wonder and a kind of sorrow.

The most important upshot to myself, however, of this demise of the crown, was the dissolution of Parliament; for the King's illness had allowed time, if it had been made use of, to undermine my interest at Frailtown; but, by some strange cause, no effort of that kind was made. I and Lord Dilldam were hand and glove; for my politics, though I adhered to the Duke's party, were not greatly adverse to his lordship's; and the pruning of the Government patronage left but little on that score to differ about. I think it was owing to this cordiality between me and his lordship, that the election at Frailtown went off so smoothly; for, no doubt, had Lord Dilldam put his shoulder to the wheel against me, I would have had a heavy pull;

for, to say the truth, his lordship was much beloved in that quarter; and although he was not a man that could be esteemed for talent, he was the best of masters and of landlords, and took sincere pleasure in putting himself on a pleasant footing with his tenantry and the inhabitants of the town. He was, indeed, one of those weak good men who so conduct themselves as to render the possession of great wisdom and ability of doubtful value.

I did not, however, in my own secret mind, relish the perfect smoothness with which I was returned for Frailtown. It seemed to me, that with a new king, and with such signs in the times as were then palpable, it was not a thing to be trusted, but, on the contrary, was very ominous, betokening rather an unripeness of purpose among the inhabitants than a party hesitation.

For some time it was well known that the growth of radicalism was spreading, and that the people were gone a degree beyond Whiggery in the malady. Now, I was a moderate Tory, that is to say, one who, when he saw repair or amendment necessary, would not object to the same, especially when the alteration was recommended by Government; and Lord Dilldam's politics were of the same colour, but a shade deeper. This I well knew, and could not but think that it was very odd how our united interests, which were so opposite to the conceits of the populace, were not resisted. And when I met his lordship in town, after the election, I spoke to him concerning the same.

'My Lord,' quo' I, 'what is your opinion of the lull that now prevails at Frailtown; I fear it augurs no good to your lordship's influence, and as little to the permanency of mine.'

'My dear Mr. Jobbry,' was his answer, 'you never were more out in your conjectures. The good people of Frailtown do not see where they could find a better member than yourself; and having an idea that I am of the same opinion, which, without compliment, I frankly acknowledge, they are content to leave the care of their political interests in our hands.'

'I wish your lordship may be correct,' was my dubious reply; 'but, throughout the land, there is an unwholesome

crave for something or another; and I have my apprehensions that Frailtown has not escaped the infection. In truth,
my lord, I jalouse that the inhabitants are no longer content
with the power of election remaining, under the old charter,
in the corporation.'

'What reason,' said his lordship, after a pause of
thoughtfulness, 'have you for that opinion? It is, however,
not to me alarming,' he added; 'for though the elections
were thrown open to the general burgesses, it would make
but little difference, my family having been so long popular
and well beloved among the inhabitants.'

I was very sorry to hear his lordship, worthy man! speaking
in such delusion; but I had not the heart to break his dream
of complacency. I saw, however, that my own reign in
Frailtown was coming to a conclusion, notwithstanding
the calm that then seemed to smile upon it. I therefore
began to debate with myself, whether I ought not to dispose
of my seat in a reasonable time; but the sort of attachment
that I had taken to the House, and the rational amusement
that was now and then to be obtained there, when discreet
men spoke of the affairs of the nation, had its weight upon
me, and I came to no determination.

There was, indeed, an interest arising from the state of
the country that had its effect upon me; and I had a kind
of a longing to wait till it would come to some result. This,
no doubt, was partly owing to the stramash that had taken
place at Paris, which had made the cocks and leaders of the
radicals among ourselves crouse and bold. At the same time,
I was not without a sense of apprehension concerning the
Duke's government, his grace having declared himself so
stubbornly devoted to the existing frame of our constitution.
That speech I ever regarded as a declaration of war against
the radicals; but I had such confidence in him, that while he
found himself able to stand in the stronghold of office, I had
no fear; still, I ought not to disguise the fact, that all things
in the country, at the meeting of the new Parliament, looked
in a very grievous condition; and I did not think the Duke
stood upon a rock, – the more especially as his ministerial
forces were not armed with weapons to contend with those
who had gained the ears of the people against them, nor

were they prepared with the measures requisite to quench the Irish kind of misrule that was raging in different parts of the kingdom. All things, indeed, had a very bad aspect; but still I was not so strongly minded to quit my public post, as perhaps a man of more prudence would have been. In this crisis I got a severe lesson.

CHAPTER THIRTY-THREE

One Friday night, or rather Saturday morning, after a husky debate, Mr. Boldero Blount invited me to go down with him, next day, to his country seat. Says he to me, 'I have had a letter from my wife, telling me that she is very uneasy on account of the state which she hears the country is in; not that any thing has yet happened, but rumours are going about which make her very unhappy; so I have resolved to go down tomorrow, and to return on Tuesday; and would be glad if you would take a corner in my post-chaise, especially as no particular business is coming on.'

I accepted Mr. Blount's offer; saying, at the same time, 'that I had heard very uncomfortable tidings from his part of the country; and nothing would give me more satisfaction than to see with my own eyes, and hear with my own ears, the truth and circumstance of the matters reported.'

Accordingly, early in the afternoon we set off for his place, and arrived in time for a late but very excellent dinner; after which, to be sure, Mrs. Blount gave us a sore account of the state of the laborous peasantry in the neighbourhood.

'They have not,' said she, 'broken out into any outrage as yet; but they hold meetings in bands in the evening, and think the scarcity of work is all owing to the tithes and the high rents, which their employers the farmers pay, in addition to their share of the taxes.'

This, as it seemed, was a brief and clear account of the discontent; and we had all the servants about the house brought in one by one, and examined on the subject anent such particulars as they had severally heard.

When this was done, Mr. Blount, who was an off-hand man, and went at once to the marrow of most things, said,

'This notion of the peasantry is plainly a thing ingrafted upon them, and not of their own induction.'

I thought so too; but I said to him,

'It is, however, not the time now to inquire from what airt this wind comes, but to think of sheltering ourselves from the blast. Tomorrow is the Sabbath day; the country folks and farmers will be at the church: let us both cast ourselves familiarly among them, and reason with them.'

The which Mr. Blount most cordially approved of; and then, as we sat over our wine, we discoursed more anent the growth of the new doctrine concerning rent.

'It rises,' said Mr. Blount, 'from that sound that has been echoing through the kingdom for a long time about the burden of our taxes.'

'No doubt of it,' replied I; 'but the weight of taxes is comparative with the means of payment, and there must be something very strange in the condition of our nation which makes us now, when we are relieved from the expenses of the war, less able than when under them to bear the public burdens.'

'That is the puzzle, Mr. Jobbry: what can it be? for no truth can be more self-evident than that there has been a withdrawing from us of some secret thing that must have counteracted the burdens of the war. Have you any notion what it can be?'

'It can be no small matter, Mr. Blount, since it is equivalent in effect to millions on millions on pounds sterling. In my opinion, it can have been no less than a great sum subtracted from the money among hands, or what the political economists call a contraction of the circulating medium.'

'By Jove!' cried Mr. Blount, 'you have hit the nail on the head. The Bank has contracted its issues to a vast amount, equal to much of the reduced taxation; the country bankers are like shelled peascods, not a tithe in their notes to what they were: no bills are circulating for the munitions of war. Upon my word, Mr. Jobbry, I do think that all our evils arise from our contracted circulation. But, although this be the root of the evil, what are we to do to get these crotchets out of the minds of the deluded commonalty?'

'That's a heavy question, and I fear cannot be answered, even by looking at those who have an interest in promoting the discontent.'

'Ay! who are these? not the poor, simple people, – they are but the instruments: for though tithes and taxes were all abolished tomorrow, they would get no more than their hire, and that hire would bring them no more than a subsistence. It is the rule of Providence and Nature that it should be so, and so it must continue until machinery comes to the head that the perfectibilians dream of, as to abridge in all things the labour of man.'

'If it's not the common people,' quo' I, 'it cannot be the landlords, nor can it be the priesthood; for the rent of the one is not better founded than the tithes of the other. If the tithes were taken off, the landlord would increase his rent, and what would the public benefit by such a change?'

'That is not the radical doctrine,' replied Mr. Blount: 'they don't want to take off the tithes altogether, but to apply them in mitigation of the taxes, and to let the churchmen make a living for themselves in the best manner they can.'

'It may be so, Mr. Blount; but I doubt the country rioters do not consider the matter so finely. Now I'm going to say a harsh thing; but don't get angry if you differ from me.'

'Well, let's hear it.'

'You see, my good friend, that the farmers are the only parties that really could expect to profit by the abolition of tithes and the reduction of rents.'

'Surely, Mr. Jobbry, you would not insinuate that the farmers are the authors of these outrages which so disgrace the country?'

'That is another question, Mr. Blount; but I mean to say, that they are interested in propagating the opinions by which the labourers are misled; and we must not disguise it from ourselves, that there begins to be a very dangerous opinion hearkened to in the world, namely, that both landlords and an established priesthood are not necessary.'

'That notion is indeed very tremendous; it strikes at the root of property: no man under it could have any thing that he might call his own.'

'I do not, Mr. Blount, at all think that the opinion is sound; but it is an opinion that is spreading abroad, – a disease, a moral cholera, if you please; but if all things are to be measured by utility, or, in other words, by their money value, what is to become of the world? In short, Mr. Blount, it's my notion, that some of our cleverest men, and those too in the highest places, have been overly eager in propagating what may be called abstract theoretical truths; and that the modification which is requisite in practice to fit them for men's different humours and characters has been too little attended to. We want men who understand the tendency of the current to stem it boldly; for there is a hurry in the course of men's thoughts that cannot be checked too soon or too steadily.'

Just as we were thus speaking, Mrs. Blount, who had for some time before retired, came flying into the room, saying that the light of three distant conflagrations was then visible, and that farmer Haselhurst's stack-yard was in flames, and a great crowd around it huzzaing and rioting.

This made us gather to our feet; but the particulars require another chapter.

CHAPTER THIRTY-FOUR

The house of Elmpark, as the country-seat of Mr. Boldero Blount was called, stood on a rising ground, and in daylight commanded a beautiful prospect down a long valley, in the bottom of which winded a broad and bright stream. Several villages, with trees and steeples, were seen on the sides of the valley, and far down the river was a mill with a bridge across; making a picture that was most delightful to contemplate in the morning or the evening, when the sun was shining. But on that night, when we sallied out in front of the house, it presented another sight. The darkness was clouded, and only a few stars could here and there be seen; but the distance was dismal. On the east, a wide and red glare was burning, – it cast no light in a manner upon any object, which made it very dreadful to behold; nearer, and in the south, there was another fire, the flames of which, licking the very clouds, could be distinctly seen, and black gables among them; and there was a window in one of the gables that shone like a star, but whether from a light within, or the reflection, nobody among us could tell. At a short distance from this great conflagration, we saw another farm-steading all in a blaze, which, although not so considerable, was yet very terrible to see; but the worst of all the spectacle was, the farm of Mr. Haselhurst. It was less than two miles off, and the fire was very vehement: every thing in and about his farm-yard was distinct, and we saw the black figures of the crowd moving to and fro in terrible shapes around it. One of the mob I could clearly see, with my own eyes, whirling a cart-wheel into the midst of the burning, and Mrs. Blount saw likewise another fling a ladder upon the flames. It was an awful sight.

Mr. Blount was very calm and collected; and he said

to his servants, and some labouring men that had come round the house, –

'Friends, these rioters will be here; but, if you are true men, they shall not burn us out both with ease and honour. Get ready the guns, and shut up the lower windows as well as you can, and prepare to receive them at those of the drawing-room floor.'

On his saying this, all the servants and labourers declared their readiness to defend the house; which, on hearing, I said to Mr. Blount, 'that as I was a stranger and unknown, I would just walk down to Mr. Haselhurst's farm, and see what the mad criminals were really about, if there was any body that he could spare to shew me the road.'

To this proposition Mr. Blount readily acceded; and, with one of his gardener's sons, a hobbletehoy of a laddie about fourteen, I walked towards the scene of destruction. I never, however, reached it; for when we were yet less than a quarter of a mile from the place, we met the crowd running and scattered, pursued by a whirlwind of dragoons, and a cloud of the county magistrates and gentlemen blowing at their heels.

Me and the laddie who was my guide stood up at a field-gate, to let the uproar pass, when, to my consternation, before I could open my mouth, a fat justice of the peace seized me, like a bull-dog, by the throat; and at the same time one of the dragoons struck the boy with the flat of his sword down into the ditch.

'Friends! in the name of peace and the king, what are you about? Unhand me!' cried I.

By this time the main body had ridden on, and I was left, with the poor greeting laddie, in the hands of the Philistines.

'Let me be,' said I to the fat magistrate; 'let us both be: we are innocent people.'

'We shall see to that,' cried a young man; and with that he caused a groom to come with a whip-cord and bind our hands behind our backs, in spite of all that I could say in remonstrance; and when I told my name, and that I was a Member of Parliament, they only tightened the cords, and caused me and my poor terrified guide to walk towards a turnpike-house, where they obliged us to mount into a cart. My heart was roasting with indignation; and the more I said to them the less would they hear. At last, we reached the borough-town, where they intended to put us in jail. The whole town was in commotion: women crying, and running dishevelled to and fro, and candles were at the windows.

When the cart stopped before the door of the Talbooth, seeing that no attention was paid to what I said to my conductors, I called quietly to a young man in the crowd hard by, and requested him to go to the mayor of the town, and tell him who I was, and that in their frenzy they had, by mistake, made a prisoner of me.

The young man was in the greatest consternation at hearing this: with nimble heels he went to the mayor; and presently a great hur got up, candles were brought, and much ado was made to lift me and the gardener's son out of the cart. But although everybody around said, any one without an eye in his head might have seen it was not probable that we were of the rioters, still the fat justice of the peace that took me so unmannerly and suddenly by the throat, maintained that I was only an imposter, and that I was no other than the old fellow Swing, that drove about the country in a gig with a gray horse, with combustibles, stirring the peasantry into rebellion.

Really, my corruption rose against that man; and if something had not restrained my arm, I would have cloven his skull with one of the council-room brass candlesticks; but a gentleman who was there pacified me, and said to the others that he would be responsible for the truth of my story. This served to moderate my wrath; but it was not till an express was sent for Mr. Boldero Blount, and he was brought there present at the midnight hour, that they were satisfied.

It is very true that Mr. Blount and me have many times since had a hearty laugh at the adventure: but I have often thought that the mistake with regard to me was a sample of real doings elsewhere; for I could observe, that more than one of the magistrates had but little command of his senses, and that even if I had been a guilty one, caught, as was thought, in the fact, there would have been no injustice in handling me with a little more consideration.

However, my case was but as a drop in the bucket compared with the calamities which began that night; and, to say the least, it would have been more creditable to the justices if, instead of watching till the nocturnal hours, and then scouring the country with dragoons before them wherever they saw a light, they had soberly, in daylight, set themselves in council, and considered the complaints of the people. My friend, Mr. Blount, in his straightforward way, was an exception. He inquired into the matter, and even, where need was, gave help, though that was not often required; and, in consequence, both his own premises and his farms sustained no damage.

CHAPTER THIRTY-FIVE

In consequence of these terrible hobbleshaws we did not return to London so soon as we intended; for Mr. Blount judiciously thought that the matter should be inquired into, and I thought the same thing. Accordingly, we spent several days on this business.

He caused the principal farmers around to be invited to his house, and several decent old gaffers from the neighbouring villages, together with a Mr. Diphthong, who was a schoolmaster, well known in that part of the country to have much to say with the common people, being a young man of parts, and both for learning and capacity above many in his line.

These guests we sifted with a scrutinising spirit; and it was very lamentable to hear how far the judgment of some of them had gone astray: indeed, it is not saying too much to assert that, with the exception of Mr. Diphthong, who really was a clever lad, scarcely one of them had a mouthful of common sense, the which made me jalouse that some of them were nigh at hand during the burnings.

However, though it was a task of some difficulty, we made out pretty plainly that the rioters were not instigated by want, which was most distressing to ascertain; for if they had, then there would have been some palliation for their mad conduct. Nor were they altogether set on by the spirit of revenge for wrongs or hardships they had sustained; but only out of a mistaken notion, that by so shewing themselves they would force on a reformation of the national abuses, as they considered them, not only in tithes and rents, but taxes and poor-rates. Against the latter, in particular, our informers said all the lower orders were just vicious.

It was not easy to see how a remedy could be applied

to such a sweeping complaint. For my part, I was greatly dumbfoundered, and Mr. Blount was no better; it being very manifest, that at the bottom of these opinions of the common people lay no less than a notion, that somehow, by the removal of oppressions, every labourer would live like a gentleman. Some, no doubt, knew better; and of them it may be said, that they only blew the coals to a certain degree, thereby hoping to achieve some mitigation of the public burdens.

One remark made by Mr. Diphthong, however, on the poor-rates, struck both me and Mr. Blount as very uncommon.

'Much,' said he, 'of this unhappy state of the country lies in a mere name; and were a little pains taken to place the matter in a proper light and ministration, a great deal of the discontent among the rural population would be appeased. There has grown up,' he continued, 'a disposition to consider all those as paupers who are employed by the parishes, as well as those who are assisted with alms by the parishes. This should be rectified.'

Mr. Blount, evidently surprised to hear him say so, inquired what he meant.

'I mean,' was his reply, 'that the money raised to mend the parish roads, and to do other parish work, ought not to be included in the poor rates; for where the parish gets work done in return for employing the labourers when work is scarce, it ought not to be considered that the wages of these labourers are alms. It would be just as equitable to call the bricklayers who are now building the new church paupers, as those poor men who are breaking stones for the improvement of the highways. And thus it is that I say the error is in a name. Why not call the fund that is made use of for parish improvements the labour fund, and keep it distinct from the poor-rates? Were this done, certain am I, from what I have observed in our own parish, there would not be found any such increase of pauperism, as it has been of late years so much the fashion to enlarge upon. Indeed, I am so well convinced of this, that I do not believe the real poor-rates are at this time so great as they were at the beginning of King George the Third's reign, if the increase of population be considered – I mean the amount paid to the aged and infirm, for whom alone they are raised.'

'I doubt,' replied Mr. Blount, 'you are making a distinction without a reason. It is employment that is wanted, and what signifies it whether the man that stands in need of employment be employed by the parish or gets alms.'

'A wide difference, Mr. Blount. What the labourer gets for his labour is his own – he has earned it with the sweat of his brow – but alms are humbling; and no man likes to be an object of pity.'

I said, 'that I thought the observation very sensible; but still I did not very clearly see how to take work for alms differed from giving them for God's sake.'

'No?' replied Mr. Diphthong: 'do not the paupers, to use an ignominious term, work on the roads to make them smoother? Compare the country roads of England with what they were only a few years ago, and say if the public has derived no advantage? Do not your waggons carry more and draw easier? And the same thing may be said of every transportable commodity. Is there no advantage in that?'

'Yes, Mr. Diphthong,' replied Mr. Blount, 'what you say is true. But were it not for the want of employment otherwise, we could do very well were our roads and hedges less trim.'

'Not so, sir: we are now a more refined nation than we were,' answered Mr. Diphthong; 'and it is needful to our improved habits, that our roads and hedges, as well as every thing we have of a public nature, should correspond with our desires. Make a LABOUR FUND, and you will at once raise the spirit of the people of England, and place the merits of our institutions on their true footing: at all events, keep the poor-rates apart for pauper purposes.'

'Still,' replied Mr. Blount, 'that would only be calling six half-a-dozen. There is a surplus population, or, in other words, a want of employment. How is that to be remedied?'

'By two ways – emigration and public works.'

'But where are the means to execute public works?'

'Circulation. Property must be taxed: the proceeds of this

tax must be devoted to the employment of the labourers, for public advantage or ornament. From them the money will flow to the dealers, thence to those they employ, and so pervade the community.'

'But, Mr. Diphthong,' quo' I, 'don't you see that the effect of that would be to bring down the large properties?'

'I do,' said he; 'but is not this better than to put an end to the rent of landlords, which is the present tendency of public opinion?'

'Really, Mr. Diphthong, you put the matter in a very alarming light: is there no alternative?'

'I think not,' said he; 'the great properties have had their day: they are the relics of the feudal system, when the land bore all public burdens. That system is in principle overthrown, and is hastening to be so in fact. The system that it will be succeeded by is one that will give employment to the people – is one that will gradually bring on an equalisation of condition.'——

At this I started, for I saw by it that he was of the liberty and equality order; and grieved I was that men of his degree could talk so glibly on subjects that puzzle the highest heads in the land. But I said nothing: his sentiments, however, remain with me; and I cannot get the better of what he propounded about the feudal system being at an end, and of the system by which he thinks it is to be succeeded. Mr. Blount was no less disturbed. We both agreed, that although Mr. Diphthong was probably very wrong, something was going on in the world that gave a colouring to his inferences, and we concluded that a time was fast coming in which prudent and elderly men ought to quit the public arena, and leave it clear to the younger and the bolder. It was this conversation which in a great measure led me to think of retiring from Parliament.

CHAPTER THIRTY-SIX

Next week, when we returned to town, the first news we heard was, that the Duke's ministry were tottering, which I was much concerned to hear, as I thought the country at the time could ill spare such a straightforward man. My concern was the more deepened, as there was also a rumour, arising from the manifold fires and turbulence throughout the kingdom, that some change would be made in the way of a Reform of Parliament, to pacify the people.

The first report was not many days in circulation till it was confirmed; and sorry was I that the occasion chosen for doing it was one of a very insignificant kind. As the ministry had made up their minds to retire, it was, I must say, a weak and poor thing of them to make their resignation turn on the snuff-money of a few old shaking-headed dowagers. Surely it would better have become the Duke's manly nature to have given a frank and fair notice of his intention to break up his ministry, than to make it seem dissolved by the results of a question in the House that was not important.

The chief cause of my dissatisfaction was, however, in the event itself: for plain it was to me that the Duke's retiring from office, and the coming in of his adversaries, was a change amounting to something like a revolution. It was not, as other changes that had taken place before, a mutation of the Tory party among themselves, but a total renunciation of that ascendancy which they had so long preserved, and during which they had raised the country to the pinnacle of glory. I had, indeed, a sore heart when I saw the Whigs and Whiglings coming louping, like the puddochs of Egypt, over among the right-hand benches of the House of Commons, greedy as corbies and chattering like pyets. It was a sad sight; and I thought of the carmagnols of France, the honours of the Sitting, and all that which made our French neighbours, forty years ago, so wicked and ridiculous.

How I should have come to this conclusion concerning the new ministry and their abettors, requires no explanation. It was manifest to the humblest understanding that the Tories, our party, to whom the country owned so much both of renown and prosperity, were overthrown. We had for many years preserved the country, both from foreign and domestic foes; and every one must allow that we could not but feel greatly discomfited at being forced to abandon our supremacy to those who had never ceased, in all our illustrious career, to be the enemies of our enlightened policy.

No doubt, the Whigs in this revolution were the leaders; but they were backed and supported by a far stronger faction than themselves, – a faction who are looking forward to frighten them from their stools at the first expedient uproar of difficulty. It is however, foreign to the principal purpose of this book, which is intended to let posterity know how those judicious supporters of Government felt and did like me, and who will, to a moral certainty, in the end be missed.

As soon as the new ministry had taken their places, I began, with the help of Mr. Tough, to cast about for a gentleman to succeed me in the representation of Frailtown: but dealers were no longer rife. The rumour of the reform made purchasers shy; and though some there were who nibbled a little, he could find none that would bite, – so much did all the land stand in awe of this new phoenix which the ministry were known to be hatching.

When at last the plan did come out, I expected no better than a total loss by my seat; for although by it the power of representing two-and-twenty millions was proposed to be given to no less than the half of one million, it yet happened that Frailtown was included in the condemned list, the which I could not but think a very great hardship, and a most unjust thing, as the borough had been guilty of no misdemeanour to deserve such a punishment.

The other mischiefs of the measure troubled me very little. I saw that the die was cast, and that my wisest course was to make the best bargain I could for the borough, and retire by times to the Girlands, well aware that the one-and-twenty millions and a half will not be long content with such a fractional representation as it is proposed to give them; for what is the reform intended to do, unless it be to work out the abolition of rents and tithes? Less than that, I fear, will not satisfy the radicals; nor less than that, sooner or later, will a reform parliament, after it has again reformed itself, be found obliged to concede.

But I must not indulge these reflections, lest I be suspected of writing under feelings of disappointment and chagrin. The suspicion, indeed, would not, perhaps, be unfounded, for I acknowledge that I am vext; and no man has as yet greater reason, for just on the very day that Mr. Tough had concluded a reasonable bargain with Mr. Mysore, to succeed me in the representation of Frailtown, notice came out, that if the Reform Bill did not pass, the Parliament would be dissolved, which caused him to draw back, and I could discover no other to take the seat off my hands. All the world knows the Parliament was dissolved, and my apprehended loss was in consequence inevitable.

It is true that Lord Dilldam wished me to stand again, upon the high Tory interest; but my moderation would not listen to the suggestion: indeed, his lordship shewed himself not very wise in this, for how could I expect to be well received in a town where my temperate politics were going out of fashion, the obstinate side? All was over; and to struggle I saw would be of no avail, so I determined, at the dissolution, to close my career, which I have accordingly done; and now, as a simple spectator, I look afar off for the coming on of what is ordained to take place.

p.1   *William Holmes:* Galt, at the outset, reinforces the
'authenticity' of his fictional hero Jobbry by having
him dedicate his autobiography to a real person, William
Holmes M.P. from 1808 till 1832. D.N.B. describes him
as 'the adroit and dexterous whip of the tory party . . . a
most skilful dispenser of patronage.' Galt thus sets the
stage for a picture of the operation of the system.
Colonel Napier: dedicated his history to Wellington
because I have served long enough under your command
to know, why the Soldiers of the Tenth Legion were
attached to Caesar'.
your old office: i.e. of Tory whip.

p.2   *a graduated property tax:* this form of income-tax, a
war-time measure and a bad memory for the well-to-do,
was not renewed by Parliament in 1816. Jobbry's fears
that it would be re-introduced were justified.
Fulham: A contemporary route-book notes that Holmes
had his residence in the rural village of Fulham (*Paterson's
Roads*, ed. E. Mogg, 1822, p. 52).

p.5   *a young friend:* a young relation. The Scots use of 'friend'
for 'close relation' (husband, wife, cousin, etc.).
in Scotland: Town Council delegates from the smaller
Scottish boroughs (which were arranged for the purpose
in 14 groups) elected a member for each group. There
was plenty of scope for bribery and the solicitation of
local and family connexions. But the open purchase of
a seat from a sitting member (which is what Jobbry has
in mind) was a simpler matter in England. See Porritt,
op. cit., on 'Seats acquired by Purchase', i, pp. 353ff.
a five-year old Parliament: One of the effects of the
1715 Septennial Act was to increase the cash-value of
a seat, since the purchaser had an assured tenure for
the seven year term. The canny Jobbry hopes for entry
to the final two years of a parliament at a bargain price
– and therefore a safe (and costless) seat.

cholera morbus: i.e. the 'plague' (of repairs).

the Indian directors: directors of the East India Company (in Leadenhall Street).

p.7   *Lord Entail:* as the major landholder in the district he controlled the election of both local members, (1) the 'county' M.P., who was elected by the freeholders, small property owners who were in their turn the creation of the Lord, and (2) the 'borough' M.P., who was elected by the three delegates of the grouped three borough councils – who in their turn were also 'under his thumb'. For another example see *The Provost,* chap. v.

p.8   *freeholders:* enfranchised small property owners. See above.

twelve hundred to fifteen hundred pounds per session: Galt's figures are accurate. In 1807, fourteen hundred guineas a year was offered for a seat, in an advertisement in the *Morning Chronicle.* See Porritt, *op. cit.,* i, p. 358.

p.9   *Ibbotson's Hotel:* the London directories of the period (e.g. Holden's) list this hotel in Vere Street, Oxford Street.

according to Hoyle: 'by the proper rules'. E. Hoyle's authoritative 'short treatises' on card games (especially his *Whist,* 1742) gave rise to the phrase.

p.11   *at the Jerusalem . . . India House:* East India House was in Leadenhall Street. The nearby Jerusalem Coffee House (in Cowper's Court, Cornhill) was a 'subscription house for merchants and others trading to the East Indies', H.B. Wheatley, *London Past and Present,* 1891, ii, p. 308.

Carbonell's claret: London directories of the period list Carbonell and Son as wine-merchants in Golden Square, later in Regent Street.

p.12   *Burns:* 'Tam o' Shanter', line 163.

man in a wig: i.e. the Speaker of the House of Commons. Jobbry is asking whether the member is expected to sit on the government or the opposition side of the House.

p.14   *Smithfield:* even the cost of a trading-place at Smithfield meat-market is rising.

p.15   *the true Simon Pure:* 'the genuine person'. A catch-phrase from Mrs. Centlivre's *A Bold Stroke for a Wife,* 1717.

p.16   *franks for letters:* Members of Parliament had the privilege of free postage, by signing the outer cover of a letter.

p.17   *petitioning:* Jobbry threatens to petition the House on the grounds of corrupt practices. See the following note.

contrary to law: though the purchase of seats remained common practice till 1832, it was contrary to an Act passed in 1809. See Porritt, *op. cit.*, i, p. 346. Jobbry is aware of both the actual law and the common practice – and can use either to his advantage.

p.21   *reported progress . . . and asked leave to sit again:* an exclusively parliamentary expression, used of adjourning committee proceedings which are to be resumed later.
my constituents: Jobbry slyly lets slip that *he* is the purchaser.
your offer: Probe accepts the gambit.

p.22   *the Chiltern Hundreds:* the legal fiction of being appointed to this 'office of profit under the King' (and so rendering oneself ineligible to be a Member of Parliament) is still the method of resigning one's seat. See Porritt, *op. cit.*, i, p. 242.

p.24   *condescension:* Galt always (both in his published works and in his letters) uses this now pejorative word in the earlier (and neutral) sense 'voluntary abnegation of the privilege of superior rank' (O.E.D.).
the state fry: (fry: 'young fish') the younger members of noble families, with junior positions in the Government.

p.25   *distributor of stamps:* one of the range of well-paid sinecures at the disposal of Government. Wordsworth's distributorship of stamps for Westmorland was worth about £500 a year in 1813 and later increased in value to about double this figure.

p.29   *a canal:* the building of canals, requiring private Acts of Parliament, led to much lobbying for support among members. Galt himself, in 1819–20, had been well-paid as a parliamentary lobbyist by the Union Canal Company. See Gordon, *op. cit.*, p. 22.

p.31   *gumflowers:* artificial flowers, used for hat-trimming.
p.34   *operatives:* artisans.
p.35   *Utilitarians:* followers of Jeremy Bentham. J.S. Mill (*Utilitarianism*) singles out Galt as having introduced the word to English usage.

p.39   *Buonaparte:* the date is c. 1811–12.
p.40   *Easyborough:* Galt's ironic name for a rotten borough.
p.44   *ora rotundas:* 'eloquent voices'. From the Latin 'ore rotundo' ('with rounded phrase'), Horace *Ars Poet.*, 323. Galt's Irvine Grammar School education had given him a facility for Horatian tags. He wrote translations of some of the *Odes*.

p.45   *pairing off:* the parliamentary practice by which the whips arranged to set off the vote of a government absentee against that of an opposition absentee.

my daily franks: abuse of the parliamentary privilege of free postage led to restrictions, in an Act of 1802; see Porritt, *op. cit.*, i, p. 288–9. A member in Jobbry's day was allowed ten franks a day, and the whole superscription (not merely the member's signature) on the 'cover' had to be in the member's handwriting – which explains Mr. Gabblon's difficulties and the details of the ensuing scene.

p.51   *my lodgings in Manchester Buildings:* a double row of private houses between Cannon Row and the Thames, a few hundred yards from the House 'principally occupied by bachelor members of parliament' (W. Thorby and E. Walford, *Old and New London*, 1873–8, iii, p. 381).

get to the north road: Mr. Tough orders the chaise to be driven south over the Thames by Westminster Bridge, then doubles back at the 'Obelisk' (where five roads converged in the Borough of Southwark), recrosses the river at Blackfriars Bridge, and resumes his original route north.

p.54   *Athens of the north:* Edinburgh.

p.55   *abstract one of the council:* Galt recounts a similar incident (based on actuality) in *The Provost*, chap. v.

p.58   *a true bill:* Galt adds a further touch of 'authenticity'.

p.65   *the Union:* Union of the Scottish and English Parliaments, 1707.

p.67   *Lord Sidmouth:* Henry Addington, Prime Minister both at the time of the Treaty of Amiens (1802) and at the renewal of the war with the French (1803).

p.71   *Abdiel:* the one faithful seraph (*Paradise Lost*, v, 896).

wally, wally: i.e. 'lamentation' (from the ballad 'O waly waly').

p.72   *Chaucer's pilgrims:* the starting-point of the *Canterbury Tales* was the Tabard Inn in Southwark ('the Borough').

p.73   *suffered . . . by an invasion of the enemy:* Mr. Selby's situation was that of the Canadian settlers, ruined by the invasion of 1812, whom Galt represented for some years. See Gordon, *op. cit.*, p. 73.

p.76   *Westminster:* franchise in this ancient 'scot and lot' borough was a function of residence and payment of municipal charges. The number of voters was consequently considerable (c. 17,000; see Oldfield, iv, p. 252) and elections were consequently Hogarthian.

p.81   *three boroughs in the West:* Cornwall and Devon contained a very high proportion of the rotten boroughs abolished in 1832.

p.87   *the plate:* wooden or metal tray carried by presbyterian elders gathering 'the collection' in church.

p.94   *The multitude . . . to conserve their rights and privileges:* ironical – they had none.

p.99   *tubs . . . to the whales:* i.e. 'diversionary tactics'. See O.E.D. and Swift's *Tale of a Tub*, Author's Preface.

p.101   *balloted a member of a committee:* by the Grenville Act of 1770 charges of corruption at an election were determined by a committee of Members chosen by ballot. See Porritt, *op. cit.*, i, pp. 540–2.

        Rhadamanthus: in Greek mythology, judge of the underworld.

p.102   *freemen:* in essence, members of trade guilds. In many boroughs, the freeman had the preponderance of voting power and were able to enjoy 'the lucrative exercise of the franchise' (Porritt, *op. cit.*, i, p. 66).

p.104   *The Melham bank . . . had stopped payment:* over sixty country banks failed in late 1825, as a result of over-issue of credit.

p.105   *Colonel Armor:* a typical Galt 'cross-reference' to one of his other novels. He is a captain in *The Provost*, chap. xxix.

p.107   *the Money Question:* during the war, gold had given way to paper currency. It was reintroduced in stages between 1820 and 1823, the pro's and con's being hotly debated in parliament and in the press.

p.108   *paired off:* see note p. 45.

p.109   *One night:* the ensuing 'night scene in London' was justly singled out for special praise by *Fraser's Magazine*, April 1832, pp. 373–4.

        politician's pillow: Galt slyly hints that Jobbry's pillow has been shared in nights gone by – but the young woman of this night's encounter is very different.

p.112   *a new canal:* see note p. 29.

        potwalloper or freeholder: two of the varieties of enfranchised voters before 1832. A potwalloper was 'every inhabitant in the borough who had a family and boiled a pot there'; a freeholder – after the forty-shilling Act of 1430 – was a small property-owner. See Porritt, *op. cit.*, i, pp. 20, 31–2.

p.116   *the Holy Alliance:* Alexander I of Russia's 'Christian' treaty of 1815, for which Jobbry professes admiration.

p.118   *Machiavelli:* 'scheming politicians'. Galt (who had a competent knowledge of Italian) makes a mock-plural of the word. In 1814 he published an article based on his reading of Machiavelli. See Gordon, pp. 18, 50, 136.

Carbonari: secret society of republicans in Naples, formed in 1819 against the French occupation.

p.121   *Catholic Relief Bill*: passed 1829.

p.122   *rules . . . for the regulation of shipping*: relaxation and modification of the restrictive navigation laws were approved by the government in 1822 and on several later occasions.

Liberals: the term had only recently become current in this sense. See O.E.D.

p.123   *corn-laws*: originally passed to support and protect agriculture, they were resented by manufacturers and the town-workers (the 'operatives') and were subject to continual modification from 1815 onwards. Galt, though a Tory, personally supported the views of the manufacturers. See his article, 'Hints to the Country Gentlemen' in *Blackwood's Magazine*, October and November, 1822, where he adopts the persona of a Glasgow merchant.

p.126   *George IV*: his death, 26 June 1830, resulted in an automatic dissolution of Parliament.

the Duke's party: i.e. the Tories, under the Duke of Wellington.

p.128   *stramash*: riot (the Paris riots of July 1830, leading to the downfall of Charles X).

p.132   *perfectibilians*: a relatively new coinage in Galt's day. O.E.D. credits Peacock (1816) with its first use.

p.136   *Talbooth*: although Jobbry is brought before a magistrate in the south of England, he uses an exclusively Scottish term. In a small Scottish borough, the Tollbooth incorporated the Town Council offices, the magistrates' court, and the jail. See *The Provost*, chap. ix and elsewhere.

p.139   *Mr. Diphthong . . . on the poor-rates*: Mr. Diphthong is expressing Galt's personal views, which he had already expounded (under a nom-de-plume) in 'Thoughts on the Times' in *Blackwood's Magazine*, October 1829, pp. 640–3. Galt – like Jobbry – was a 'moderate tory' but some of his personal political opinions were much more 'liberal' than Jobbry's.

p.143   *the country owned so much*: 'the country acknowledged so great a debt'; 'owned' here is a Scotticism.

the condemned list: the Schedule to the 1832 Act which contained the list of boroughs which would lose their right of electing members.

JOHN GALT

THE RADICAL:
An Autobiography

WITH NOTES BY
PAUL H. SCOTT

TO

The Right Honourable

BARON BROUGHAM AND VAUX

Late Lord High Chancellor of England

*To you, my Lord, 'the head and front' of our party, I inscribe
these sketches.*

*No individual has, with equal vehemence, done so much to
rescue first principles from prejudice, or to release property from
that obsolete stability into which it has long been the object of
society to constrain its natural freedom.*

*To you belongs the singular glory of having had the courage to
state, even in the British Parliament, 'that there are things which
cannot be holden in property;' thus asserting the supremacy of
Nature over Law, and also the right of man to determine for himself
the extent of his social privileges. What dogma of greater
importance to liberty had been before promulgated? What
opinion, more intrepidly declared, has so well deserved the
applause and admiration of*

NATHAN BUTT!

9th May, 1832.

The darkest hour is ever before the dawn. This the disappointed and the unfortunate should bear in mind, and
cherish their hearts, in despondency, with the consideration,
that if a man can afford to wait, he never fails in the end to
obtain much of the object of his wishes. These reflections
come with encouragement; for now, thank Heaven, our
long-deferred hopes are about to be realised, – let no one
despair when his fortunes seem most disastrous! Who,
in this long-afflicted nation, could have indulged in the
glorious anticipations that now brighten in our prospect?
What man, who has tasted the bitter of Tory exultation,
and been forced to stoop to that abasement which, like
iron, entered every Whig soul, when the arrogant official
faction, in its high and palmy state, trampled on our sacred
rights? But our pearls are about to be rescued from the
hooves of the tramplers. The day begins to dawn, in
which all honest men, with emancipated immunities, will,
in the free natural exercise of their faculties, vindicate the
perfectable greatness of the human character, and lift it
above those circumstances of oppression, privation, and
servitude, which it has from the beginning endured.

But enough of this; I must repress the enthusiasm with
which my feelings are excited by that which is at this moment
the theme of all tongues, all heads, and all hearts. I allude
not to the Cholera, but to the Reform Bill. I speak not of
laudanum, or rhubarb and brandy, or of any drug that
has been found efficacious in the pestilence; but of that
alone which the contemptuous Tories have denominated
the 'Russell purge.'

To return, however, to the subject of these pages – the
history of my own life: – I am sure that I cannot adopt

any better course to secure to me the sympathy of the reader, and his participation in my joy, than by simply relating my experience during that bondage and servility from which we are all on the point of being relieved. In my sufferings I have had many companions; and a naked recital of what we have undergone together, is sufficient to demonstrate the iniquity of that frame of society now ordained to be destroyed. Happy posterity! in vain shall ye, with all the invention of your future genius, attempt to conceive the calamities of that condition from which we, your ancestors, now intend to save you. It is reserved for you and yours to employ, with proper truth and effect, that precious expression, which the Tories of these days have so perversely used – 'the wisdom of our ancestors!'

I shall not waste my reader's time with a particular account of my pedigree. Things of that sort, like other ancient errors, are fast becoming obsolete. A plain narrative of facts is all that my purpose requires; and these I shall record with a manly and undaunted pen.

My father was an attorney. In his mind the rubbish of ancient law was often inconveniently manifest: he had strange unwholesome notions of the reverence in which the decisions of tribunals should be held; and it was his intention that I should be adulterated, in the very purity of youth, with similar respect for the same dogmas, and with the conclusions of understandings trammelled by precedents; but Fate willed it otherwise. There was, indeed, an elastic principle of resistance within me even from my childhood; and I have never ceased, supported by it, to regard political shackles with unabashed antipathy. My spirit was nerved with irrepressible energy against every symptom of pretension, no matter in how dear or venerable a form it menaced me.

Well do I recollect, that while yet a mere baby, playing on the hearth-rug with a kitten, which in its gambols scratched my hands, how I seized it by the throat, and how my grandmother, then sitting by, took me up in the most tyrannical manner, and, before I would forego my grasp, shook me; but it was not with impunity. The spirit of independence I have ever largely shared, and it was roused by her injustice. One of her fingers, to the day of her death, bore witness to the indignation with which my four earliest teeth avenged her intervention in behalf of the feline aggressor.

It would, however, be a tedious and vain task to recount the manifold instances in which my childhood was molested by misrule, the lot of all, under the old system. Reciprocal oppression was the very spirit of that system; and it is no exaggeration to say, that the whole human race now in existence can verify this fact. But I allude only to the anecdote of the cat, to shew my precocious sentiment of the divine right of resistance. The circumstance, indeed, proves with what a lively discernment I was in that innocent period awakened to the sense of wrong, and the instinctive alacrity with which I resented the violence of the old woman, who, without discrimination, took the adversary's part, but she has gone to her audit, if audit there be, and I shall say no more: I have only brought it in here as my earliest recollection of my antipathy to injustice.

I might multiply domestic injuries of the same kind, of which I was the victim, especially as my mother was a person who never allowed any of her children to evince the slightest independence; on the contrary, she often irresponsibly ruled them with a rod of iron. Perhaps, however, her discipline was inseparable from her situation, for it must be conceded, that her offspring were not always of the most pliant and submissive humour: my brothers and sisters were brats of the most wilful kind, and were ever endeavouring to make a slave of me; but with a firmness of fortitude singular for my age, I resisted all their attempts to domineer. I shall not, therefore, animadvert with any particular rancour on the memory of "all the ills I bore" during that juvenile persecution wherein I was the martyr.

The courteous reader, after this, will not object to follow me to school. On that calamitous arena it is impossible to describe what I suffered. Lenient were the lions that the Roman gladiators had to encounter in the amphitheatre, compared to the wild bipeds that I was compelled to fight with in the play-ground. O Nero and Caligula! and thou sullen Tiberius! were ye not amiable compared to the autocrats of the birchen sceptre, under whose jurisdiction I sustained the thraldom of so many grievous years? But example is better than precept; and it belongs to the nature of this undertaking that I should describe one or two of those instances of despotism, which, in their effect, have been more durable on my mind than all the lessons I then learnt. The recollection of them, it is true, no longer excites that flush and throbbing of the spirit which I felt at their advent; but as the boy is father to the man, I cannot entirely forget that such things were. My school-master was, what every boy well knows, of course a perfect brute, and it is needless to say more about him; universal sympathy awakens at the justness of the epithet. Listen, kind reader, and I will give you a taste, by example, of that peremptory pedagogue.

It has from time immemorial been the artful aim of all education to obscure the sense of natural right. To education, therefore, I am inclined, with Mr. Owen, to ascribe all the vice and distress which deform our human condition. The antipathy, indeed, which we are taught to foster in ourselves against those ebullitions of feelings misnamed crimes, is purely conventional. The opulent and aristocratical, who have usurped the possession of property, and who by a strange fraud have wrested the privilege of legislation from the general human race, have found this essential to their interests; and, accordingly, the indulgence of even the most ordinary feelings is branded in their vocabularies with epithets of iniquity.

I had not been a twelvemonth at school when I made this discovery; the consequences were striking; but I must describe the story as it came to pass.

There was at that time a boy of the name of Billy Pert at our school: he was my chum and fag, and, allowing for the subordination arising from the latter circumstance, he was also my comrade and friend. It happened one day that Billy and I strolled towards the village by a foot-path we had never before frequented; it led to the back-gate of the Rector's garden, which we approached without very well knowing the temptation into which it led.

On reaching the gate, we beheld, over the hedge that surrounded the garden, trees loaded with blushing and inviting fruit; our mouths watered at the sight; and Billy observed to me, that it was a shame apples should be so beautiful and not free to all who longed to taste them. The remark was philosophical; and having heard somehow that church lands were national property, I ingeniously observed, which was to him delicious, that whatever, therefore, grew on such lands was public property: we accordingly, after a little reciprocal comparison of ideas, agreed between ourselves, that we, being of the nation, could commit no moral offence in helping ourselves to those beautiful apples. With the intent to do so, but still having a dread before our eyes of the prejudices of society, we looked cautiously for an aperture in the hedge. Our search was successful; but we observed that a window of the house stared upon the gap; and we resolved, in consequence, to postpone the gratification of our wishes till night, when the moon, who was then in her first quarter, would assist us.

After having reconnoitered the environs, we returned to the school, and there arranged with several other boys who slept in the same dormitory, on the mode by which we should be most likely to accomplish our desire. We went earlier than usual to bed, but we did not undress; on the contrary, with the assistance of one of our sheets, we lowered ourselves down from the window, and with silent footsteps ran to pluck the forbidden fruit.

On our arrival at the breach in the hedge, we stood, however, appalled; a candle was in the window, and the Rector behind was shaving himself, as it was Saturday night, and he deemed that task unbefitting the solemnity of the Sabbath morn. But our wits readily supplied an expedient to overcome the difficulty; one of the boys suggesting that he and two others should go round to the front of the Rectory, and there shout and with a great noise alarm the inmates; assured that Dr. Drowser, as the rector was called, would hasten to the scene of turbulence; while Bill Pert with two others and I should ravage the garden.

This stratagem was speedily carried into effect: Bill and another boy scrambled through the hedge, mounted the tree, and threw us lots of apples, till we deemed that we had acquired enough; but in descending from amidst the boughs, Bill's foot slipped, and he fell to the ground, sprained his ankle, and was with the greatest difficulty hauled through the hole in the hedge. As he was excellent at whistling, it had been agreed that he was to give the signal to recall the confederates from the front of the house; but, alas, the best-concerted schemes are often frustrated! The pain of his ankle rendered him unable to give his lips the needful expression, and I was obliged to go round and call the others off from their part in the enterprise.

It might have been supposed that in the performance of this duty no particular risk was likely to be incurred; but Fate was inauspicious and ruined all; for not receiving from our companions a reply to my first shout, I cried aloud, 'Jem Stealth, come home!'

The Reverend Doctor was by this time looking out at one of the windows, and immediately recognising my voice, called out, with exultation, ''Tis Mr. Skelper's mischiefs.' The whole party heard this, and scampered home as fast as possible, leaving poor lame Billy Pert and the apples behind them.

Billy, on finding himself deserted, bellowed as loud as possible to the Rectory, and presently the whole family, with Doctor Drowser himself in his dressing-gown and night-cap, and a candle in his hand, issued forth, and laid hold of the culprit, as they denounced that unfortunate child of nature.

I shall not bestow my tediousness on the reader with what happened that night; but on the Monday morning – (Sabbath passed innocently) – when Mr. Skelper came into the school-room, there was silence, and solemnity, and dread. All those who were engaged in the assertion of genuine principle sat conning their lesson with downcast eyes and exemplary assiduity, – serious were their faces, and timid were their eyes; my heart rattled in my breast like a die in a dice-box: the other boys were under the malignant influence that was characteristic of the then state of the world – their laughter, though stifled and sinister, was provoking; and for the side-long looks which they now and then glanced at us, their malicious eyes ought to have been quenched.

The master advanced with sounding footsteps to his desk; his countenance was eclipsed: – never shall I forget his frown.

Having said prayers with particular emphasis, he then

stepped forward, and summoned all who had been engaged in the nocturnal exploit, by name. With trembling knees we obeyed; and I chanced to be the first whom he addressed.

'Nathan Butt,' said he, with a hoarse austere voice, (for he was a corpulent man) 'Nathan Butt, what have you been engaged in?'

This was a puzzler; but I replied, 'that I had just been reading my lesson.'

'You varlet!' cried he; 'don't tell me of lessons: what lessons could you learn in robbing Dr. Drowser's garden?'

'I could not help it, sir,' was my diffident answer; 'we were tempted, and could not resist: the Doctor should not put such temptations in our way; he is more to blame than we are;' and waxing bolder, I at last ventured to say, 'we only tried to get our share.'

Mr. Skelper was astonished, and exclaimed, 'What can the boy mean? You audacious rascal! these are the sentiments of a highwayman;' and with that he hit me over the shoulders with his cane, as if he had been a public lictor, and I a malefactor. In a word, no more questions were asked, nor the truth of our opinions attempted to be ascertained; but each and all of us were compelled, after receiving a cruel caning, to sit on a form by ourselves, ruminating indignantly on our wrongs, a spectacle to the whole school. The sequel is still more illustrative of the bold character of my companions, and the free and noble principles which from that day have continued to animate my abhorrence of coercive expedients in the management of mankind.

Situation develops character; and the little adventure which I have just described illustrates this truth. School-boys before, and school-boys hereafter, have been, and may be, subjected to punishment for stealing apples; but few, I suspect, were ever animated in such an exploit by motives so exalted as mine. It was not the sordid feelings of the covetous thief that drew me into that enterprise; but an innate perception of natural right; and the consequence has been indelible: it rivetted my young determination to reform a system of society which took so little cognisance of the extent of temptation. The tale itself has often served, by its incidents, to brighten the social hour; but the effects have ever been like molten sulphur in my indignant 'heart of hearts.'

For days and nights after that morn of retribution, I burned with resentment: my meals were unrelished; my tasks, which were never pleasant, became odious; one time I thought of flying from the school – of playing the Roman fool; I roamed about the common, moody and vindictive; and when the fit was strong upon me, I could have put the master to death; but I was afraid of what the eloquent and energetic Caleb Williams calls 'the gore-dropping fangs of the law.'

From the greatest depths of despair the elastic spirit often rebounds; and accordingly, from that ultimate abasement of purpose to which it is the nature of revenge to sink us, my spirit recoiled – I became animated with the noblest impulses: instead of subjecting Mr. Skelper to penalties, I resolved to rouse the school to a glorious Reformation. It is impossible to describe the rapture with which the conception entered into my mind. The ecstasy of Jean

Jacques Rousseau, when he imagined his essay against the Arts and Sciences, was flat and stale compared with mine, which descended upon me with the enthusiasm of a passion; and I saw that the vindication of the privileges of my young companions opened a career illustrious and sublime.

No sooner had the animating idea revealed to me its beauty, than with youthful ardour I obeyed the impulse. Sagacity taught me that my companions and partners in suffering were already prepared by Destiny to listen to my suggestions with glad ears; and it was so; for when I took occasion to speak my purpose, they declared their willingness

'To share the triumph, and partake the gale.'

It was on the Sunday week from the day of our punishment that I first broke my mind. The scene was in the churchyard, after sermon; the bumpkin crowd had dispersed: around us were the tombs of the dead! Had we been companions of Catiline, meditating the overthrow of Rome, we could not have been more grim at first in our determinations of revenge; but as we proceeded to plan the operations, our awe of failure gradually diminished, insomuch that in the end we relished in anticipation the result of the undertaking, and revelled in the assurance of success: – a clear proof, as it has ever since seemed to me, that man has not that innate and gloomy abhorrence of those bold risks by which liberty must be conquered from the few who have an interest in maintaining general servitude and poverty.

Our first resolution was vengeance on Mr. Skelper; and our next was a unanimous determination to quit the school in a body, with three triumphant cheers, at the consummation of our success. Some of the boys, with a true republican spirit, proposed to tar-and-feather the despot; but my humanity revolted at the idea, and I endeavoured to assuage their animosity by an exhortation to a philanthropical suggestion: others thought that he should be seized in his easy chair, and carried out of his study, at the dead of night, and plunged into a gravel-pit that was

near the house and full of water. But these extremities were
congenial only to the few; and, after a long discussion, it
was agreed, over a new grave, with a mutual shaking of
hands, that on the next Saturday night every edible and
drinkable in the house should be taken away from larder,
closet, and cellar, by the avengers; and that when all was
fairly removed out of the house, the boys should assemble
in front and give three brave farewell huzzas.

Alas! in this contrivance we counted not on the weather.
The fatal night came on as wet as it could pour, and
our preparations were so far advanced that discovery was
inevitable; my good genius, however, pointed out a way of
rendering this disaster subservient to our gratification.

As was the case in rainy weather, we had that night the
use of the school-room. There, mounted on a form, I
harangued my compeers on the exigency. They received
my oration with shouts of applause. I pointed out to
them that it would be a confession of cowardice to be
baffled by Fate, and on such a night it could not fail to
be otherwise, if we attempted our original purpose; 'but,'
said I, dilating as I spoke, 'we are in this but urged to a
greater undertaking: forth we cannot go in such a night; it
would drench us to the skin, and frustrate our ingenuity:
let us, therefore, invoke the spirits of justice and the demon
of revenge; let us use the cords of our beds, not to hang
him, but to tie the arms of the tyrant and the myrmidons
of his household; and when we have done so, let us put
candles in every candlestick and empty bottle in the house,
and fill his devoted mansion with illumination; then let us
place ourselves round the table, before his eyes, and riot
upon every savoury article beneath his roof; when we are
satisfied, let us drink his health, and place regular watches
over him for the night: in the morning, as it cannot rain
always, we shall be ready to depart at an early hour.'

With exultation this suggestion was adopted. A party was
sent to the dormitories to uncord the beds; and when the
nightly bell was tolled as a signal for us all to go to sleep,
we gave a roof-rending huzza, and each well-appointed
phalanx proceeded in the execution of their several hests.

I led that band by which our dreadful retribution on the

master was to be executed. He submitted to our cords without uttering a word; but on one occasion he gave me a look that withered my heart. By this time the outcries of the maids were shrill and piercing, mingled with horrible giggling and screams. Old Mrs. Dawson the housekeeper, who had retired, before the bell rang, to her own chamber, hearing the uproar, came to the banisters of the stair, and inquired with alarm what was the matter; we, however, respected her sex: she was a good-natured body, and a favourite with all the boys; in consequence she was only ordered into her own room.

The revolution was now irresistible; but in the midst of the fury, a cry from Mrs. Dawson's window, wild as that of fire, was heard, and presently a knocking thundered at the door. From what hand that knocking came, none stayed to question; but all, with a simultaneous rush, fled by the back door, despite the rain, and sought refuge in the Goose and Goslings Inn at the village. The arrival of so many juvenile guests terrified the landlord. The news of the insurrection spread like wildfire; the whole town was presently afoot; and before we could rally our scattered senses, we were led captive by beadles and constables back to our fetters.

But mark with what singular emphasis Destiny spoke her will to me: all the other boys were received back, and on the spot decimated for punishment on Monday morning, all save me; me Mr. Skelper would not again receive: he called me the ringleader, a boy of incurable audacity, and ignominiously inflicting his toe on a tender part, bade the constable take me out of his sight.

A transaction of this kind needs no comment. I saw the full iniquity of that system in which such irresponsible power was allowed to be exercised. No prayers I said that night; but I made a solemn vow, that the overthrow of that organisation of things in which man durst so treat his fellow-man, even though he were a child, ought to be the intrepid business of my life.

In the morning I was sent home by the stage-coach, the guard of which was the bearer of a libellous letter to my father. What ensued on my arrival, when the old gentleman read the nefarious epistle, cannot be told; but it gave me both black and blue reasons to resent the ruthlessness of that false position in which children and parents stand, with respect to each other. Who ever heard that, in a state of nature, where all is beneficent and beautiful, the cruel hyæna, which so well deserves the epithet, inflicts coercive manipulations on her young?

For several days after my return home, my situation might have drawn sympathy from statues. My father never spoke; my mother looked at me in silence and shook her head: I was as a tainted thing; and my meals, with a refinement of cruelty, were made solitary, in another room from the family parlour. The impression of such iron-hearted conduct, to a generous high-minded lad of fifteen, may be guessed, but cannot be described. My heart swelled with grudging; and I could see no remedy for my deplorable condition, but only supplications for pardon. To this meanness, however, I strengthened myself with the sternest resolutions never to stoop; and, in the end, my tenacity of purpose was rewarded as virtue ought always to be.

My mother, on the third or fourth day, began to relent. The first symptom of the thaw was evinced by her presenting me with a pear, and saying that she hoped I had received a lesson that would serve me for life. My father, however, remained still inexorable; and his first speech, on the morning of the fifth day, was appalling. 'Nathan Butt,' said he, 'you have been from your infancy a turbulent child, ordained to break the heart of your parents, and send their gray hairs with sorrow to the grave. The offence that you have been guilty of to Mr. Skelper can never be forgiven; it is a blot upon your character which can never be effaced; but you were not sent into the world to sulk in idleness all the days of your life; I have therefore resolved that you shall go to another school, where you may learn something, and redeem, by endeavour, the past. To-morrow morning you shall come with me by the stage-coach to Witherington school: you may have heard that the Rev. Dr. Gnarl, who keeps it, is a very different person from the lenient

Mr. Skelper. He is a man that will make you stand in awe of him; the audacity of such a thought as tying him in his chair, you will find dare not there enter your head. I say no more; but be ready when the coach passes at daylight to-morrow, to come with me.'

There was something cool and steady in the severity of this speech that I did not much like, and destiny presented to me no alternative but only to submit; accordingly, in the course of the day, I began my preparations; and in the evening, much to my surprise – for I had been all these dismal days a stepson in the family – my mother invited me to sup with the rest; and I observed that the supper on this occasion was distinguished with a spacious florentine, which I lacked not the discernment to perceive had been consecrated for the celebration of my departure; but, with the same fortitude and forbearance that have ever distinguished me in life, I resolved not to taste it, enticing and savoury-smelling as it was. In this masculine resolution I persevered, my father and mother exchanging rueful looks.

Without taking any part in the conversation, I retired early to bed, though not sleepy; and as I lay tossing in the dark, I heard my mother come stepping softly into the room, and take a seat at my pillow, where she had not sat long till she began to sigh and sob. The room was dark, and I could not see; but I have no doubt she was indulging in a fit of tears; for she had not the spirit of a Volumnia, though her son had so much in him of Coriolanus.

When she had given way for some time to her sensibility, she inquired if I was sleeping. My innate respect for truth would not suffer me to disguise the fact, though I had an apprehension of what would follow.

On receiving my answer, she began to exhort me to change my behaviour, adding a great deal of motherly weakness and affection, more than I could endure, inso-much that, while she was speaking in the most earnest manner, I found it expedient to give a great snore, and pretend that I had fallen fast asleep. At this she rose with a heart-felt sigh, and pronouncing a benediction, went away.

Early next morning I embarked with my father in the coach for Witherington, where we arrived in time for breakfast, which we took at the Black Bull Inn, and afterwards proceeded to the residence of Dr. Gnarl.

His house stood on the edge of a green common, within a white-painted railing, many palisades of which were broken, and all around wore an aspect of the ruin that is more akin to destruction than decay; indeed, though we saw none of the doctor's pupils; it was quite evident, from the appearance of the place, that it was the domicile of numerous school-boys; and so I soon found; for, instead of the thirty blithe and bounding boys that I had left at Mr. Skelper's, there were upwards of a hundred lads, of various ages, all of whom possessed a particular artificial character, the effect of the doctor's austere discipline, through which, however, as I afterwards observed, their natural tempers and buoyancy broke out with an amiable brilliancy. They consisted chiefly of youths who had been, like me, expelled from other seminaries, but for causes of bravery which, when we became more acquainted, they were proud to relate. They were, indeed, notwithstanding their submission to the authority of the doctor, gallant and congenial companions, and had a just sense of the thraldom to which they had been consigned by their parents and guardians, in obedience to those prejudices with which society has been so long oppressed and deformed.

My introduction to Dr. Gnarl was an epochal event, never by me to be forgotten – an era in my life. My father and I were shewn into a raw, unfrequented kind of a drawing-room, where soon after the reverend doctor came to us, and to whom my father said, at his entrance, 'I have brought you Nathan Butt, my son, who I trust will, in your hands, be reclaimed from his audacious courses.'

I looked at the doctor. He was a little, stumpy, red-faced man, with austere eyes, and as erect as it was possible to be; dressed in black, neatly I must say. His legs were thick, and his feet small, on which he wore bright and glittering shoes, fastened by little round silver buckles. He also wore a trim close wig, slightly powdered, with his spectacles up; and spoke with a lisp, which inspired me at the first hearing with no reverential sentiment.

My father having some business to transact in the borough, which returned two members to Parliament, and it was then the eve of a general election, soon after left me alone with the doctor, by whom I was immediately treated in a manner that made my blood boil. Having seen my father to the porch, he bowed; and bidding him good morning, returned into the drawing-room, where I was standing, by no means comfortable; nor was my felicity in the slightest degree increased by the manner in which he said, –

'Nathan Butt, follow me into the school-room; and when the other boys have said their lessons, I shall see what progress you have made.'

With these words he twirled on his heel, and marching with an air of consequence on before me, led the way to the school. I followed with a palpitating heart; for it was impossible to conceal from myself that his accent and appearance betokened humiliation to me.

As we approached the school, which was behind the house, I heard a dreadful clamour within, which recruited my faded energies, and I took fresh heart from the music of the din; but the moment we entered, all was silence, and my courage instantly sank, for it was a sudden and ominous tranquillity, that told, with more emphasis than words, the power with which the master ruled, and the terror with which the adolescents obeyed.

Although I had now turned my fifteenth year, I was not at all aware of the state of society. The blind gropings of instinct had, indeed, instructed me of something wrong in the habits and usages of mankind; but nothing very precise could be said to have obtained my serious attention. I could see around me the hand of oppression ever visible, and I felt in my own case that power rather than justice was consulted by those who regarded my independence with jealousy. But the time was drawing nigh when the inductions of reason were to ratify the apprehensions of instinct, and the nebulæ of sentiment to assume the clearness and distinct forms of rational conclusions.

I have mentioned that the ancient borough of Witherington returned two members to Parliament, and that a general election was soon expected. In less than a month after my arrival at Dr. Gnarl's school, the dissolution of Parliament took place; and at the same time it was made known that one of the old members, a Whig, retired, and that two new candidates, a Radical and a moderate Tory, intended a contest for the vacant seat. The tidings of this struggle were received with gladness by all the school; and in the course of a few days the pupils declared themselves resolute adherents of the liberal cause. Dr. Gnarl, however, with a strange sagacity, inspired by his fears, foresaw this result; and accordingly announced that he would punish, as guilty of a gross offence, every boy who presumed to take a part in the election.

This decision was fatal to the joyful thoughts with which we were animated, especially as he declared that on the days of election the doors of the school would be shut, and no egress allowed while the poll continued open. But arbitrary absolutism has ever been defeated; – the boys held a consultation together in the play-ground; and it was resolved to address a round-robin to the Doctor, and remonstrate with him for so interdicting us in the exercise of our undoubted rights as Britons. Some of the bigger lads advised a different course, and suggested that we should dissimulate our principles, and pretend to be of the Tory party. This, however, was scouted by those who knew the Doctor best and longest. They asserted, that, notwithstanding all his Tory predilections within the school, he was out of it an inveterate Whig, and the most pontifical of living things, – maintaining that no apparent change on our part would cajole him.

This opinion soon became universal; and the majority of the boys declaring that it would be equivalent to an abandonment of principle to disguise our feelings, the expedient of the round-robin was adopted, drawn out, and signed. It was to the following effect: –

'Sir, – Glorying in the name of Britons, we have been astonished at your prohibition of our privileges; but we will assert our native and immutable rights. Give us, then, freedom to attend at the hustings, or prepare yourself to endure the consequences of a refusal.'

Six boys, including me, at my own request, were appointed to present to the potentate this Spartan epistle; and next morning, when the election was to begin, the ceremony of giving the round-robin was to be performed.

Never did an incident of the kind exhibit the corruption of nature in man more impressively than this ceremony. At eight o'clock in the morning the deputation went to present the remonstrative robin. Whether we had been betrayed by any sinister adherent, I know not; but the Doctor was seated in his elbow-chair, and beside him stood a gigantic horse-whip. He received us, however, coolly, with a smiling countenance; and having taken the paper in his hand, he read it aloud, carefully looking over the names. His sneers were satanic; in the most irresponsible manner he flung the paper into the fire, and suddenly grasping his whip, he laid on the shoulders of the deputation, as if they had been each an obstinate waggon-horse. We fled before him, and sought refuge elsewhere; but his tyranny was only exasperated by our flight. One by one he called up the other boys, and treated them with as little mercy. Their cries and screams, which ascended from beneath his dreadful flagellation, for the whipping made him fiercer, filled us with sympathetic anguish and sorrow; till one of our number, called Jack Scamp, cried out, that the cowardly rascals deserved it all, for sitting silent spectators of the outrage committed on us. This led to a change of operations. We instinctively gave three huzzas; and with indefatigable zeal, and being on the outside of the school, broke every pane of glass in the windows. The lion at this came rushing forth, pale and ghastly, followed by the whole school, who immediately joined our party, and assisted to envelop the little man in a cloud and whirlwind of missiles, snatched from the ground. By what partial God he was borne away from our vengeance, still remains undivulged; but when the storm abated, he was no where to be seen.

Our triumph was complete. We arranged ourselves in a body on the spot, and marched in regular array to the hustings. To crown the éclat of our noble assertion of independence, we happened to fall in by the way with an old fiddler, who was playing to obtain charity. Him we instantly impressed and placed at our head, astonishing the assembled multitude at the hustings, who made way for our procession!

I have been the more particular in these details, because they are associated with the hallowed doctrines that Mr. Chase, the popular candidate, impressed me with on that memorable day. It was, indeed, the birthday of my soul's freedom; for the manner in which he described the malefactions of the Whigs and Tories (he spared the delinquency of neither) was congenial to my best feelings; and the tale he unfolded of the usurpations of their aristocracies, not only in legislation, but in property, froze the very marrow in my bones. It seemed to me as if the world had been, from time immemorial, in backsliding confusion; and my heart burned with a vehement ardour to arrest the chaos into which it was fatally hurrying. But in that moment, the demon of the age – that genius of the oppression which so saddens the earth – was hovering at hand; and in the very flame and passion of my antipathy to the afflictions of the world, a numerous band of constables surrounded the whole of Dr. Gnarl's resolute youths, and, in the most shameful and lawless manner, compelled us to return with them to the school; where the despot, with a courage that would have done honour to a better cause, welcomed us back, hoped we had been well edified by the trash we had heard, and with undaunted sobriety ordered us apart in threes and fours to our respective rooms, where he kept us on bread and water for two days; at the end of which, to our amazement, when summoned into the school-room, we beheld our fathers and guardians assembled.

'Gentlemen,' said the Doctor to them, when we were arranged before them – 'is it your pleasure to remove these rebellious youths from under my jurisdiction? or am I free to let them feel a weight of discipline equivalent to the offence they have committed?'

The courteous reader need not be told what answer the fiend of the existing order of things taught them to give; but from that hour the law went forth; and for the next twelve months never more than three of the boys were allowed to be seen talking, or in any manner associating together, under the penalty of a severe horsing. Thus, with a harshness that would have disgraced the worst of all the Caesars, he re-established the discipline of the school; peace was restored, – peace, did I say? Alas! can it, therefore, be wondered, that I am so animated against a system in which crimes so obnoxious to the freedom of rational beings can with impunity be committed? On that day I swore never to abate in my desire to crush a social organisation whose natural secretions evolved such suffering and guilt.

The remainder of that year of bondage, worse than Egyptian bondage, which I breathed under the iron rule of Dr. Gnarl, completed my epoch of youth. At the end of it my father summoned me home; and though I carried with me the reputation of being subdued, I know that in my heart I was none altered. The true complexion and the right side of things were revealed to me, and, I need not add, with no increase of admiration for either. Some of our neighbours acknowledged that they saw a change upon me; but with that inherent predilection for detraction which belongs to morbid sentiment, they described it as something which could not be understood, and never railed to call it malignant. My stern and manly contempt of oppression, in whatsoever form it appeared, they spoke of as sullenness.

The effect of their calumnious insinuations was soon visible. Many lads of my own age and station, who had been originally my playmates, and whom I again expected to be the associates of my riper years, became prejudiced against me; and the first years that I spent in my father's office after my return, for he placed me on the lofty tripod stool, were well calculated to nourish morose determinations.

I soon discovered, by that perspicacity with which I was naturally endowed, that I could only hope to be received into fellowship by the young men whom I had expected would be my friends, by a submission, on my part, of the erectness of my principles, and a pliancy of conduct towards theirs, the bare idea of which was revolting; and accordingly, with a decision of mind, which their contumely and manifest aversion made no sacrifice, I turned from those who should have been my companions, and soon found a congenial refuge among spirits of a more generous philanthropy.

The town in which my father's house was situated, had, a few years before, been a listless village; but the accident of a wealthy manufacturer ascertaining that the brook which bounded the green was practicable for mills, induced him to build a large factory there, and doomed

'Sweet Auburn, loveliest village of the plains,'

to the hectic prosperity of the cotton trade.

Among the spinners and weavers which this insalubrious change introduced, was an aspiring band of young men, with pale faces and benevolent principles. In their society I found an agreeable solace and compensation for my abandonment of those whose station was more on a par with my own. We held frequent nocturnal meetings, at which they always treated me with the greatest respect, and made me their president; but this honour, I felt, was, like all others, most incommodious: seldom an opportunity arose, while in the chair, to give utterance, by opinion or argument, to the inductions of my understanding; and, in consequence, I resolved to abdicate the pre-eminence to which that portion of the old leaven with which they were yet leavened inspired them to raise me. After this abdication, I found myself in all my energy; a free gladiator in the arena, my strength and superiority were then displayed.

During the first winter we discussed general topics and the speculative conjectures of erudite men; but when the rumours os what was then taking place at Paris reached our rural haunts, and the London mail brought daily news as it passed through our town, patriotism and curiosity constrained us to club together for a newspaper.

If the orations of Mr. Chase, on the hustings of Witherington, roused my latent feelings, that newspaper gave them tendency and purpose. It was soon evident to those brave philosophers – who were such indeed, though by profession but weavers and cotton-spinners – my companions, that mankind had incurred a fearful arrear in their duties to one another; and in vain we endeavoured to discover by what right, sanctioned by the equity of nature, lords were lordly, and the poor man doomed to drudge. That something was wrong, and destructive of natural rights, in the unequal existing division of property, could not be questioned. The speeches of the illustrious great of the French Convention, confirmed by the eloquence of some of the brightest stars in the constellation of the British senate, enlightened our understandings. It required, indeed, but little other reasoning to convince us all, that the world had been led by some pernicious undiscoverable influence in the olden time to prefer the artificial maxims of society to those natural first principles which ought ever to be paramount with man.

When we had arrived, self-taught, at this conclusion, the majority of our association held resolute language, and began to nerve themselves for enterprise. A few, however, among us, tainted with a base diffidence, listened with alarm to our distinction between the institutions which originate in the frame of the social state, and those absolute rights which man has inherited from nature, anterior to the operation of the gregarious sympathies that have led to the organisation of society – an organisation which gives forth the grievances of the world.

Debates for some time ran high and warm: at last we became so fervent towards our respective adversaries, that a breach was inevitable. Soon after, several of those who were considered as the champions of the existing social order, married, and became church-goers. I do not insinuate, however, by this, that they recanted their former notions of the ecclesiastical usurpations; but I thought of what Lord Bacon says about men who give hostages to society, and ceased, in consequence, to have any intercourse with them.

Whilst I was thus, in obedience to Destiny, developing my faculties, and fitting myself to take a part in those great purposes in which I am, to all appearance appointed to be drawn forth, it is necessary I should here relate a personal incident that has had some influence on my subsequent career, and in the adjustment of my feelings between nature and society.

About the time of which I have been speaking, an amiable young woman and I were brought into a very awkward position by the parish officers. Perhaps, as the affair was altogether private, I ought not to have mentioned it in these pages; but as my chief object is to exhibit the perverted world as I found it, I can do no less than narrate some of the circumstances; especially as they serve to shew how widely that artificial system, which has so long been predominant, is different from the beauty, the simplicity, and the integrity of nature.

For some weeks there had been a shy and diffident acquaintanceship between Alice Hardy and me, insomuch that, before we exchanged words, we had looked ourselves into familiarity with one another. She was not, however, in that rank of life which my father, in his subserviency to the prejudices of society, would approve of as a fit match for me; and therefore I resolved to seek no closer communion with her. Nevertheless, it came to pass, I cannot well tell how, that one day we happened to fall into speaking terms; and, from less to more, grew into a pleasant reciprocity. Nothing could be more pure and natural than our mutual regard; it was the promptings of an affection simple, darling, and congenial.

While in this crisis of enjoyment, malignant Fortune

influenced the parish, and we were undone. One morning the beadle, wearing his cocked hat, big blue coat with red capes trimmed with broad gold lace, appeared at the door of Alice's mother, and calling her forth by name, impertinently inquired respecting some alteration that he had been told was visible in her appearance. To this she gave a spirited answer; at which the intrusive old man struck the floor with his silver-headed staff in a magisterial manner, and said, with a gruff voice, which alarmed the poor girl, that if she refused to answer his question, he would have her pulled up before her betters.

This threat she related to me in the evening, when we met, as our custom was, to walk in my lord's park; and next morning I went to the saucy beadle myself, and demanded why he had presumed to molest her with his impertinence. But instead of replying as he ought to have done, he said, with a look which I shall never forget, that he was coming for me to give security that the parish should not be burthened, as he called it, with a job.

This was strange tidings; and I was so confounded, that I did not know what answer to make. I assured him, however, that it had all come of an unaccountable accident, and should be so treated; for that neither Alice nor I had the least idea of the consequence – indeed, we never thought of it at all. But I spoke to a post; and, by what ensued, it was plain to me how much parochial beadles are opposed to the fondest blandishments of nature.

In some respects, the affair, in the end, as far as the parish and the beadle were concerned, was amicably settled; but my father, highly exasperated that I could not discern, or would not confess, a fault resolved that I should no longer remain in that country side. Accordingly, I was sent off very soon to my uncle, in one of the principal manufacturing towns of the kingdom, to be placed in his counting-house; it being deemed of no use to think I could ever make any figure in the law; my mind, as the old man asserted, was doggedly set against the most valued institutions of the country, and altogether of an odd and strange revolutionary way of thinking.

'Nathan Butt,' said he, on the evening previous to my

departure, 'you go from your father's house – what he says with sorrow and apprehension – an incorrigible young man: you have, from your youth upward, been contumacious to reproof, and in your nature opposed, as with an instinctive antipathy, to every thing that has been endeared by experience.'

This address a little disconcerted me; but in the end my independence gave me fortitude to say, – 'Sir, that I have not been submissive to the opinions of the world and to yours is certain; but it is not in my character to be other than I am. Fate has ordained me to discern the manifold forms which oppression takes in the present organisation of society——'

'Oppression!' cried the old gentleman, with vehemence, 'do you call it oppression, to have been, from your childhood, the cause of no common grief to your parents; to have been kicked out of one school, and the rebel ringleader in another? – Nathan Butt! Nathan Butt! unless you change your conduct, society will soon let you know, with a pin in your nose, what it is to set her laws and establishments at defiance.'

'Alas! sir, pardon me for the observation – but you have lived too long; the world now is far ahead of the age which respected your prejudices. I am but one of the present time; all its influences act strongly on me, and, like my contemporaries, I feel the shackles and resent the thraldom to which we have been born.'

'You stiff-necked boy!' exclaimed my father, starting up in a passion; 'but I ought not to be surprised at such pestiferous jargon. And so you are one of those, I suppose, destined to be a regenerator of the world! Come, come, Mahomet Butt, as I should call you, no doubt this expulsion to your uncle's will be renowned hereafter as your Hegira. I have seen young men, it is true, in my time – that which you say is now past – who, with a due reverence for antiquity, and a hallowed respect for whatever age and use had proved beneficial – but the lesson is lost on you: however, let me tell you, my young Mahomet, that we had in those days mettlesome lads, that did no worse than your pranks; but——'

'Well then, sir, what was the difference between them and me?'

'Just this, you graceless vagabond! – what they did, was in fun and frolic, and careless juvenility; but you, ye reprobate! do your mischief from instinct; and evil, the devil's motive, is, to your eyes and feelings, good! You – ye ingrained heretic to law, gospel, and morality, as I may justly say you are – have the same satisfaction in committing mischief, that those to whom I allude had, in after-life, in acts of virtue and benevolence.'

It was of no use to answer a man who could express such doctrine; so I just said to him, that I claimed no more from him than the privilege of nature. 'The beasts and birds,' said I, 'when they have come to maturity, leave their lairs and nests, and take their places in the world.'

The old man, in something like a frenzy, caught me by the tuft of hair on my forehead by the one hand, and seizing a candle with the other, pored in my face, at first sternly, and then softening a little, he flung me, as it were, from him, and said, – 'Go, get out of my sight, thou beast or bird of prey!'

I shall make no animadversions on such a domestic life; the reader will clearly see that it belonged to that state of society which soon, thanks be and praise, is about to be crushed. It will no longer be in the power of one, dressed in a little brief authority, to play such fantastic tricks with those in whom the impulses of nature are justly acknowledged as superior to all artificial maxims and regulations.

My uncle, Mr. Thrive, was a brother of my mother, and the toppingest merchant in all the town of Slates. He was a bustling, easy-natured man, indulgent to the foibles of others, yet, at the same time, regular and respectable in his own habits. His reception of me was familiar and jocose. He had previously been prepared for my arrival by a letter from my father; and I delivered him one from my mother, which he read over before he spoke to me; and as he read, I could perceive a temperate smile dawn and brighten on his countenance. He, however, at the conclusion, affected a droll austerity, which was to me as relishing as pleasantry.

'You scamp,' said he, 'you have too good a mother; – here is my soft sister beseeching me for all manner of kindness towards you, and mitigating, with a deal of fond and motherly palaver, the impression which she fears your father, in his anger, may have produced upon me. But I will make no promises, – if you do well, it will be better for yourself; but if you be abandoned to the follies your father speaks of, Nathan, my nephew, you are a gone Dick!'

There was certainly something in the manner of this address that I did like; but there was also a firmness of tone in the utterance of the latter part, that fell upon my spirit with the constraint of a magic spell. I perceived that Mr. Thrive was a stout and steady man of the world; though a merchant, he was yet less indulgent than my father, who was an attorney.

There was a great difference in their appearance too. My uncle was a portly, well-dressed person, of an urbane, gentlemanly air: my father, who had been more than five-and-thirty years the legal adviser of Lord Woodbury, one of the greatest beaux of his time, was, in his appearance, the opposite of all ever deemed fashionable and favour-bespeaking. His clothes were of a strange and odd cut: he wore half-boots, light-blue stockings, and brown kerseymere inexpressibles, with large silver knee-buckles; commonly a black satin waistcoat with spacious pockets, a bluish-grey coat with broad brass buttons, a tye-wig well powdered; and his face was red as with the setting glow of a departed passion.

But the difference was most remarkable in their tempers. Mr. Thrive was a shrewd, sharp observer, who saw many things with a glance, which he afterwards recollected apparently without effort. My father, on the contrary, possessed but little of that alert faculty, and somehow was as little inclined to remember whatever he observed objectionable. This much I am bound to say in candour; for it was the general opinion of those who had known him longest. Towards myself, however, I do think his character was an exception; for my least faults he uniformly noticed severely, and never forgot; my most piquant remarks he often scouted with derision, or blamed with animadversion in no measured terms: in short, he was an aristocrat of the Tory tribe, and I in those days gloried in being a thorough democrat. It requires, therefore, nothing additional, to assure the reader that we did not live on the best of terms. My removal to Slates was, in consequence, really an agreeable translation; for my uncle, what with his business, and bustling, and jocose disposition, seemed to look lightly on my pecularities; and for some time I spent with him the happiest halcyon days of my life; – and yet Mr. Thrive was a stanch Government man.

When I had been a few weeks at Slates, I gradually fell into acquaintance with several spirited liberal young men, more distinguished in the town for their philosophical principles than for those aberrations in conduct, which made others of the same class less eminent for decorum. It would ill become me, indeed, to speak lightly of those to whom I allude; but I soon was led to notice that there was something of an organic difference between my companions and them.

We were of a sedate and methodical character, addicted

to books more than to bottles, – thoughtful, inquisitive, and in our way of life sober and reasonable. Our adversaries, for such in truth they were, gave themselves up, in many respects, to wild and dissolute habits, possessed little information, and, with a kind of irreverent ribaldry, professed themselves the champions of those institutions of which we, on our part, considered it the greatest of duties to work the overthrow. They were, indeed, like the drunken soldier who in the Puritan war swore to a church, that he would stand by her old soul while he had a drop of blood in his veins.

It was during my intercourse with those enlightened associates, that my crude reflections on the causes of unhappiness in the world assumed form and consistency. At that time the war of the French revolution was raging; the Great nation, having got rid of their ancient government, and having cured their country of all its hereditary scrofula, was renewed in vigour; every thing they undertook was consolatory to the oppressed of the earth; and they exhibited to astonished Europe the amazing effects of that enlarged philanthropy which they had so long cherished, and by which they had become the foremost people in the universe. It was delightful to contemplate the triumphs of liberty among them, and how they hallowed their cause with blood. But the contrast, when I looked around me, was deplorable. Never can I forget the indignant feelings with which I regarded the obstinacy of the infatuated Pitt, and the audacity with which his sordid adherents resisted the progress of knowledge, and arrested the perfectability of man.

In the midst, however, of the humiliation which that weak and wicked statesman and his colleagues made me suffer, I was cheered, as the mariner in the storm is with the sight of a beacon shining bright and high. The disasters which so often overwhelmed their measures gave confidence to my hopes that, shipwreck was their doom. But it would be to weary the intelligent reader, to descant on this theme. It is sufficient to observe, that the ruling demon of society and the genius of nature were then fighting in the mid heavens; and the latter could not but sooner or later prevail. 'Thrones and sovereignties,' said I, 'the resources of empires, hierarchies, and orders, and the progeny of artificial life, may for a time withstand the eternal goddess; but as sure as the moon waxes to the round bright full, she will vindicate her jurisdiction, and gladden the earth.'

It is not my intention, as I have already intimated, to record in these pages my private memoirs; but I cannot adequately describe the impressions which I received from many circumstances, originating exclusively in that state of society which there is now the happy prospect of living to see dissolved and abrogated, without now and then departing from the strict rule prescribed to myself, and touching a little on the incidents of my domestic history.

When I had resided some time, better than a year, with my uncle, he said to me, as we were sitting together one Sunday evening by the fire-side, he looking over some family papers, and I reading Godwin's Political Justice, a work in the highest style of man:

'Nathan Butt,' said he, 'our family is not very numerous, and in course of nature, bating my sister, you are the nearest, as the eldest of her children, to me of kin; and should you survive me, I have thought that it would be a prudent thing of you, and a great satisfaction to me, were you to make a prudent marriage. I see it is not necessary that fortune should be an essential ingredient in the choice, but it can be no detriment.'

To this I replied, 'That I was very sensible of the kindness with which he treated me; but, sir,' I added, 'marriage is what I have never thought of: indeed, to speak plainly, I have great objections to incur an obligation, to which the world has attached so many restraints, at variance with the freedom which mankind have derived from nature.'

'Pooh, pooh, Nathan,' cried my uncle, 'I am serious; don't talk such stuff now; we are not on an argument, but an important business of life.'

'I assure you, sir,' was my sedate answer, 'I have never

been more serious. Marriage, sir, is one of those artificial compacts invented by priests and ecclesiastics to strengthen their moral dominion.'

'I shall not dispute with you, Nathan,' replied my uncle, 'that marriage does bring grist to the church's mill; but we are not to judge of it merely by the tax which we pay for its blessings; therefore say nothing on that head. Men and women must have some law to regulate them in their domicile, and as no better has yet been enacted, we must conform to what is.'

'In Paris, sir,' said I, 'it is no longer——'

'Nathan Butt,' said my uncle, rather sternly, 'I am speaking to you on a very important subject; therefore don't trouble me with any thing about your French trash, and the utility of living in common like the beasts that perish.'

I had never heard Mr. Thrive express himself in this manner before: hitherto he had only laughed, as it were, at what he called my Jacobin crotchets; but I could discern that a feeling of a more sensitive kind affected him on this occasion. He was a rich man – his favour was therefore worth cultivating; and I frankly acknowledge that this consideration had great weight with me. But principle should be above corruption; and I felt at the moment that I was yielding to the deleterious influences of the artificial social state, when, for a moment, I thought it might be for my interests to accede to what was evidently his intention. However, I rallied, and frankly told him that I never intended to marry.

'You are a fool,' cried he, 'and may live to repent it:' and abruptly gathering up his papers and rising, said, before leaving the room, 'Reflect, Nathan, well on this short conversation. I do not look for an old head on young shoulders, and you are not destitute, on some occasions, of common sense; reflect on this, I say, for a week, and next Sunday evening we shall resume the conversation.'

He then went away; and as his remarks had disturbed the philosophic equanimity with which I had been pondering over the sound and sane maxims and apothegms of the book before me, I closed it; and drawing my chair close to the fire, placed my feet on the fender, and began to ruminate on my uncle's worldly dogmas.

It was clear to me, that, with all his ability as a man of business – and in that he was considered eminent – Mr. Thrive had no right conception of the difference between man in a state of nature, and as a member of society which is in so many things opposed to nature. 'What good, I would ask,' said I to myself, 'can he expect to reap, by alluring me, with pecuniary considerations, to hazard all that is valuable to a rational being, by taking on me the fetters of an obligation that is not only fast becoming obsolete, but is acknowledged by so many as the most vexatious that can be incurred;' and I thought of Doctors' Commons.

For several days I did reflect on the conversation just recited, and felt, even to the Thursday night, that all my principles remonstrated, as it were, against a compliance with the wishes of my uncle; but from that evening I certainly underwent some change.

I then thought, for the first time, of the shortness of life – no elixir or expedient having been discovered by which it could be prolonged. I reflected also, with a sigh, on the uncertainty of fortune, how often the best-laid schemes were frustrated, and the seeds of industry and skill blighted in their growth, affording no harvest. I became sad; a feeling of grief, more intense than melancholy, occupied my heart; and I said to myself, 'Man is but a cog on a wheel, a little wheel in the great enginery of Fate.'

This nothingness of individual man in the universal system of things had a great effect upon me, and at last I began to think, who among all the females of our circle would make the best wife: but this was unsatisfactory. Over and over again I meditated on the subject; but the more I meditated respecting them, the faults of each became more conspicuous to me; insomuch that by the Sunday evening, although I had resolved, in submission to circumstances, to assent to an occultation of principle, I was embarrassed, and could determine on no choice. Thus it happened, when the hour came round, I was exceedingly perplexed, and, contrary to custom, instead of taking a book, as was my wont, I sat idle; while my uncle, I could perceive, eyed me with occasional sinister glances, that made me thrill, as if I felt that he suspected me of some delinquency. At last he broke silence:

'Well, Nathan Butt,' said he, 'I observe by your manner that you have been giving some heed to what I said last Sunday night; what is your determination?'

'Truly, sir,' was my diffident answer, 'I know not what to say: marriage itself I consider as one of the incidental evils of the social state, and until that undergoes a thorough reformation, it appears to me, all things considered, that, out of a philosophical respect for the opinions of others, it must be tolerated.'

'Well, Nathan, I do not say that your remark, which looks so like philosophy, is altogether nonsense; but the matter in hand is, Are you, then, disposed to take a wife?'

'I cannot exactly answer that question, because I am acquainted with no young lady that I would prefer more than another; and therefore, as I have little inclination for the state, and no motive of preference, I am very likely to remain a bachelor.'

'Well, I must say, Nathan, you are a young man of very odd notions; but as I am convinced marriage is the best thing that can happen to you, my endeavour shall not be wanting to discover a proper match. What think you of Miss Shuttle, the daughter of my old friend? I have long considered that she would make you a very suitable wife, being largely endowed with good common sense, with which you are not overburdened, and a cheerful social temper, in which you are greatly deficient.'

Now, Miss Shuttle had never blithened my cogitations; but the moment my uncle mentioned her name, I was sensible of an attractive bias towards her. Not, however, to trouble the courteous reader with further particulars, let it suffice that we were in due time made man and wife, according to the most approved forms of the Establishment; though I, being the son of a Dissenter (for my father was a Presbyterian), would have preferred a ceremony less ostentatious.

My wife certainly possessed those qualities for which she had been recommended; her only fault was, indeed, of the most blameless description. She had not the slightest predilection for ratiocination; but, on the contrary, she was living effigy of passive obedience; and it was only in this supple compliance that I ever found her tiresome. Once, however, she did evince a capability of sustaining an argument – the highest faculty in man; and I have never since ceased to wonder at it, for on that occasion she was triumphant.

She had changed our cook; at which, as the woman was civil and managing, I expressed some surprise, it being my habit to partake of my philosophical share of dinner without remark.

'What you say, my dear, is very true,' was her answer; 'she is an excellent creature, but a very bad cook, and I hired her for a cook.'

'But,' replied I, 'you should have balanced her good qualities against her defects.'

'That would not have mended her cookery – it would still have been as bad as ever; and you cannot deny, Nathan Butt that good eating is one of the greatest comforts in life.'

'Is it? I'm sure, Mrs. Butt, I pay no attention to it: it is a subject – an animal subject – beneath the dignity of an intellectual being.'

'It may, sir; but when one thing at table happens to be better than another, I observe you instinctively prefer the best; and it is only by having a good cook that we can be sure of enjoying a comfortable life.'

This silenced me; it being evident that the enjoyment we have in eating, especially in good eating, is one of the few unimpaired innate immunities of the species; and that my wife was quite right in her estimate of a cook.

With the single exception of this brief discussion, we never had a word which shewed the least difference of opinion between us: indeed, I had no occasion to contradict her; she always submitted to my pleasure and so maintained in an amiable manner, the peace of our house.

Although the accordance of my conduct to the prompting of nature, was generally, I may truly say always, reciprocated by Mrs. Butt, we yet had one serious controversy; all others were uniformly of the most amicable kind. It only required a little firmness on my part to see that every thing was done as I desired; for I never could abide to debate first principles in such trifles as household particularities. I anticipated all objections by the judicious serenity with which I announce my will and orders. But uniform tranquillity belongs not to man in his social condition.

In the course of the second year after our marriage, my first-born in wedlock, a son, came to light. At that epoch there was a moderation in men's minds such as had not been experienced for some years. The French, under the fatal dominion of Napoleon, had lost much of their interesting character. He had degraded himself by a union with the sentenced blood of Austria; and those who had once thought they saw in him the deliverer of the human race, were mortified by his apostacy. The effect of this made me, as well as all of my way of thinking, shrink back into ourselves, and seek to obscure our particular opinions by a practical adherence to the existing customs of the world – errors and prejudices which we never forgot they were.

It thus happened, when Mrs. Butt proposed to me that our child should be baptized, I made no objection; only remarking, that it was a usage to which we must submit, and the expense being inconsiderable, it was not a case in which we should shew ourselves different from our neighbours.

Sometimes before, I had observed that she was not very well satisfied with an occasional word which dropped from me respecting priestcraft and ecclesiastical usurpation; but as my father was a Presbyterian, she ascribed those accidental strictures to the tenets of his sect, supposing me of the same persuasion. But that I should speak of baptism as deserving of consideration only on account of the fees, produced an effect for which I was not prepared.

She was standing when she put the question, and I was reading the book of a recent continental traveller, a man of liberal principles, who had shrewdly inspected the world, and correctly discerned its prevalent errors and abuses; for it was, indeed, chiefly from such travellers that I obtained right expositions of these controverted topics. Without raising my eyes over the edge of the leaves, I gave her the answer quoted; to which she made no reply, but, retreating backwards to the elbow-chair opposite, sat down and drew a deep sigh.

Not expecting that any thing particular was about to take place, I took no other notice of her consternation than by casting a glance over the top of the book; which she observed, and, wiping her eyes, suddenly rose and went away, and wrote to my mother on the subject. In the course of two or three days, on the evening before the day appointed for the christening, the old lady made her appearance; having come, as she unhesitatingly declared, to witness the solemnity.

I welcomed her as she justly merited to be from me; for although in some things she was wilful, as most parents are, she nevertheless had made herself, by her kindnesses, a cosy corner in my bosom, and I was sincerely glad to see her, – a little surprised, however, at her unexpected visit.

Early next morning my father also arrived by the mail. He had travelled all night, and seemed in rather an irksome humour. After swallowing a hasty breakfast, he went directly to my uncle; saying, in a manner that struck me as emphatical, that they would both dine with us, adding, 'The ceremony must be deferred till the evening;' and, grinning with vehemence, he shook his stick at me as he left the room, adding, 'You blasphemer, to break my heart in this manner!'

The secret motive of the visit was thus immediately disclosed; for no sooner was his back turned, than my mother and Mrs. Butt took out their handkerchiefs – as evidently preparatory to a scene, as the drawing up of the curtain is to a tragedy.

'Much has your poor wife, Nathan Butt, endured; but this is beyond pardon. I have come a long journey, and your worthy father has travelled all night – a dreadful thing at his age. We can, however, forgive all that; but who will forgive you for making the baptism of your first-born a consideration of parish fees, with no more reverence for religion than if you were a sucking turkey?'

'Do turkeys suck?' said I: 'that they are irreligious is doubtful. I have often myself noticed that they, as well as other poultry, never take even a drink of water from the dub, without lifting their heads and eyes towards the heavens in thankfulness.'

'Oh, Nathan, Nathan!' was her exclamation, in an accent of grief that smote my very heart, 'what will become of you and your poor baby? for now ye're the head of a family. Oh, oh!'

I made no answer; but I could not help wondering at the folly of the general world in thinking religion something different from the forms and genuflexions in which its offices are performed; or that there was aught in it beyond the ingenuity of those who in different ages had invented its several rites, as a mode of levying taxes for the maintenance of their order. And I turned to my wife, who was sitting hard by, and, with really more asperity than I ever made use of to her before, said, 'What is the meaning of this? Surely you very well knew that I was quite neutral in my wishes on the subject. If you desired our boy to be made a Christian, I had no objection: by making him undergo the ceremony, he could not therefore be less a man. You might have spared me from the reproaches of my father and mother, whose prejudices, at their time of life, it is vain to assail, and allowed the infant to be baptized quietly, and without more ado.'

Her reply filled me with amazement: 'In all temporal things, Nathan Butt, I considered it a duty – a sworn duty – to obey you, and never till this occasion have I ever felt a wish to depart from the strictness of my marriage vow. But, Nathan, this is not an earthly and mortal matter; the soul may be in danger of hell-fire by us; and religion admonishes me, yes strengthens me, poor, weak, and silly thing that I am, to give this sentenced scion of a fallen race the chance of salvation.'

I was confounded by her energy, and I pricked up my ears, for her manner was full of a fine enthusiasm, and she spoke like the Pythia. My mother then took up the strain, but with more familiar rhythm.

'She entreated your father and me,' said the old lady, 'to come to her aid; for she could not in conscience allow you, in your present state of unbelief, to take upon you the baptismal vows. Your father and uncle are to be the sponsors.'

'And am not I to have any thing to say in this affair?' replied I, a little fervently; for it seemed to me then, as it has done ever since, something beyond all toleration, that a father should, by any occult influence of the theocracy, be thus deprived of his natural right.

'Do you deserve to have any?' cried my mother.

My answer was sedate: 'I do not reckon on what I may deserve, but only on what is due to me as a parent.'

'This, Nathan,' said my wife, 'is not what is due to a parent. God has revealed that by baptism the condemned souls of the tainted race of Adam will again be rendered acceptable to his love; but wherefore it has been made the qualification for that election is a mystery. Yes, Nathan, I may in this be a disobedient wife, but there is holiness in the disobedience; and I hope that our dear baby, by receiving the sign and impress required by the Redeemer, will become eligible to partake of the blessing.'

'Why should there be mysteries in the world?' said I.

'Why should you be in the world?' exclaimed my mother.

'Hem!' was all I could say to this jargon; but, to do my wife justice, she spoke as it were with the voice of an oracle. At other times the terms of her phrases were like those of other women – simple, and not more to the point than needful; but that day her mien and elocution were impassioned, and her accent high, yet melancholy, like that of the afflicting spirit in a painful task of mercy.

I grew uneasy with her exhortations, and being irked too by my mother's vituperative persuasion, rose and went away.

I have no reminiscence of my carly life that still affects me like the recollections of that discussion; for although many arguments of the women were feminine enough, there was a solemnity about my wife that I had never seen any thing like before. I saw clearly that she was not only resolved to have the child christened, but that she meditated something more – what that was, the sequel will shew; but I could not help reflecting, as I walked along, on the inveteracy of religious prejudice, which could so disguise the various taxes by which it was upheld, that even very shrewd persons were unable to discern its object or tendency.

Instead of strolling towards the town on this occasion, although it was near the hour when the London mail and news usually arrived, I bent my steps towards the fields.

At all times since my childhood I have been a lover of Nature; and when my feelings have been chafed by the effects of the existing system, I have sought solace and soothing from the beauty and calm of the landscape. But on this occasion its wonted sweet influences were stale; for in my bosom there was a bitter controversy, in which conscious rectitude, and adherence to my own notions of the right, would not intermingle. Something decisive was, however, requisite; and at last calling to mind how much nobler it is to sacrifice one's own sentiments to those which are dear to others, I resolved to make no farther objection either to the fees or the baptismal performance; and accordingly returned home in this benevolent resolution, where, finding my wife alone in our bed-chamber, I bade her wipe her tears, and do in the whole affair as she thought fit, adding, 'I am ready to do my part – the father's part in the ceremony – since to you and the old people it is so important.'

Instead of returning me any answer, she began to weep still more grievously, which seemed very inexplicable; and I expressed my regret, with some surprise, that she should receive my concession with so little satisfaction.

'O Nathan!' cried she, 'speak not to me in that manner: although you are my husband, the father of my child, and one whom I have vowed at the holy altar to love and obey – it will yet make me turn from you with feelings that I dare not entertain. Your concession fills me with horror. In the ceremony you have no part; and it is the dreadful thought, that it is I who must object to you, which makes these tears to flow.'

'What do you mean?' cried I; 'you are incomprehensible.'

'Ah! in that lies much of my grief. Your irreligious opinions – I will call them by no harsher name – disqualify you to take the Christian vows. Your father and uncle are to stand in your place.'

'Come, come,' said I, somewhat disconcerted; 'this is carrying the joke too far: I assure you, my dear, that I will do what I ought, and all that you can desire.'

'But you shall not. No, Nathan Butt, it is I that bar you from the altar. You are not fit to take upon you the sacred obligations for your own child. Your father and uncle must incur them for you.'

I was not pleased to hear this bigotry, and was on the point of replying with more sternness than I had ever felt towards her before; but at that moment a housemaid announced that the two gentlemen, with a third, the Rev. Mr. Trial, a Presbyterian preacher, whose church my uncle regularly attended, had returned.

I went immediately to the drawing-room, into which they had been shewn; and on making my appearance, my father came towards me, and taking me by the hand, in a manner which affected me with sadness, said: 'We have brought with us a religious man, who will converse with you alone before dinner. The ceremony is to be performed in the evening by Dr. Colridge, the rector. Your wife being of the Establishment, surely you will not object: I am willing to indulge her in this little matter of mere form.'

'The whole affair,' said I, 'is a matter of no importance to me.'

'So I see,' rejoined my father, with a severe accent; and taking my uncle by the arm, led him out of the room, and left me with the Presbyterian minister.

It would be a tedious story to relate the conversation that then ensued between us; for he was a narrow-minded man, and spoke of a future state as confidently as of tomorrow; which shewed how little his mind had been accustomed to examine opinions unsupported by fact. But, saving this weak credulity, he was not so austere in his notions as many others of his cloth that I have met with; for, in answer to a remark of mine, expressive of wonder that he should so readily consent that Dr. Colridge should receive all the fees, he in a very gentlemantly manner said, these were of no importance in the question; 'the point of difference,' he added, 'between Dr. Colridge and me is a mere etiquette; and no sensible man, either of the Scottish or English persuasion, attaches to it much importance. In the scruples of Mrs. Butt, however, we are both deeply interested: she is a pious woman; and to reason with her respecting the state of her conscience in this matter, would be to disturb her, yea, perhaps, to shake the foundation of her faith.'

Language of this sort, seeming so liberal, on a subject that is any thing but liberal, perplexed me not a little; but when I called to mind that the poor man's stipend and welfare were at stake in his doctrine, I so far complied with what at the time appeared as a domestic duty, that I said he was very right.

'Mr. Trial, what you have expressed,' said I, 'is very edifying; but you know in a matter of this sort a man cannot be too delicate; and I would not altogether like to take upon me obligations, which in my conscience I felt were susceptible of doubt.'

I could perceive by his manner that the reverend gentleman was much troubled with the force of my observations; for, after a pause of some time, he rose and said, 'We had better join the company; our respective opinions are not to be easily reconciled I perceive, Mr. Butt; only it is some sign of a promise of grace, that you are not so strongly opposed to the principles of your wife, as to resist her in this solemn matter.'

We then joined the company in the drawing-room, where I observed Mr. Trial and Dr. Colridge soon after enter into conversation by themselves, which I could not fail to discern, by their side-long glances, was all about me. Nevertheless, dinner passed over with a little less pleasantry on all hands than might have been expected on such an occasion; and in the evening the ceremony took place, my father, uncle, and mother, being the sponsors. I stood a mere spectator, not very well comprehending the utility of what passed. But from that time till our son had come to years of discretion, his mother ingrained him, I am sorry to say, with such obsolete notions that I doubt, now when our moral courage ought to be lively and alert that he is not among the number of those who will prove themselves the emancipators of the human race.

But to return to the effect which public measures and events had upon me, I must beg the intrepid reader to attend to what I felt at the progress of Napoleon – that great bad man, who so singularly threw away the world.

When Napoleon came upon the scene as a monarch, it was an epoch of the drama wherein he bore the principal part. From the moment in which he assumed the imperial attributes, I had my doubts of his integrity; for I beheld then that the star of ancient things was again in the ascendant. I trembled at his restorations – I grieved at his institutions; and I saw only a revival of thraldom for mankind, especially when he blended his fortunes, by marriage, with the fated progeny of the doomed. But when, after that lapse, he again stepped forth in his glory, conquering and to conquer, a new hope dawned upon me. Alas! it proved but the glare of that false light, which streams up in the northern sky, and is succeeded by no day. The Russian campaign disappointed my dreams; and the havoc and storm which pursued him to the Isle of Elba, smote me with consternation. All around seemed blasted; and my sad ears heard no sound but the riveting again of shackles and fetters on the wrists and ankles of man.

In this dismal crisis, when the cry arose that the captive Eagle was again on the wing, and the wrens and sparrows cowering and flying before him, inadequate is the utterance of my pen to express what I then felt. The primeval energy of my spirit blazed up, and I anticipated the renewal of all those fond illusions which I had cherished with enthusiasm in former years. But the fortune of the world is like the destiny of individuals – a very shuttlecock. Brief indeed was the flattering hope that the return of Napoleon to the Tuileries, and the flight of Louis to Ghent, inspired.

The battle of Waterloo blighted my expectations; and with a sick and humbled heart, I acknowledged that the cause of philanthropy was, in consequence, suspended. But

I had yet the embers of secret consolation unquenched at the bottom of my heart.

'The cause of man,' said I to myself, 'is a sacred cause – a cause to which the heavens themselves are propitious; and this very eclipse that has darkened its splendour, is a proof that it is in progress, and will hereafter shine forth with more refulgent lustre. It is to make the world sensible of the blessing shed by the French revolution, that the restoration of malevolent things is permitted. Another revolution – the bright breaking of another – and all will go well!'

The comfort I derived from the foresight of these reflections was soon realised. The revulsion which took place after the peace, was, in its calamities, convincing to me that I had thought with sagacity; and the rumours which then began to rise of discontents in the manufacturing districts, assured me that the great cause still lived, and that the candle, though low in the socket, was not extinct.

'Even in their ashes live their wonted fires,'

said I to myself, when I considered the bold front with which men, determined to have their wrongs redressed, assembled at the convocations of those advocates of reform who vindicated the rights of their brethren.

The adversaries of freedom and equality were not blind to the danger kindling around them. With the same disregard of eternal principles which had enabled them to come victors out of the war, they exerted their utmost to stifle the rising spirit – and undoubtedly for a time they succeeded. Smother it they could not, for it is a divine flame; but they certainly did manage for a while to put down what they sarcastically called the 'Radical uproar.' I shall not, however, speak of the promiscuous blood which, at their instigation, was shed, nor of the persecution to which the bold and free were consigned. The reader will recollect them all.

Still, even in those triumphs and victories, as the adversaries of emancipation deemed them, there was consolation to the subdued and oppressed. It was clearly visible that the champions of freedom were not yet in circumstances to contend with the usurpers of property, and the possessors of power. Measures, therefore, more consonant to our condition, were forced upon our consideration by the ineffectuality of the Scottish Radical campaign. To strive with those who in the field commanded the sinews of war, required a peculiar, and new as peculiar, system of tactics. But the same untired genius that ever delighted to re-illume our darkening hopes, was still amongst us. Taught by it, we retired from the battle of blows, and with a unanimity that will be remarked by posterity as among the wonders of the time, we had recourse to the weapons of reason, and the intellectual contests of argument. Yet in this retreat we did not escape contumely. On the contrary, we were treated as if we had been subjugated; and in the endurance of that exultation, we acquired the patience which is now giving us a foretaste of at last becoming in our turn the conquerors.

Well do I recollect the ineffable sneer with which my father, at this time an old man, attempted to rebuke me while describing to a party at his table the glories of the French revolution, and how much the world had lost by its failure, – the effect of the unprepared elements it had to work with.

'It was,' said I, 'a new era – the revelation of better truths and dogmas, when the spirit of liberty, which had long struggled in the bowels of despotism, burst forth at Paris with an explosion that astonished the whole earth.'

'Truly, Nathan,' interposed my father, 'French liberty was indeed a fundamental error.'

'Experience teaches fools;' and her lessons were not lost upon me, nor upon those who, like me, were stimulated by an innate antipathy to that oppression which it is the effect of the social state, in its existing structure, to entail on man.

It was evident that Nature, ever wise and beneficent, rejected the design of advocating her cause by force. Nothing but this palpable truth can explain the disasters which befell our arms. But, though late, instruction came at last; we saw that our weapons were arguments, and our artillery reasons; and accordingly we suited our belligerency to our means.

After the fatal turbulence displayed in the manufacturing districts, and the apparently subdued bravery with which we retired from the hostile demonstration of mobs with clubs, we instinctively turned our valour to intellectual controversy.

No man could deny the burdens of the nation – all felt them, and augmented the general cry. Nothing could be more galling to the latent indignation of the country, than that so many should enjoy the fruit of the taxes – should revel in elegance, or wallow in opulence, on the hard-won earnings of the industrious poor; and we took up this obvious truth as our theme.

'What did it avail,' we said, 'that these persons, supported by the taxes, had either served the state by themselves or relations? More honourable it had been for them, had they employed themselves in the arts or honest trades, and provided for their friends from their individual gains, rather than have deemed themselves, from the accident of their being servants of the public, entitled to pasture their kindred near them on the same common.'

This argument took: Whigs and Tories, subdued by its plausibility, joined in the cry; and retrenchment became the universal shout. It never once occurred to these witlings, that retrenchment could not be made to touch the public establishments without affecting individuals; and they both, regardless of consequences, urged and clamoured for it as an unmingled blessing.

This was serving our purpose, and recruiting our ranks. Every one who was cast upon his own resources by retrenchment, became added to the phalanx of Reform. The more the cry for it prevailed, the stronger we waxed in numbers; while the two poor, short-sighted, rival factions were devouring each other – the Tories, by yielding to the representations of the Whigs, and the Whigs, by goading on the Tories into measures that were one day to leave them both without that influence in society, which it is the nature of patronage to ensure, and of property to beget. The more that the one was provoked by the taunts of the other to sanction retrenchment, their respective powers were diminished. But the infatuated saw not this. The Whigs cried out for reduction; the Tories, in their ineffectual endeavours to appease them, discharged and reduced the adherents of Government, or, in other words, lessened the number of the mercenaries in the system of oppression, and made it in some sort defenceless.

A rational war like this was the only war we ever should have waged. But at first, – as the child, who grows conscious of strength, instinctively employs it in mischief, – we unfortunately were not aware that physical coercion never could accomplish moral purposes; and yet to attain them we had recourse to physical means. When our reason, however, grew to maturity, we saw our error; and the indefatigable use of the mere word 'retrenchment,' did more for the restoration of natural privileges than all the crimson struggles of the early French revolution – the insubordination of the manufacturing districts – and the abortive endeavours of embodied multitudes to intimidate the law. It enchanted the Tories to part with their guards

– it left the Whigs without a pretext to take them into their service; and the victims of what was considered national policy, in their destitution and bereavement, flocked to our standard. It was this, thank Heaven, that made us what we now are – that put us in a condition to render the Whigs subservient to our will, and the Tories, in their astonishment, the objects of our derision. Too late have the latter discovered, that in yielding to retrenchment, they but multiplied discontent. But in vain is all their bravery; we have wrested from them the sceptre – one struggle more, and it is broken for ever.

When the effect of the cry for retrenchment became visible, I remember a discussion that I had at the time with my old friend Mr. Grudger – a true man he was, with all his feelings palpitating and obvious: Spagnoletti never painted one of his skinless subjects with muscles more strikingly articulated than Mr. Grudger, with his throbbing sensibilities, always appeared to me.

'No doubt, Mr. Butt,' said he, 'from the manner in which retrenchment is administered, as you observe, the general interests of the human race may derive great advantage; but think how very nearly it has endangered the Radical cause. Had the aristocracy of the Tories seen the thing in its true light, they would have made a stout stand against retrenchment in the very beginning, or would have begun their reductions with plucking, what one of the most strenuous advocates of retrenchment calls 'the birds of prey.' Instead, however, of doing so, they have always regarded the desire in man for the re-establishment of equality as a temporary cholera; and, partly from folly mixed with sordidness, they began their reductions with their dependants. Had they set about lopping their own salaries and sinecures, and given up to their inferiors something, instead of taking from them every thing, the feeling towards them would have been very different. The age required that men who had large private properties should have resigned what they drew from the public purse. But the Tories have acted otherwise; and as they have sown, so shall they reap. As for the Whigs, their conduct has, in principle, been still more efficacious, though unintended.

They have never lost an occasion on which they could decry the cupidity of their adversaries, and thus have fought our battles; little aware, that, when the time should come that office was to be at their acceptance, the very words which they employed against the grasping of the Tories, would be used as javelins and barbed arrows against themselves. By their arguments they have advocated our cause; and the Tories by their conduct were also, unconsciously, our auxiliaries.'

'What you remark, Mr. Grudger, is very true; had the Tories done, as you say they might have done, the very course of proceeding that makes for us, might have been otherwise; for then retrenchment, in that case, would have taken the sacred character of sacrifice, and the hearts of men might have rallied to uphold a system productive of such beautiful results. But, my dear sir, you forget that corruption, which it is the aim of every philanthropist to remove, prevented the Tories from doing what you say; and the Whigs in employing the means they have done to drive their rivals from place, happily forgot that the school-master was abroad, and in oblivion of that circumstance, they spoke to his unwashen pupils, the populace, as their predecessors, the Whigs of other days, cajoled the country gentlemen. The commonalty now are at least equal in understanding to the De Coverleys and Westerns of other years.'

My friend seemed a little thoughtful as I said this, and, disinclined to continue the conversation, subjoined, 'It would take a wiser head than mine to say what course would now be most salutary for the world; but let us hope that it cannot be an evil thing which so many are pursuing with such ardour.'

Subsequently to the discussion with Mr. Grudger, it often occurred to me that retrenchment alone was not sufficient to account for the visible strengthening of our cause; and I began, in consequence, to look into the secret workings of the world, both as they affected man, and man affected them. The result was consolatory.

It appeared to me, by this study, that a moral transmutation was taking place, at least equal in importance to that political change which had at first attracted my attention. The olden and the reverenced were no longer regarded with the same sentiment as in other times; and men's minds, instead of considering what might be for the good of society, began to question whether society itself, organised as it was with error, could be of any good at all. I frequently wondered how it came to pass that mankind ever consented to endure artificial arrangements subversive of the rights of nature; for there can be no doubt that the arrangements which result from the social structure are corrosive of individual powers and endowments. Privilege is but a poor substitute for faculty; and it is as much the nature of society to subvert individual faculty, as it is of education to extinguish original genius.

Not, however, to enlarge on this interesting subject, I perceived a growing doubt in the world as to the utility of many things which our ancestors held in veneration; and to search out the root of that doubt was, for some time, with me an object of peculiar solicitude. In the investigation I was well rewarded; for it afforded me a striking assurance that prejudice was becoming obsolete.

Among other changes, at the same time, which I observed taking place in society, was an ebb or subsidence of anxiety for the interests of posterity, – an ancestral error in the feeling of patriotism or public spirit, which occupied a high station in the minds of our predecessors. For example, it had been deemed the very acme of human wisdom to put off the evil day always as far as possible; and accordingly the nation incurred debt, and the more freely, too, as posterity could not complain of the condition to which it would by it be borne, not having any experience of better circumstances. But when the truth of the case was discerned, it became the general opinion that we should remove the taxes that were to relieve, by the Sinking Fund, our progeny from the debt, to enjoy the fruits of that removal ourselves. Many taxes were, in consequence, reduced and taken off, and the debt left for posterity to deal with as might be seen fit. But, strange enough, it came to pass, that as the taxes were extinguished, both public and private distress increased, – a phenomenon that has yet to be explained.

The distress which flowed from retrenchment was obvious and explicable; but that a similar result should be a consequence of reducing the public burdens, puzzled many sound heads; nor could it be deemed accounted for, when it was said, that the greater the amount of taxation, the quicker is the circulation of money; and in proportion to the velocity of the circulation is the vivacity of prosperity.

I did not, however, perplex myself with investigating the causes of this effect. I was pleased with the moral issues to which it tended, inasmuch as with them was a more legitimate progress of right thinking, than from the sordid discontent generated by retrenchment. But with many of my friends the satisfaction was not so decided. They saw in the afflictions occasioned by the stagnation, only evils, which I regarded but as the calamities of a battle, where victory promotes a righteous cause, – for it seems to be an ordinance of Nature, that evil should be ever the precursor of good.

One day as I was speaking on this topic with a neighbour, and expressing my wonder to Mr. Thole, how it so happened that the community became in all its manifold interests more and more depressed by the measures intended to repair its elasticity, he, who was not altogether of a sound and sane way of thinking on many points, said, after some cogitation, that he thought I made a mistake, by attributing the distress to one cause, which by its results was evidently the consequence of another.

'It is manifest, Mr. Butt,' continued he, 'that if the taxes be burdensome and a grievance, their removal should lighten a load; and therefore I do think it stands to reason, that if when they are removed an increased weight be felt, and a grievance becomes more galling, something else than the taxes must be in fault.'

I was a little in doubt as to the answer I should make to this, which looked so like reason, and said, 'Very true, Mr. Thole; but as Radicalism thrives by it, and the general world is turned more towards the question of permitting property to continue in such large masses, we need not trouble ourselves as to what may be the real source of that suffering, which seems to come of reducing the taxes. It is sufficient that it does come, and if not the spring of the distress, it is certainly a sign.'

'I cannot be of that opinion,' replied Mr. Thole; 'for although I have in many cases great reliance on your judgement, it startles me to hear you ascribe to one cause an effect which clearly belongs to another: I cannot away with that.'

'Then what do you think,' said I, 'can be the origin of the distress, which, if it does not arise from abridging the circulation by taking off the taxes, is coeval with it? for I am willing to admit that the phenomenon is perplexing.'

'I am not a man, Mr. Butt, as you know well, much addicted to abstruse matters; I have, however, a notion, that unless rents are reduced in an equal degree universally with the taxes, much of the distress may be owing to that circumstance. The newspapers now and then tell us of this gentleman, and that nobleman, who on his audit-day remitted so many per cents to his tenantry; but I doubt if the fashion has yet become common.'

'Then, Mr. Thole, does not that convince you of the badness of that state of things wherein the few have the power of producing such affliction to the many? No, sir: whatever be the cause of so much and such general distress, it cannot be doubted that the breaking into pieces of the great masses of property would essentially contribute to alleviate the grievances. Get change for a shilling, and you may relieve four-and-twenty beggars; but while you have only the shilling entire, where is your charity? Let the great properties be smashed, what will then be the effect of the fragments distributed among the million?'

I had him here on the hip – he could not controvert the inference; and I added, as a clencher, which for that time closed the discussion, 'Is it not something to know the cause of the distress of the world? for knowing the cause, we may bethink ourselves of removing it. Yes: you are right. The taxes have nothing to do with the distress; the rents! – the rents! should be looked to! and can that be done without looking to the land that yields them? Tell me, sir, why it is that the world permits the continuation of such an abuse as the existence of that class or order called 'landlords?' What is the origin of their property? How was it derived? For what purpose was it given to them? – Look to that, Master Brook – look to that!'

But while I was thus occasionally indulging speculative opinions with my friends, and had hitherto in no particular degree felt the severity of the times, the hour of visitation was drawing nearer and nearer. The business in which I was engaged with my uncle was one of those sober and methodical trades which are less subject to vicissitudes than others sometimes more profitable. We experienced the flush of prosperity in more moderation than many of our neighbours, and, in like manner, the blight of adversity fell milder on our industry, when it reached to the roots and often withered the branches of theirs.

That very regularity in our business, which may be said to have had a moral influence in attaching the old gentleman to the existing form of things, and caused him to dislike changes, as fraught with danger, was destined, in the shock of commerce, to sustain molestation. He had retired from active life; but he left his name and a large portion of his capital in the concern, of which I of course became the head and manager. The system worked well, and I had only to see that the wheels were properly oiled. The course of Nature in the seasons was not more trustworthy than the regularity with which our affairs produced their accustomed harvest; but as in the former the Universal Mother sometimes goes awry, we had also to endure accidents; and thus it happened, that an old and esteemed correspondent, who was deeply in our debt, and of whose solvency we had never a doubt, suddenly died; and on examining his books, it appeared that the general decay of trade had so preyed upon his means for some years, that his assets were not adequate, by a considerable sum, to the discharge of his obligations. Our loss was great, so great that it materially injured our fortune, and caused a depression of spirits, and the most gloomy forebodings, to fasten on my uncle's mind.

For some time he bore up against the calamity with an energy that was encouraging to contemplate in an aged man, and I was nerved by his example; but in the course of the following winter his health began to give way, and he fell into a black and pale despondency of the most funereal kind. The disease slowly but still increasing, grew apace as his strength declined; and at last the doctor told me that he could not live long.

At this period my uncle resided a few miles from the town, in a country-house which he had purchased to enjoy his freedom when he quitted active life, and I had not seen him for some time. On receiving the physician's intimation, however, I went to him immediately – for I was more affected by the tidings than a strict philosophy could justify. Nature had, by old age, so plainly served her writ upon him, that he could no longer postpone the payment of her debt.

It was the evening – a winter night – as I approached his dwelling, a handsome mansion, situated in a respectable park. The leaves were all fallen, and the wind blew gusty through the branches, as I rode up the avenue. I saw a light in his bed-room as I approached the house, and by several of the windows I could perceive persons with candles in their hands moving to and fro in the house. From my earliest years I have been accustomed, by some inscrutable association, to connect such numerous and moving lights, dimly gleaming from the windows of silent houses, with ideas of anguish and misfortune, and the mysteries of death. My mind was, accordingly, at the time full of these solemnities, to which the warning of the doctor had given the most saddening probability. I alighted at the door with awe and sorrow; for the old man had always been very kind to me.

The servant, who took my horse, answered to my eager inquiry, that my uncle, his master, was still alive; and without ceremony, I softly ascended the stairs and hastened into his bed-chamber; but a feeling of uncontrollable dread seized me as I entered, and I could not advance towards the couch, – and yet I shall never forget the scene that was before me.

On a table, with a shaded lamp, stood a mass of Esculapian mummery – labelled phials, open papers of the apothecary, with pill-boxes, tea-cups, and a small basin with a spoon. A Presbyterian clergyman, an old friend of the dying man, sat at his pillow, and on the coverlet lay the New Testament open; while Mrs. Guidance, the venerable housekeeper, grasping the curtain with one hand, and holding a handkerchief in the other, stood gazing in the old man's face, whose fixed and glassy eye glittered as with the reflection of a ray – but it was not of the mind.

My consternation, for I have no other name to give to what I felt, dissolved away, and I advanced. The suppressed noise of my movement for a moment excited attention. The minister looked up; Mrs. Guidance towards me behind her; and as I bent forward, the good old man, whose time was come, turned his eye upon me with a gleam of intelligence, and expired.

For some time I was so agitated with the thought of having been almost too late, that I could not recover my scattered senses. I had never been so impressively affected before; and though it is impossible to say wherefore, I sat down on a chair, and my tears began to flow. At this crisis, Mr. Trial, the clergyman alluded to, left his seat beside the dead man's pillow, and coming towards me, took me in a merciful manner by the hand.

'You must go with me,' said he; 'the women are coming, and it is not meet that we should at this time remain longer here: let us go down stairs. He has had a pleasant departure, and has been blessed with that hope in death which can only be earned by a well-spent life. Come, let us go together; his latest words were of pity concerning you, and I promised to repeat to you his last request.'

Having, all my days, had a judicious suspicion of ecclesiastical craftiness, this expression put me on my guard; and I replied, 'At some more convenient season, Mr. Trial, I shall be most happy to receive any communication you may have to make; but at present the fatigue of my ride, and the mournful spectacle we have just witnessed, render me unfit to give proper attention.'

'It was his wish,' said Mr. Trial, 'that I should take the very first moment, when the impression of his death was strongest, to deliver to you his last solemn advice.'

I felt this as a little importunate, and replied, 'No doubt it is natural that you, Mr. Trial, should be eager to perform your duty; you are a sensible man, and know well that the wisest in the crisis of death are not in the best situation to give advice.'

'Sir,' cried he, drawing up, as if I had offended him, 'men in all ages have ever deemed a death-bed admonition deserving of more than common consideration.'

'I know what you say is the prevalent opinion of the world,' replied I, 'and the gentlemen of your cloth have found an advantage in upholding it; but the truth, notwithstanding, is, that a man in the throes of death has quite enough to do with his own pains and fears, without thinking much about what may be for the benefit of others. I shall, however, in the morning be in a better condition to hear what you have to say to me from my uncle, than I am at this moment.'

Without making any answer, he looked at me for a short space of time with the wonted self-sufficiency of his order; and seeing I was serious, and indisposed to farther conversation, he turned on his heel, and with an air that would have become a pope or metropolitan, bade me good night, and immediately left the house.

Since that incident, I have studiously kept myself aloof from all the different denominations of the priesthood; for I never so clearly saw as I did on that occasion, that there is something in their office which leads them to imagine themselves superior to the commonalty of mankind, or prompts them to desire that the world should believe so. It is only by individuals commencing in their respective spheres the work of reformation, that it ever can be accomplished. Were all men to treat the members of the privileged orders as I have done, the nuisance of being troubled with them would soon be abated.

The natural extinction of my uncle, as may be easily deduced from the foregoing chapter, forms an era in my life. The cause which hastened on the event had great influence on my conduct; and the event itself, as I have shewn, induced me to determine on finally separating myself from the ecclesiastical order. With the aristocracy I had never much communion, and accordingly no particular estrangement was requisite towards them.

The same cause which accelerated the exit of the worthy old man, acted on me in a twofold manner. It abridged my means, and, by obliging me to attend with more sordid eagerness to mercantile concerns, diminished the time I had to spare for loftier pursuits. The result was manifest on my fortune; and I soon saw that I must abandon trade or politics. The election to a liberal mind was not difficult: I retired with a competency below what, had I continued, would probably have been my portion; small, however, is the enough for a philosopher:

> 'Man wants but little here below,
> Nor wants that little long.'

But the domestic tribulation which I still suffered, from the effects of the ecclesiastical dogmas on the mind of my wife, was not so easily alleviated; for she never ceased to express her grief at the insensibility with which she alleged I treated my eternal interests.

In vain did I often tell her, that marriage was but a temporal arrangement, the necessary consequence of those laws of inheritance which the mistaken founders of society had imposed upon the innate freedom of the species; and that beyond the duration of the legal tie there could be no reciprocal obligation on the one to care for the other. 'Besides, Mrs. Butt,' said I, 'why do you think I regard my soul less, if I have one, than you do yours? Truly you give yourself too much thought on this head.'

Thus it happened, though I cleared myself of that occasional interference of the priests, with which I had been molested from the baptism of my son, I was yet compelled to endure from Mrs. Butt a constancy of remonstrance on the subject, the more afflicting, as the poor woman was really sincere, and seemed to think that belief in her doctrines could be brought about by exhortation. But her error in this respect at last became intolerable; my instinctive sense of liberty revolted at such unvaried anxiety concerning matters of which the evidence, to say the least of it, is concealed in mystery; and I resolved to revert to first principles, and rid myself of the grievance.

'Mrs. Butt,' said I, one night as we were sitting by the parlour fire-side, 'it is a very extraordinary thing, that now, when I am free from the cares of business, and can give my full attention to the solicitudes of philanthropy, I experience no increase of ease.'

'How, indeed, Nathan, can you ever expect it – you whose only trust is in the things of this world – things, too, that are but possibilities in the future time? Were you, Nathan, to set your heart on the stabilities of that future which lies beyond time, the ease would be far different with you.'

'That, Mrs. Butt, is just a repetition of what you have said times without number; and you would not lower yourself in my good opinion, were you to forbear such reiteration; for, let me tell you, I begin to think that much of the molestation of my condition comes of your incessant probing and pricking of what you are pleased to call my infidelity. There must be an end of the plague.'

'What end, Nathan? Can I ever give up my regard for your immortal welfare?'

'If that is your opinion, Mrs. Butt, the sooner we come to a right understanding the better.'

'What mean you?'

'It is needless,' said I, 'to repeat, that I am too much of

a philosopher to think of enduring afflictions which may be shunned.'

'Would indeed that you were less in some things! But what is it in the troubles of human life that you can shun?'

'You,' was my court reply.

To this she made no answer; but looking in my face with a smile tinctured with sadness, she took hold of my hand; I had, however, fortitude to add, 'It is not to be disguised, Mrs. Butt, that your way of thinking – indeed the very substance of your thoughts – is different from mine; and we should both act prudently, before coming to an open quarrel, were we to break up our domicile.'

I need not relate what then ensued; but she said that surely I was beside myself, to carry my phantastical notions to such an extremity; and concluded, 'But I will never consent, – I am your wedded wife:' and then she added, jocularly, – 'the law will not allow it.'

'You do not suppose,' replied I, 'that in a rational matter of this kind I would have recourse to the law; I only put it to you, as a sensible woman, how much more expedient it would be for us to live in different houses, than to be worrying the life out of one another in this way.'

'And who do you intend to put in my place?'

'That's a very feminine suspicion,' said I, coolly; and seeing she was at the time in a very irrational mood, I rose and left her to ruminate on what we had been talking of.

As usual, when disturbed, I walked into the garden; for although the season was advanced, the night was clear and pleasant – the stars were all out, and the new moon, the sickle of time, in its brightest polish, hung sharp on the horizon. The still air was bracing, without being cold; and, after I had taken two or three turns, I felt myself in a composed and judicious mood and course for calm reflection.

'Without question,' said I to myself, as I paced the walk, 'the woman is in the right; and the yoke that galls me is not of her nature, but is plainly one of those evils which result from the institutions of property, as well as from the ascendency of the pontifical order, whose influence, more or less, pervades in all things the condition of man. By those fatal laws which have rivetted husband and wife together, a dependency is induced of the weaker on the stronger; and, to make it the more indissoluble, it has been consecrated. As a general institution it may perhaps be susceptible of some defence; but between two enlightened and intellectual beings, like my wife and me, surely neither of us should set so much store on an ancient custom, as to punish ourselves by adhering to it.'

Having thus reasoned myself into the fullest conviction, that in our case there was manifest folly in doing as the world did, I went into the house with the intent of coming to an explicit understanding; but, much to my surprise, I found Mrs. Butt sitting in the dark, in her own chamber, and weeping very bitterly. I had at the time a candle in my hand, and I placed it on the dressing-table, and inquired, in a soft voice, what had happened.

'Need you ask, Nathan?' was her reply. 'But it is not the first time I have noticed, with awe, that you have allowed light words to drop from you concerning the marriage-vow. What have I done, that you should speak of sending me away? Am not I your wife, the mother of your children? And, in all things save the claim of Heaven, I have been ever to you true and faithful. Your conscience cannot accuse me of any deficiency. Why, then, do you harbour such cruel and disreputable thoughts against me?'

'You take a wrong view of the matter altogether, my dear,' was my considerate reply. 'I am only anxious that we both should try our natural rights; and your very blamelessness is with me a reason for proposing it; for there is nothing which the world can impute to you in disparagement, but every thing to render the step respectable in the eyes of our neighbours. It is just such a pair as we have ever been, that should shew an example of superiority to prejudice.'

'Nathan Butt,' was her answer, wiping her eyes – 'if I had not always heard you spoken of as a man of talents – nay, a man of genius, with nothing more to object to than a few of those innocent crotchets inseparable from that temperament, I should think you either a bad or a mad man. Just content yourself with me; for I'll never consent

to a separation, which only crime or necessity can justify
– and neither of us has a plea of that sort to set up.'

Seeing that she was thus so obstinate in her prejudices, I
refrained from pressing the subject; for there is much good
reason in forbearance, when you see your argument falls
ineffectual, like water spilt on the ground.

If I did not in every thing meet with that compliancy in my domestic circle, after I quitted business, that I had so much cause, from my philosophical sobriety, to expect, out of doors my character and name were increasing; and I perceived that many of my neighbours were inclined to my way of thinking. We did not, as on former occasions, hold meetings to display our strength and numbers: we pursued a more effectual and impressive course, and saw clearly before us, that, even if we failed to vindicate the jurisdiction of Nature over society, we should yet better the condition of mankind, by persevering in our efforts to procure reform.

I ought, however, in justice to the unaltered integrity of my principles, to mention, that I was not quite satisfied to concur in the compromise which this implied. I still remained as convinced as ever, that the prize and goal of our pursuit should be nothing less than the emancipation of the human race from the trammels and bondage of the social law; although, certainly, I did abet rational undertakings to procure parliamentary reform, as among the means by which my own great and high purpose might be attained. It thus came to pass that, notwithstanding the celebrity I acquired among the Reformers, I was not, in fact, a strict member of the sect: my heart beat warmly towards them, but my hopes went far beyond their desires. I saw in the accomplishment of their objects that a new stepping-stone would be established to help on to mine.

The truth is, that the Reformers and the Radicals are two very different parties. It is not impossible – and I say so, having studied their predilections – that the former may hereafter amalgamate themselves with the Whigs and

Tories, which the latter never can. Radicalism is an organic passion, and cannot be changed in its tendencies; it goes to the root of the evil that is in the world, and discerns that, without an abolition of the laws and institutes which it has been so long the erroneous object of society to uphold, the resuscitation of first principles can never be effected; and nothing less than that resuscitation will be satisfactory.

Once, when I happened to say so to my neighbour Mr. Cobble, who was not a Radical, but only a Reformer, he made a remarkable observation, which I have never been able properly to digest.

'Radicalism, then,' said he, 'is but that desire for further improvement which is the result of improvement, and can have no end or limitation: whereas the reform that I seek is a moderate measure of amendment in things that have fallen into abuse. Yours is a new system – a revolution; but we seek no overthrow; we only would repair the dilapidation of ages, and the tear and wear of time. We would not have society put on a new aspect, or greatly depart from her wont; but you behold evil in all things, and aim at their total removal. I doubt, Mr. Butt, that if the Reformers once suspect your party of being actuated by such ambition, they will make no scruple of joining our common adversaries to repress them.'

I pondered on this speech; and being unable to understand it properly, I exclaimed to myself, 'Can any two things be more dissimilar than society and a state of nature? Is not society the creation of mere human wisdom, and therefore defective? but is not nature endowed with a divine fatality, which is constantly operating to the confusion and overthrow of the artificial state? What is meant by the spirit of one age being milder than that of another, but that the progress of knowledge has taught men to relax the fetters that society has placed on nature?'

In short, the remark of Mr. Cobble troubled me, and opened my eyes to many things which perhaps my sanguine temper had made me overlook. Hitherto it had been too much my habit to consider the simple Reformers as of our party, and only a lukewarm class of them; but from his expressions I discerned the inherent difference but did not perceive for some time how much that difference was intrinsic; and when I did discover that it was vital and elementary, my mind was far from content. In fact, it was obvious that if the Radicals were under the influence of a misconception, the Reformers committed no very hazardous mistake in reckoning them in their association; but the case was unfortunately otherwise, when the Radicals imagined that the Reformers were with them: a difference to be remembered.

This detection, as I would call it, gave me great uneasiness, for as soon as the suggestion was confirmed, by what may be described as auricular demonstration, I was sensible of the necessity of changing our course.

'Sooner or later,' said I, 'these timid Reformers will be absorbed by the Whigs and Tories; and out of the amalgamation a fourth party will be coagulated, stronger than either, the denomination of which is as yet dormant in the womb of time. It behoves us, therefore, to be wary; and as the Whigs have used the Reformers for their own ends, and the Reformers have treated us with as little principle, we must, in our great cause, make no scruple of fighting them all with their own weapons.'

The force of this opinion I took an early opportunity of testing among friends who were thorough philanthropists; and, by its effect on them, I saw that the true course which we ought to take, was to intermingle ourselves still more, and systematically, with the Reformers, and avail ourselves of every judicious opportunity of sowing among them the seeds of our regenerative philosophy. This esoteric doctrine, or rather the practice directed by it, soon became general in the country, and it is since quite extraordinary with what rapidity it has spread. I do not, however, say that all Reformers now are in their hearts Radicals; but many who did at first believe that a reform of the Commons' House would extinguish all grievances, are now fully persuaded that it will not even lessen them; and that, unless there shall be some perennial fount of first principles established, at which legislation can be refreshed, – the reform will have only the effect of substracting from the wise few that power which, in the possession of the foolish many, may lead to interminable consequences.

It is, however, more in accordance with the scope of these sketches, to illustrate by incidents than to enforce by theory; I shall therefore abstain, at present, from farther dissertation, to give some account of the result on the conduct, both of my friends and myself, as it came to pass, when we discovered how much the Reformers, those ephemeral philosophers, were making tools of us, whose principles are as indestructible as the atoms of light – for truth is light – moral light, and its particles eternal!

In this state of doubtful opinion as to the strength of parties, I had a few confidential friends one day to dinner; and our conversation, after Mrs. Butt had retired, was in the highest style of philosophy. Few topics connected with the condition of man were left untouched: the West India question of slavery; the inconvenience arising to the boldest and the best men, by the political subdivision of the world; and the insurmountable barrier which so many different languages present to the progress of knowledge, – were all discussed as they should be, and in some instances with an intrepidity of argument that was quite invigorating.

Mr. Blazon was particularly eloquent on that most abominable tax on knowledge, which renders the newspapers, those oracles of a wisdom not materially manacled by education, so costly, that seven pence is demanded for what would be dear at a penny; concluding his peroration with a prophetic vista of the time when the English language, by the American States, and the Oriental Colonies, would be universal over all the earth; maintaining that we should regard it as one of our greatest duties to promote a consummation so devoutly to be wished.

Often have I thought since, that the Society for the Diffusion of Useful Knowledge had its origin from what passed on that occasion; for soon after, one of the party visited London, where he no doubt met with many remarkable men, to whom, as a matter of course, he probably related what he had heard, and thus sowed the seeds of that most pregnant institution; an institution which may with propriety be referred to as a well-head of the human mind, which it is now purifying. Its cheap tracts are worth the recondite quartos of a former age.

Can philosophy desire a better proof of the perfectibility of man?

On the occasion alluded to, after we had handled several interesting topics with powerful effect, Mr. Asper, a shrewd but cautious man, most invaluable as a neighbour for his suggestions, though little inclined to take a very active part in the measures of which he was the father, said the time was come in which it was befitting our cause that we should assume more ostentation in the world; and proposed that we should for the future advocate the enterprises of the Reformers, but in such a manner as to leaven them to our own purposes. On this proposition there was a great deal of sound opinion offered; but it took no effect with any of the party till the middle of the summer following, when it was determined that three of us, a post-chaise full, should together visit some of the most excited parts of the country, and place ourselves before the people.

When this was determined on, I resolved to be one of the three; for my talent lay in the hardihood with which I always, from my very youth, went through adventures of bravery. Not that I was either froward or forward; but it delighted me to have a task of stratagem or difficulty – a spirit which lay dormant while I was in business, but awakened and came forth in revived vigour when I became my own independent master.

Accordingly, when the fixed period arrived, Mr. Blazon, Mr. Asper, and I, set out for the north. It was concerted among us that we should be a considerable distance from our own neighbourhood before we entered on our vocation. Not that any particular diffidence affected us; but we called to mind the old saying, that prophets are not respected in their own countries; and on the hint of Mr. Asper, resolved to keep our lantern shut till we were in a proper situation.

At this time we had received some information, which led us to believe that the men of Old-Port were verging to a right way of thinking; and we resolved to begin with them. Two reasons led to this. The first was, that in the neighbourhood of that town lived a Whig gentleman, whose house and board were ever open and free to men earnest in the good work; and the other was no less cogent, – the corporation of the place, however liberal and enlightened the citizens, was strictly Tory. But it was apprehended a change would soon come to pass; as the chief magistrate, who had been particularly fierce in his opinions, had recently died; and the other who survived was reported to be an easy man, and not very stern in his opposition to the display of popular feeling. We were therefore induced to select Old-Port as our first scene for these reasons, that if a change in the sentiments of the town were manifested, we might have the credit of being instrumental in producing it. The result, however, was not exactly as we had anticipated.

Mr. Greedison, our Whig friend, lived about a couple of miles from the town. His mansion was one of the best in that part of the country; but his servants were rather notorious for their arrogance; indeed, he was a man himself of an austere temperament, and perhaps encouraged them a little in their failing, by his example. Nevertheless, he received us in the most hospitable manner, and it was evident that our arrival was an epoch to his household.

We had purposely so arranged it that we should reach Mr. Greedison's some time before dinner, having announced to him by letter, that in our tour to ascertain the state of public opinion in that quarter, we intended to hold a meeting next day in Old-Port. It accordingly happened, that being thus apprised of our intention, he had sent notice concerning us to the town, where a great expectation was awakened, and every heart beat high with the most exalted feelings. 'It is truly delightful,' said Mr. Greedison, 'to see the enthusiasm which awaits you; but I am rather surprised that no answer has been sent to the letter I wrote to the magistrate to announce the object of your visit.'

In this, however, he was not long left to marvel; for while we were at dinner, a letter came from the town-clerk, announcing that the surviving magistrate had not altogether made up his mind to let the meeting take place at all. Such a communication was most provoking; but Mr. Greedison declared that he would not be disappointed; and with great manfulness, he upon the instant sent two servants to the town to give notice that the meeting should still take place next day in his park, which should be open to every British subject that chose to attend.

This was, no doubt, spirited of him; but it was not just what we wanted. We could not say in his park what we intended – we felt that the genius of the place would compel us to say more of Reform and Whiggery than consisted with our design. But it could not be helped; and Mr. Asper suggested, during the evening, that the two orators, Mr. Blazon and myself, could enlarge on many grievances without difficulty, and give such a turn to them as would help our own cause. But it will be as well to relate what took place next day, rather than to enter into a description of what passed among ourselves.

Next morning a cart was drawn out to the bottom of a rising ground in the park, and the congregation both of men and women, in their best apparel, from Old-Port, was extraordinary. Mr. Greedison, who, like all the Whigs, was accustomed to open-air meetings, estimated the multitude at some thousands. This was highly gratifying; it would indeed have been a great disappointment had the assembly that day been thin: fortunately it was otherwise; for the good people of Old-Port, never having had before a reform meeting, were moved alike by principle and curiosity to come forward on this occasion.

Mr. Greedison himself announced the object of our visit, stating that the time was come when every man should boldly stand forth in the defence of his own and of his neighbours' rights. His sentences were pithily put – as all of his party well know how to do, when addressing a multitude; and he was listened to with the greatest attention, and concluded amidst the loudest applauses.

Mr. Blazon followed: his speech was much to the purpose. He likened the nation to Christian in *Pilgrim's Progress*, plunging, and struggling, and staggering through the Slough of Despond, with a grievous burden on his back. His description was most pathetic; and many in the crowd shed tears of sympathy with the ineffectual endeavours of poor oppressed John Bull to reach a steadfast footing. But it is not for me to describe the effect of the different topics on which he descanted: one thing, however, is certain, that all his auditors were fully convinced by his oration – as, indeed, how could it be otherwise? – that the British people were the most deluded and oppressed of the earth. No demonstration could be clearer, than that we stood in a false position with respect to our situation. In our prosperity there was no soundness – it was but a hectic glow, foreboding decay – a crimson cloudy morning, that betokened a tempest: even our national improvements were all of the most fatal description – expensive to prodigality – and when executed, destitute of use. These facts were detailed with energy and a graphic precision: no one could listen to the least of them without alarm. But it is useless for me to attempt even a summary of what he said; let it suffice, that it was most eloquent and striking, affording his hearers the utmost satisfaction. They were sensible that as a nation we were the derision of the world, and that our name was become a by-word and reproach in foreign countries.

When the cheering which attended his peroration had subsided, I presented myself, with a downcast look and modest air, to the attention of the multitude. I spoke with gentle accents, and in a conciliatory manner. Truth was my object, and truth needs no heralding where she asserts her dominion. I told the crowd that I was a man plain in speech, sober in my philosophy, and had all my days been addicted to the contemplation of the right side of things.

'That we are a ruined people,' said I, 'there can be no doubt. You have heard from my friend that we are so; and after what he has stated so perspicuously, who can question the fact? In truth, fellow-countrymen, even language amongst us is corrupted to the core; its meaning is perverted, and by that perversion we are credulous to the most amazing improbabilities. Has it not been an axiom, from the beginning of time, that the wise are few, and the foolish numerous? and yet how little does the opinion of the few avail in our public affairs? – the majority rules all. If there be any truth in the remark – and who shall deny it? – that the minority of mankind are the wise, what but some unspeakable metamorphosis causes, in every stage of our legislation, the judicious sentiments of the wise to be rejected, while the blazing declamations of the foolish are received with plaudits and invested with power. Yes! my fellow-subjects, till on this point a right understanding is established, violence and outrage will continue to rule the earth. Let, then, your first efforts in the sacred cause of reform be directed to this point; for, until all questions, whether of public or of private life, are determined by the opinion of the few, it is in vain to expect that we shall be able to accomplish any consequential change.'

This clause of my speech was heard with the most profound attention – to myself that attention was delightful; and the moveless eyes and open mouths before me, were signs that would have made a Demosthenes proud on the Areopagus.

Then, after a brief pause, I applied the sense of what I had been stating to the condition of those who were, like myself, impressed with its truth. 'We are, my friends, probably but a small party in this great nation,' I resumed; 'but each of you must be conscious that we are therefore not the less correct in our opinions. That consideration should be encouragement to our perseverance; for even were we fewer in number than we are, the conviction that wisdom is with the few, should alone make us superior to our adversaries. But, let us not be deceived, even by the clearest conclusions of our understandings. The world is ruled by force, which is by nature clothed with physical means, and therefore, however wise, or just, or right, we may be, still we must employ the physical means to attain our ends.'——

Just as I said this, a kind of burr and clattering of hoofs was heard, and I discovered a squadron of cavalry coming furiously up the avenue; and in the same moment the crowd began to disperse, like chaff before the wind; insomuch that in the twinkling of an eye only the triumvirate of visitors, with Mr. Greedison, were left on the spot; all the park was dotted with fugitives.

In this crisis, and before we had time to alight and run, the dragoons surrounded our rostrum. In the course of a few seconds a post-chaise hove in sight, and from it descended the surviving magistrate, attended by the town-clerk, and, with terror in his looks and trepidation in his limbs, read the riot-act, and at the conclusion called to the officer commanding the troops, with a fearful voice, to do his duty; whereupon he directed his men to return their swords into the scabbards, and they rode back with an easy canter to Old-Port.

When the dragoons had disappeared, Mr. Greedison went to the surviving magistrate of Old-Port, and reproached him for his intemperate conduct; and without shewing him the slightest courtesy, allowed him and the town-clerk, with the riot-act in his pocket, to depart in their post-chaise, while we returned into the house.

That we were all indignant at having been so interrupted, the reader does not require to be told; and the aggression on the liberty of the subject was justly condemned in the most veracious London papers. But it was a mistake both in the Government journals and in those on our side, to say that the massacre was appalling. There was in fact no massacre at all; and I have a suspicion that our adversaries only made their statement to insinuate that we were turbulent, and that in consequence a massacre was probable; while our friends – those at least who conceived they were so – made their representation to awaken sympathy for our cause, and to enhance the public antipathy against our foes. Be this, however, as it may, it must be allowed that the whole affair proved nugatory; for the people in the neighbourhood talked so much about the uproar created by the dragoons, that no one seemed to have received any impression whatever from the doctrines we attempted to inculcate.

But although we had failed, and been frustrated in our intent, the effect on that part of the country was most salutary. Several respectable persons from Old-Port came to Mr. Greedison's house in the evening, and, complaining bitterly of the contumelious treatment we had received from the surviving magistrate, proposed that we should hold another meeting of the same kind in a timber-yard belonging to one of them, and in which, being enclosed and private property, he assured us the magistrate would not dare to shew his face. An offer of this kind was truly patriotic, and we accordingly accepted it; but nothing in human affairs ever runs smooth in its anticipated channel.

By the post, on the morning of the appointed day, I received a letter, requesting me to return immediately home, as my mother lay at the point of death, and was anxious to see me before she closed her eyes. Public spirit and personal affection were thus set at war in my bosom. 'If I delay obedience to the summons,' thought I, 'till after the meeting, I shall justly incur the imputation of neglecting private predilections for public duties; but then, though in the eye of affection I may incur blame, the action will rank me with the Bruti; but if I obey the summons, and fly as it were from the performance of the public obligations, the case will be quite the reverse.'

I hesitated; and it was not till the multitude had begun to assemble, that I recollected how in all things the incitements of nature should be held in reverence above the usages of society. 'It is true,' said I to myself, when I reflected on the dilemma in which I was placed, 'that there always must be something wrong where nature in the heart goes against the calls of society. Were not the social state egregiously perverted, there could exist no cause for the public meeting we intend to hold; and as that public meeting springs rather from a wish to avenge the wrongs of nature than from a direct suggestion of the goddess herself, the claim upon me to visit my expiring parent is clearly more direct, and in so far ought to be allowed a proper predominance.' This reflection decided my hesitation; I resolved not to go to the timber-yard, but to return immediately home.

I was afterwards informed that Mr. Blazon made a very affecting use of the incident, and thereby greatly ingratiated both himself and me with his numerous auditors.

Singular as it may appear, it is to this simple circumstance that I owe my enviable situation in the House of Commons. Had I attended the meeting, many would have thought that the report of my mother's illness was not so alarming, and would not have given me credit for that abstinence of feeling which I really might have deserved; but when the struggle with which natural and social duty agitated my bosom was represented by Mr. Blazon, it was moving to hear how much the multitude were touched with commiseration.

The report that Mr. Greedison sent me, by the next post, of what had taken place, was wonderfully interesting. The neighbouring borough of Mothy, in which the elective franchise was in the potwallopers, was softened, as he said, so much in my favour, that it was openly spoken of at a public supper, which was held the same evening in Old-Port, in a manner so gratifying, that Mr. Asper, in proposing my health, suggested that no borough, which possessed its proper freedom, could choose for its representative a more amiable man, or one more pure in principle or firm in purpose.

'I am well persuaded,' added Mr. Greedison, 'that, as a dissolution of parliament is soon expected, were you to allow yourself to be put in nomination on the popular interest at Mothy, you would be assuredly returned.'

But this letter did not reach me in an auspicious moment; it came when my feelings were racked, and I threw it into my scrutoire as a trifle, to be examined at a more convenient season: – indeed, it could not have come upon me at a worse period; for, as I have already prepared the reader to expect, when I reached my father's house, I found the good lady just upon the point of making her exit from the mortal stage.

On leaving Old-Port, instead of proceeding to my own home, the letters I had received concerning the condition of my mother induced me to go straight to her residence. My father being dead some time before, and his end in no way remarkable, it was not necessary to be noticed when it took place; but the poor good lady's departure happened in a crisis which rendered it particularly impressive. In truth, the death of a mother is always much more affecting to her children than that of a father, and I felt the influence of the universal rule.

On my arrival at the door, I requested the aged servant who admitted me, and who had from time out of mind been in the family, to conduct me to her mistress. Without reply, she did so at once, and, on entering the room, I found the invalid sitting in her bed supported by pillows; in her appearance less, however, as one on the eve of embarking for another world than I had prepared myself to see.

As she had always been very kind to me, ever seeking to discover some gentle excuse for many of those actions which my father, of a severer humour, loudly condemned, I was in rather an unphilosophical state of agitation at the sight of her emaciated features, and the ghastly satisfaction with which she glared on me when she discovered my approach.

It required no long contemplation to perceive that her last sands were nearly all ebbed; and yet there was a speculation in her eyes which shewed that the undying spirit, as she called it herself, was still vivid within.

She raised her hand when she saw me, and stretched it out to welcome me; but her decayed strength would not second the effort, and it fell in feebleness on the coverlet, before I could reach forward to snatch it. This touched with coldness my heart; but her voice, weak and broken, had still consistency enough to sustain the maternal sentiment that she endeavoured to convey: my feelings were then irrationally strong.

'Nathan Butt,' said she, 'I am glad to see you. It was my prayer that you might be at my death-bed, and the goodness of Heaven is manifested, – you are here: – sit down. You have ever been a wayward and ungracious lad, with a warmer heart than you were conscious of possessing, and a weaker head than you ever suspected. Nothing but his conviction of that made your poor father remain, to his death, your kind friend, though rough was the husk in which, no doubt, you often thought he shewed himself.'

Not knowing what she intended to add, I said, in the pause which occurred after she had thus spoken, 'Madam, I never was insensible to my father's kindness; – but what would you say? – although I have often had reason to think he was not the most enlightened of mankind.'

'He was the best of fathers!' was her emphatic reply. 'The only dregs in his cup of life were the fears that he entertained lest your recklessness would draw you into danger. But, Nathan, I have not strength left to tell you how sincerely he was your father.'

By this effort her strength was exhausted, and her head dropped on her bosom, in which position she continued so long that my heart became sore with looking at her. At last she again rallied, and added, 'But, Nathan, I have not time to importune you with exhortations. I must bid you farewell. You have been from your childhood a better-hearted creature than the world, from your actions, has a plea to think; and if you reflect on this truth, you will soon discover that riding up and down the land, making a street-talk of yourself, is not the way to raise a respectable character. Nathan, my dear, as you are a lad but of an indifferent understanding, and the part you have chosen for yourself in the world is not exactly the one that befits your talents and capacity, I would advise you——'

I was rather surprised to hear my mother disparage me in this manner; but I remained silent, for I saw she was seized with the throes of death, and in that crisis the reason is not in the best of conditions. When she had some time spoken to me in the irrelevant manner that I have described, and during which I was very strangely affected, she then pronounced a blessing, and said,

'Now, Nathan, go away, leave me; for I have not long to live, and I have an account to reckon up before I quit this inn – for such has the world ever been. I have always felt in it that I was on a journey to another country – my home in this but a stage.'

I could say nothing; and for a minute she looked in my face very tenderly,

'Oh! Nathan Butt, are you that blithe and innocent boy that gladdened my heart so long ago?' – and she turned her face aside from me, and, after a few words murmured in pity, she became still.

I then left the room, and went to my own chamber, where, after a season, I grew impatient at my softness, and cried out, with a grudge, 'Why is it that man alone should be molested with such scenes?' But, do what I would, and resolutely as I nerved myself, I could not check the current of my thoughts and tears. This was undoubtedly an unbecoming imbecility; and for a time, in spite of myself, I was obliged to give way to the mood that fell upon me. In the sequel, however, I recovered my self-possession; and it is salutary to reflect how soon, after the grave has closed on the truest of friends – a parent – a man regains his accustomed wont. No doubt, the shrinking sense of grief is afterwards felt occasionally in the lone and the sad hour, and I have not been without the experience of its icy touch; but sorrow is not a habitude of nature, and, to confess the fact, I really felt that the demise of my worthy mother left me freer to pursue the course of my endeavours to improve the condition of man; for while she lived, my dread of giving any cause of uneasiness to her made me shy to undertake many enterprises of pith and moment that the heritage of the world so wofully requires.

During the space of time that I was employed in settling the domestic affairs which the demise of my mother had occasioned, my friends in Old-Port, and their connexions in the neighbouring borough of Mothy, were not idle. Mr. Asper, who had considerable influence in that quarter, went about among his relations, and represented me to them as a man of no ordinary calibre of understanding; and Mr. Blazon held frequent meetings with influential persons in Mothy, where he made earnest speeches, and persuaded his hearers that they could not, in the event of an election, choose a better man to represent them in parliament.

From time to time I heard what was going on; and, to say the truth, was none displeased to observe that my reputation was rising amongst them; and the natural exultation produced by this was most pleasant, especially when I read the following paragraph in the county newspaper, then published weekly in the borough of Mothy.

'We have great satisfaction in announcing to our readers and this part of the kingdom in general, that Mr. Butt, whose remarkable oratory made so great an impression at the Chevy Chase of Greedison Park, is likely to offer himself, on the popular interest, as a candidate to represent our venerable borough in the next parliament.'

This notification was, in many respects, highly conciliatory to my feelings; it delicately insinuated that my powers of elocution were duly appreciated, and that they had been exerted with impressive effect on a memorable occasion. But no man is deservedly an object of praise, in this corrupted world, without at the same time being an object of animadversion.

In the town of Old-Port there was at this time a detractive newspaper, published also weekly. The sale, to be sure, was not considerable; for it was a Tory concern, and supported by certain gentlemen of large fortunes and little ideas, who resided in the neighbourhood. No sooner had the Mothy weekly 'Oracle' published its unprejudiced opinion of my qualifications, in the paragraph quoted, than the malignant editor of the Old-Port 'Champion' resolved to give, not me, but the Oracle itself, a most unmannerly thrust. Accordingly, in his very next Number, he had the following most impertinent remarks on the subject:

'A neighbouring contemporary, not distinguished for his perspicacity, has, in the playful vagaries of his lively imagination, actually conceived that there was some chance of the ancient and respectable borough of Mothy electing one Butt to represent it in the next parliament. We have some reason to believe that the protégé of our friend is the same individual that proved himself such a theoretical fool at the hurly-burly in Greedison Park. Poor man! his return will be an emphatic lesson to the community at large, of the kind of representatives that may be expected in Parliament if the popular influence is allowed to predominate. We recollect that the speech of this sage personage went to shew the abstruse fact, that the majority ought always to rule the world.'

Now, could a greater perversion be made of what I maintained ought to be the ascendency of the few? The vulgar abuse, however, left no impression upon me – I was above that, and, moreover, I expected it: but for the purblind scribe to charge me with opinions so diametrically opposite to what I had ever cherished, was really a little too much. Nor was my indignation at the calumny at all appeased by the manner in which the weak man, unconsciously to himself, advocated my very doctrine. It was plain, by his expression, that he meant the very reverse of what he uttered; for, in ascribing to me, with a sneer, the absurdity of asserting the superiority of the irrational many over the enlightened few, he clearly, unknown to himself, was secretly of my opinion. I therefore pardoned him the sneer, certain that by it he would mitigate that antipathy which the soundness and novelty of my speculations were calculated to awaken.

Still – though, upon consideration, the nefarious paragraph fell like an ineffectual javelin from the mail of philosophical temper in which I had encased myself – yet it was exceedingly provoking to be annoyed by one who had only impudence to recommend him.

But, whatever were my own sentiments on this undeserved and unprovoked attack, the effect on my friends was most stimulative. They saw that I was ordained to be a subject of Tory persecution, and they came forward in a most manful manner in my defence.

No sooner was the Old-Port Champion published, with its most aggressive paragraph, than my friends, both in Mothy and Old-Port, and in the vicinity, met, as it were with one accord, and at once, without any correspondence with me, nominated me a candidate, and sent, by the next post, an invitation to stand at the election, which they declared should not cost me a penny; adding, they were determined to bring in a member who should prove himself at once a man of integrity in principle, of talent in endowment, and in virtue that honour to human nature, which I had so courageously shewn myself to be.

Such a solicitation, I frankly confess, I felt myself unable to withstand. My reply overflowed with feelings of gratitude: but, to avoid the expression of sentiments that might be construed as egotistical, I reserve for another chapter the details of the transactions in which I was in consequence soon after engaged.

The dissolution of parliament took place more abruptly than we were quite prepared for; but still I was none daunted. Immediately on receiving the news, I hurried off to Mothy, where I lost no time in apprising my friends there of my arrival: nor had I to long for their presence; for they immediately came flocking around, and all was hurry, talk, and activity, instantly, in the town.

That evening I was rather fatigued with my journey, which had been performed with uncommon celerity; but Mr. Greedison proposed that we should convene some of the leading characters in the place, men of well-known Whig principles and intrepid patriotism. To this, tired as I was, I offered no objection; because I had made up my mind to be, during the election, all things to all men; for it is necessary, on such occasions, to swerve a little from the straightforwardness of principles.

I acknowledge this, because, in fact, I never have been very partial to the Whigs, not being endowed with sagacity enough to discern in what respect they differed essentially from the Tories; farther than that, while the latter endeavoured to preserve things as they are, the Whigs have only been anxious to make changes in forms, without altering the substance, merely to contrive new places and employments for their partisans.

The distinction between the Radicals and the rival factions is obvious. By us, anxious to restore to mankind the salutary operation of primitive principles, an honesty and simplicity of purpose are strikingly evinced. Our object is not to preserve old things, or to recast them into new shapes; but to remove them entirely away: in this respect we differ. It were as easy for a Radical, without infringing his integrity, to unite with the Tories, who admit of no change, as for him to join the Whigs, who are for all change, – they both look only to the bullion.

The Tories are of opinion that the ancient gorgeous cups and cans are of a taste and pattern that cannot be improved; and the Whigs think the bullion in them would be more useful were it converted into forks and spoons. The Radicals are of a wiser caste: such luxuries we justly condemn; and our intent is, if we can, to make the material into coin, and add it to the circulating medium. But I forget that it was not of our respective opinions I intended to speak, but only relative to what happened that night in the Red Lion inn at Mothy.

In the course of a short time, by the means and emissaries of Mr. Greedison, a considerable company was assembled; and, as it was expected I should in some sort make an exposition of my public motives, I was requested to ascend a table and address the crowd. This I did with good humour.

I reminded them of our early longings for the epoch that had at last come to pass, and that the object of all our wishes seemed to be now within our reach. 'Reform,' said I, 'which a few years ago was the unsubstantial vision of a dream, has taken consistency, and become a thing of flesh and blood. It is no longer a phantom – but a friend and a visitor. Every one recognises it – all welcome it: it blithens our hearths; it gives hilarity to our boards; and realises the beautiful mythology of antiquity, which describes the gods as holding familiar intercourse with man, and the heavens on visiting terms with the earth.'——

By some accident, a rank Tory, one Mr. Rivet, had got in among us, and, just as I said this, being standing opposite to me, he looked, in my face, and, with satirical sobriety, inquired whether, on these occasions, tea, or punch together was the go? Another, then, of the same inordinate sect, whose name I never learnt – for I did not afterwards choose to make him of so much importance, as to seem that I had noticed him – also looked up and said, derisively, that the earth, however, never returned the visit.

This interruption was resented by my friends; and

ultimately the two intrusive strangers were compelled to withdraw; and when order was restored, I resumed my speech, which, by cheers and applause, was acknowledged to be very much to the point. I concluded by assuring the company, that it was my fixed determination, if returned to parliament, to support every measure of reform, without scruple; so much did I regard that great desideratum paramount to every other measure.

The orators who followed were, in their respective strains, to the same effect. But it was not till late, and towards the close of the business, that the name of the opposing candidate to me was ascertained. It had been known for some time, that the anti-reformers were resolved to contest the borough; that they had applied, without success, to Lord James Feudal to stand against me; and that old Sir Vicary Stale had also been entreated in vain. Several other Tory gentlemen were likewise solicited; but at last they persuaded Sir Ormsby Carcase to venture.

Their choice excited some surprise; for, although he was undoubtedly a Tory, addicted to the society and parties of the neighbouring aristocracy, it was thought that he could not be otherwise than a friend of the people at heart – being a new man; his father, the first baronet of the family, having raised himself by mud-larking, as it was called, in the common sewers of trade; and he himself was more distinguished for the round, bold shape of his head than for the specimens he now and then produced of its contents. However, not to dwell on personalities, the announcement of Sir Ormsby Carcase as my adversary was heard with evident surprise and some tokens of disapprobation; but when the first emotion subsided, the effect was cheering; a faint murmur ran round the room – a more audible buzz succeeded – and at last, from all sides, vehement voices broke out, declaring resolutions that would overwhelm him with disgrace.

'Had he been of the old gentry,' cried one, 'it would have been nothing, for they are naturally Tories.' 'It is an insult to the people of England,' exclaimed another, 'that such a man dares to think he may resist their unanimous will!' 'He shall rue, with punishment, his presumption,' said a lean little man, grinning with acrimony, and shaking his fist. In short, the indignation which the intelligence kindled was individualised in its symptoms by the characteristics of every man present; and before the meeting broke up, there was a mutual pledge given, to exert both heart and hand to procure my return. A subscription opened on the spot for that purpose was surprisingly liberal.

This affair of the subscription was not, however, entirely satisfactory to me. I could not see why it should be deemed requisite; for it certainly implied something not quite so sound among us as might have been wished among men zealous in a good cause, and resolute to assert their rights.

I had always, till the subscription was mentioned, believed the Tories to be the only party in the state who generally made use of bribery. Now and then I did, indeed, hear of Whig elections having cost a ruinous deal of money; but that the Radicals were to have recourse to the same delinquent expedients was distressing; and I told Mr. Asper, who was there, and who was the author of the subscription, that I was reluctant to lend myself to men who thought their principles stood in need of corrupt operations. He, however, said that it was not until reform should be established, that we could venture to trust only to virtue.

'Recollect, Mr. Butt, that we must fight our battles with weapons as effective as those of the enemy. In physical war, the best moral argument falls effectless, compared to the energy of a cannon-ball; and, depend upon't, if we do not employ as good reasons as those of our foes, we shall be beaten. No, no, Mr. Butt; purity of election is a blessing of future days. In the meantime, our wisdom is to use the world as we find it.'

These remarks very solemnly affected me; and when I retired to sleep, fatigued as I then was, I could not shut my eyes for reflecting on the deleterious influence of these principles on society; since here, in my own case, was a striking example of the force of custom in practice over precept in principle.

'Oh, world,' said I to myself, 'how corrupt thou art! The

globe itself is but one foul pustule – a pimple on the face
and beauty of Universal Nature.' Soon after, I fell asleep,
murmuring to myself, with a pathetic subsidence of sense,
from one of my friend John Galt's unfortunate tragedies,
which, like many other good things in the world, have only
been distinguished for their blemishes:

> 'Oh, holy Nature! thee I do acquit
> Of all the foul that stains thy minion here:
> How fair, how nobly hast thou done thy part!
> How bright and glorious shines the generous sun!
> How rich and soft earth's carpeting of flowers!
> How fresh and joyous to the corporal sense
> The all-embracing dalliance of the air!
> Contrasted with the base device of courts,
> The dire cabal, and midnight craft of guilt!'

From that moment of my early life in which I first discerned that all the evils inherited by man spring from the impediments opposed by the institutions of society to the eternal workings of nature – as pure streams and flowing currents are interrupted by rocks and cataracts in their course – I studiously endeavoured to obey the sympathies and antipathies implanted in my bosom. Often and often have I said to myself – 'Of what use are penal laws? Is not the remorse with which bad and wicked actions are remembered, sufficient of itself to deter every well-regulated mind from committing them, without the artifice of legal penalties? And do not the kind feelings of affection constitute a motive to cherish it with constancy and in purity?'

I will not, however, deny that, independently of the instigations which the institutions of society excite in the human race, there are individuals of that species who receive from nature malignant propensities. But the adder and the malevolent man are of similar naturalities: the one can no more prevent death from following its bite, than the other mischief from his practice – both are alike unconscious of the ill within them. Such men are as little apt to be improved by punishment, as the venemous reptile is by the missiles with which children, in their innate aversion, attempt its destruction.

I am led to make this observation, owing to a very trifling incident, which might have changed the entire complexion of my subsequent life.

It has been mentioned, that I received the invitation to be a candidate for the borough of Mothy at a time when my mind was disturbed by the death of my mother, and the anxieties which that event entailed upon my attention. The letter, as I said, was thrown carelessly from me; and I forgot to acknowledge the receipt, till one day the recollection of it flashed like lightning across my mind. I was absolutely thunderstruck at my own negligence; I had no words to express my vexation; and was just on the point of sitting down to answer it, with heartfelt contrition – when, lo! at the very instant, the postman brought another letter on the same subject from Mr. Greedison, expressing the sincerest apprehension lest the original letter had miscarried. Thus was I, by a stroke of good fortune, relieved from a most embarrassing predicament.

I immediately again took up my pen, which I had laid down when the letter was brought in; and, instead of the penitential eloquence which I had prepared myself to utter, I merely informed him, that I had received his letter of the 29th current, and would be with him, with all my heart and the resolution that every honest man should feel in a good cause, on the 2d proximo.

On the same day that this happened, Parliament was dissolved, and I hastened to the contest.

The interval which had taken place between the date of the first and second letter was so much lost time to me; to the rival candidate it was all gain: nevertheless, with undismayed courage, my friends and I proceeded to the canvass, in which, certainly, we were very successful; but my rival being ahead, it was by no means a decided case – indeed, it was almost desperate: insomuch that Mr. Greedison proposed, that, as the sessions were near at hand, and the jail full of prisoners, chiefly the paper-capt potentates of the town, we should make a demand for them to be allowed to vote at the election.

This ingenious suggestion was proposed in conclave; but it was deemed expedient that the real political leaning of the prisoners should be first ascertained; because, as Mr. Greedison justly said, if they are men of Tory principles, as all rogues necessarily are, then it would only be to strengthen the cause of our adversary to require them. But Mr. Asper, who was with me – a sly and dry old man – remarked, that he had no doubt they were all

Whigs, inasmuch as they had a particular predilection for the property of others; for what else can be said of taking away from the possessors pensions and places, to help themselves or their friends from the plunder? I saw Mr. Greedison redden with displeasure at this insinuation; and I said, that although the election was vested in the pot-wallopers and inhabitants at large of the borough, a stronger objection might be urged against the stratagem, – as it could not be maintained that such of the freemen as were then incarcerated could be described as inhabitants at large of the borough.

The other gentlemen of the committee were of the same opinion; but Mr. Greedison argued, that by the ancient and common law of England: (a Whig doctrine), every man was deemed innocent until found guilty, and could not therefore be deprived of any of his legitimate rights before trial and conviction: all the prisoners were in this state. 'None of them,' said he, 'have yet been brought to trial, and therefore they are all innocent, and in the full possession of every privilege which belongs to a British subject.'

'You had better try,' said Mr. Cannykin, a fat old justice of the peace, a Whig by profession, but in practice a vitriolic Tory; adding, 'My good friends, let us not waste time; for whether the inmates of the prison be or be not inhabitants of the town at large, no magistrate will venture to send them to us for their votes.'

I was greatly struck with this most shrewd remark: – can any thing, indeed, be more absurd than to consider a delinquent innocent until he is proved guilty? It may be well enough in the eye of a lawyer to see this untruth on paper; but the moral sense of mankind revolts at the preposterous supposition. However, not to become tedious with details, – in the end, after a neck and neck race, I was returned duly elected.

Every body knows that soon after the general election, the new Parliament was assembled. Great expectations were entertained of the good it would do; and all the members repaired to their posts with the utmost alacrity. I, of course, went to mine also; and my feelings on the occasion were, no doubt, in unison with those of the others who had been returned for the first time. But, whatever may have been the state of theirs, mine were not of the most harmonious tenor.

The thought of the House was constantly present with me. I heard the voice of great orators in the ear of my spirit, round, sweet, and vehement. I was afraid; and when I went down to see the halls of Parliament, on the day before they were opened for business, a chilly dread overawed me. I beheld the green leathern cushions on the benches of the House of Commons as things that betokened a mystery; and in the shape of the speaker's chair there was a phantasma that inspired me with a strange imagination of something as it were begotten between a pulpit and a tomb.

Mr. Greedison had kindly taken me under his wing, and came to town with me, that there might be no lack in the respectability of my introduction; for he had great influence with the ministers, and several of the most distinguished orators among the Whigs were his friends. Accordingly I went into the House between Mr. Bletherington, that popular man, and Mr. Assert, than whom there is not in Parliament a member of greater talent at the invention of facts.

On the third day after Parliament had met, I took the oaths and my seat.

In the meantime, my rival, who had so nearly been

triumphant, Mr. Oakdale, a Tory, had not been idle. A rumour had gone forth, from the close of the poll, that not only he intended to petition against my return, but that even some of his friends were no less resolved. Against this menace, the party on my side were equally determined: but as it did not consort with the notions that I entertain of what the purity of election should be, I told them frankly that I would not myself take any step in the business, stating my reasons, which won from them great applause, and nerved them to be intrepid in supporting my cause.

It is but fair, however, to acknowledge that I was not thoroughly content at hearing my rival was every day growing bolder; and little was I prepared for such a shock as I received, when, about an hour after I had taken my seat, an old member came to the bar with a paper in his hand, which he almost immediately, in the body of the House, announced was a petition, respectably signed, against my return, as effected – not by bribery and corruption, for that's the Tory practice – but by perjury of the grossest kind.

I shook like the aspen on hearing this; for it instantly struck me that there was some probability in the charge; inasmuch as the party which I represented were not in obvious circumstances to practise much bribery; which rendered it the more likely that perjury had been employed. Not, however, to waste time in needless narration, a committee was appointed to try the merits of the case; and as it was necessary to meet the petition bravely, I announced the event by the post of that evening to many of my friends.

I cannot describe the exact effect which the incident of the petition had upon me; but I said to Mr. Greedison, who called at my lodgings in Abingdon Street, the same evening, that I was perplexed and uneasy. 'I cannot conceive,' observed I to him, 'the use of the rules of Parliament concerning bribery or perjury at elections. Things are bad according to the circumstances in which they arise; but nothing can be more obnoxious to common sense than the hair-on-end looks which Parliament puts on, when that old woman hears either of the one term or the other. If a man has a vote, has he not a property, and may he not sell that property? In what respect, then, can the voter be more unconstitutional than the votee, who buys it, and in turn takes a place for himself or kindred of a satisfactory value? And then,' said I, 'this horror of perjury is only a proof of the inveteracy of the evil which springs from our unnatural system of government; for, if it be abstractly true that every man should have a vote, it is as clear as the sun at noonday, that society is to blame for any ill that may be in the perjury by which he asserts his natural right.'

'Very true,' said Mr. Greedison, 'very true, Mr. Butt; but, nevertheless, the law makes both offences heinous, and we must submit to the law while it exists. It therefore signifies very little to you or me whether the thing be right or wrong in principle – our task is to fight with our adversaries as dexterously, by law, as possible. Who is in the right? is not the question; but who can be proved to have violated the law?'

'Ah! Mr. Greedison,' replied I, 'you make a sad comment on the ways of the world: for my part, the right is what I will always stand by. The expedient in legislation is an abuse that I shall ever stoutly resist; but, as you say, it is the way of the world. The man that robs a crown with violence, is, in the eyes of the world, raised into worship; but the poor fool that filches only half-a-crown, is sent to the correction-house. No, no, Mr. Greedison; when the time arrives that I shall be heard fulminating, many are the preposterous customs that deform legislation, which it shall be my study to blight, overwhelm, and extirpate.'

During the time that my election committee was sitting, the Reform Bill, which the unanimous nation so loudly applauds and so vehemently demands, was introduced into the House. Wearied, troubled, and irritated as I was in the forenoon with the inquiries of the Committee, I never missed my place in the evening. Night after night I attended there; uniform was my support of the great measure; but I was not so well seconded as I expected. The main body of the Tories were to the full as frightened as any rational person could expect. The Whigs, over against them, were no less loquacious, though in a different strain, on the merits of the bill. A few country gentlemen were as short-sightedly selfish as the squirarchy in general are on all questions of national improvement; only a very few were truly of my way of thinking. Several, no doubt, sported opinions not unlike those that I have ever entertained; but none – no, not one – courageously struck at the root of the evil.

I was disconcerted at observing how far the House was influenced in its deliberations by obsolete maxims, which, in this enlightened age, should have been discarded; and for some time I was unaffectedly in doubt whether the bill was, indeed, that salutary panacea so much the theme of universal applause. But, after considering the subject carefully, I began to form a different opinion of its efficacy.

'The bill,' said I to myself, 'is not to be regarded as the medicine which the state requires; the consequences that must flow from it, when it shall have passed, are the ingredients of the purge that will renovate the hopes and brighten the anticipations of man.

'When this bill is passed, and a new Parliament under

it is assembled, will not that Parliament be more in a condition to pass another liberal bill than the present Parliament is to pass this one? Well, what next? for after the second bill, is it not consistent with nature, that the new Parliament assembled under it should pass another, still more congenial to the oppressed and the needful?'

'Under that third bill,' said I to a gentleman one night in the lobby, who had been instrumental in returning me to Parliament, 'it is my opinion, the scourge of the poor-laws will be abolished; no reformed Parliament, of the third degree, will be daring enough to sanction such a preposterous measure, as supporting the poor by a tax upon those who are themselves in difficulties, while the parks, palaces, and grandeur of the aristocracy exist. No, my friend; in the bright vista of the future I perceive what must, of a natural necessity, come to pass. Last Sunday I was up the river; and I saw, in passing, Zion House and its magnificent conservatory. Why, said I, should such environment be maintained for an individual? The reflection brought in array before me all the blessed successive reforms which are destined to be the consequences of this bill.'

'I doubt,' replied the gentleman, 'that you extend your views too far: there may be a time when all things concurring shall effect such an alteration on the phasis of society; but that is a work for posterity. If we get a measure of reform that will better our condition, we ought to be thankful and content.'

I started aghast to hear this, for he had the reputation of being an indefatigable Reformer; and I replied, with unaffected astonishment, that I was surprised to hear him say so. 'I thought, sir, your views were of a braver kind, and that, like me, you considered this bill but as a forerunner – "the morning star, day's harbinger".'

'I will not deny,' was his answer, 'that I have been strenuous in urging a greater reformation than even what is proposed to be accomplished by the bill; but it was because I was well aware, that if we did not demand a great deal, we should only receive very little. The world, Mr. Butt, is far from being so ripely philosophical as you seem to think; and I fear, from what I have observed in the spirit of the late debates, that, make what reform, by act of Parliament, the ministers choose, no more of that act will be carried into effect than the nation is prepared to receive. However, let us get what we can; and if it be too little to satisfy the age, we must struggle for more.'

Something at this moment drew me aside from the friend with whom I was conversing, and he went away. I felt, however, that he had left his mantle behind. I thought and cogitated much on what he had said; and it did then seem to me that there was great truth in his remark; for the human mind, in welling itself clear, purifies the law. No member of Parliament would now venture to propose some of those Draco enactments which still disgrace the statute-book. Even the late Lord Londonderry, who was not easily daunted by circumstances, facetiously proposed the abolition of the statutes against witchcraft – yea, at the witching time of night. The law is an oracle that speaks only the will of the majority.

Next morning, however, I was able to investigate the subject more coolly; and it did not appear that it could, for a moment, be admitted that legislation should be regulated by expediency, or made subservient to temporary exigencies. 'It must,' I exclaimed, 'be regulated by eternal principles; and it is because it has been for so many ages adapted to the wants of occasion, rather than to the necessities of nature, that it has been, instead of a protection to mankind, an everflowing fountain of bitter waters.'

The investigation of my case proceeded in a parallel with that of the Reform bill; but as the probability of the latter passing the House was more and more developed, I am sorry to say my chance of success diminished. This was altogether owing to those obsolete and artificial restrictions which the laws of the realm and the rules of Parliament have imposed for the regulation of elections, – a consideration not the more consolatory to me, who might be among the last victims; and for two reasons.

First, it is not congenial to the human mind to be in any thing disappointed; and secondly, I was most earnest in wishing to give my vote at the third reading of the bill, that I might go down to posterity, in red ink on Ridgway the bookseller's list, as an illustrious benefactor of the human race. No doubt, the number of those ambitious of this distinction was rather too great to make the honour remarkable; but few, in their aim, were actuated, like me, by a pure and noble passion. Many, indeed, were under the influence of sordid fear, and thought more of obtaining a seat in the next Parliament, than a niche in the temple of fame. Yet there certainly was no want of members about the House – chiefly of the Tory temperament, however – who were exceedingly provoking by their constant reiteration of the old proverb, that only foul birds file their own nests – alluding to the manner in which many had declared the House of Commons naught; but with such I entertained no communion of sentiment. It was not on account of any thing in the House itself that I supported the bill through thick and thin; but solely and entirely because I foresaw it would be the parent of a more comprehensive measure, destructive of those pernicious inheritances that I had been born to abominate.

The day before the bill was to be read a third time, the committee on my election decided, on grounds which no rational man could approve, that I had been returned by most flagitious perjury. And what greatly surprised me – which it should not have done, considering how such things are administered – although bribery and corruption was clearly proven against my rival's party in several instances, not a word was said on that head in mitigation of the delinquency with which my friends had been charged. However, I was not entirely forlorn nor discomfited by the result, as I had the best assurances from those who acted with and for me, that at the first election under the Reform Bill, I might count on being returned with triumph and glory.

The anticipation of this result has, undoubtedly, sweetened the bitterness of my regrets. The bill is an era – a mile-stone in the highway of perfectibility, and is worthy of all acceptation. To the Tories, unquestionably, it is objectionable, inasmuch as it may have the effect of strengthening the legislative influence of their rivals, who have availed themselves of the means of office to achieve a great advantage. To some of the Radicals, likewise, it may not be quite satisfactory, being, in fact, greatly short of what we desire. But, nevertheless, as a resting-place, from which we may look far along the future road, it affords an exhilarating prospect; even although it be not easy to describe in what the benefit expected shall consist. I cannot therefore, deficient as it may be, resist the delight of congratulating my countrymen in particular, and mankind in general, on the boon which at last awaits us. For certain it is, or ought to be, that every relaxation in law is a concession to freedom; and I regard the bill as, in its tendencies on the nature of things, calculated to promote that irresponsible liberty of action, without which man is but the slave of statutes and the thrall of individual caprice and arrogance.

Alas! how fluctuating are human hopes! The bill – the

immortal elixir that was to renovate liberty into its pristine vigour, is spilled in the very act of being poured from the phial into the spoon. Dark clouds have again fallen on our prospects. The sun is eclipsed. But still let us not despair. Neither Peers nor prejudices can extinguish Nature. The vestal fire is eternal, for it is an element; and the time is still coming on when every man shall sit under his own vine and fig-tree. This should console us; and with this assurance at heart I am none daunted by the disaster. My only apprehension lest it may never be destined to come to pass in this country, is, that in the cold climate of England the fig-tree grows not to such a size as to afford shelter or enjoyment in the shadow of its branches.

p. 153   *Baron Brougham and Vaux:* As in *The Member*, Galt gives an air of authenticity by means of a dedication in the name of his fictional narrator to a real person. Henry Brougham (1778–1868) was a Scot, born in Edinburgh and educated at the High School and University. He was called to both the Scottish and English bars and entered Parliament as a Whig. He was one of the most effective advocates of parliamentary reform, and became Lord Chancellor of England and 1st Baron Brougham and Vaux.

p. 153   *Nathan Butt:* The name suggests the Scots phrase, 'naethan but', the equivalent of 'nothing else' or 'nothing less', and therefore the character of the narrator as an extremist who will not be content with a compromise.

p. 155   *Russell purge:* Lord John Russell, 1st Earl (1792–1878). He studied at Edinburgh University and then entered Parliament in 1813. He was the chief architect of the Reform Act of 1832, but for some years before that he struggled to 'purge' the Commons of members who had been corruptly elected. Afterwards Prime Minister 1846–1852 and 1865–1866.

p. 157   *Divine right of resistance:* Galt as an enthusiast for the Covenanters was fond of this concept, even if it is hardly consistent with the defence of conservatism which *The Radical* implies.

p. 157   *Nero, Caligula, Tiberius:* Roman Emperors who were notorious for their cruelty.

p. 159   *Mr Owen:* Robert Owen (1771–1858) was the reformer and philanthropist who ran the mills at New Lanark on principles designed to improve the living standards, education and morals of the workers and their children. His book, *New View of Society* of 1813, argued that the right formation of character depended on early influences and that existing educational practices were generally harmful.

p. 161   *Mr Skelper:* From the Scots verb, skelp (beat or strike). In other words, the Scots equivalent of Mr Thawckum.

p. 162   *a public lictor:* In ancient Rome the lictors carried the fasces, a bundle of rods and an axe, as a symbol of authority and the power of punishment.

p. 163   *playing the Roman fool:* i.e. commit suicide. Macbeth in Shakespeare's play says (Act V, Sc. viii, 11. 1 and 2):
> 'Why should I play the Roman fool, and die
> On mine own sword?'

p. 163   *Caleb Williams:* The hero of William Godwin's novel, *Caleb Williams, or Things as they are* (1794). See note to page 187 below.

p. 164   *Jean Jacques Rousseau:* In Book VIII of his *Confessions,* Rousseau (1712–1778) describes the 'agitation bordering on madness' with which he conceived the ideas behind his *Essay on Science and the Arts.* His argument was that they had corrupted morals.

p. 164   *'To share the triumph' etc.:* Alexander Pope (1688–1744). *An Essay On Man,* l. 386.

p. 164   *Catiline:* Lucius and Sergius Catalina plotted unsuccessfully to seize power in Rome in 65 and 63 BC. He fled and was defeated and killed in 62.

p. 169   *florentine:* A meat pie with pastry only on the top.

p. 169   *Coriolanus:* According to tradition, a Roman general of the 5th century BC. He was exiled from Rome because he was suspected of aspirations to take power as a tyrant. He led an attack on the city but was persuaded to withdraw by his mother and his wife, Volumnia.

p. 176   *Egyptian bondage:* The persecution of the Jews in Egypt in the 13th century BC before they were led in exodus by Moses.

p. 177   *'Sweet Auburn' etc.:* Oliver Goldsmith (1728-1774), *The Deserted Village* (1770) 1. 1.

p. 177   *then taking place in Paris:* The French Revolution.

p. 178   *Lord Bacon:* Francis Bacon, Baron Verulam and Viscount St Albans (1561–1626), says in his essay, *Of Marriage and Single Life:* 'He that hath wife and children hath given hostages to fortune; for they are impediments to great enterprises, either of virtue or mischief.'

p. 180   *The beadle:* A parish officer with the power to punish petty offenders.

p. 181   *Hegira:* The starting point of the Mohammedan era (AD 622) when Mohammed left Mecca for Medina.

p. 182   *dressed in a little brief authority:* Isabella in Shakespeare's *Measure for Measure* (Act II, Sc. ii, 11. 117-19) says:
> '. . . but man, proud man,
> Drest in a little brief authority,

Most ignorant of what he's most assur'd.'

p. 184   *inexpressibles:* breeches.

p. 185   *'the drunken soldier':* I have not been able to trace this allusion.

p. 185   *the infatuated Pitt:* William Pitt (1759–1806). British Prime Minister 1783–1801 and 1804–1806 and therefore in office during the war with revolutionary France.

p. 187   *Godwin's Political Justice: The Enquiry Concerning the Principles of Political Justice* (1793) was the most important of the political writings of William Godwin (1756–1826). He was an influential rationalist and anarchist and rejected all contemporary forms of government, especially monarchy.

p. 195   *the Pythia:.* In ancient Greece the Pythia was the priestess of Apollo at Delphi and the voice of the oracle which she uttered in a state of divine ecstasy.

p. 201   *marriage, with the fated progeny:* Napoleon's marriage in 1810 to Marie Louise, Archduchess of Austria and daughter of Francis II, a Hapsburg Holy Roman Emperor.

p. 202   *'Even in their ashes'* etc.: Slightly misquoted ('their' for 'our') from Thomas Gray (1716–1771), *Elegy in a Country Churchyard* (St. 23).

p. 202   *promiscuous blood:* The 'Peterloo Massacre' of 1819 when troops dispersed a radical demonstration in Manchester, killing 11 people and wounding about 500.

p. 202   *Scottish Radical campaign:* The 'Radical War' of 1820 in the west of Scotland, probably provoked by Government agents, which led to the execution of three of the leaders.

p. 204   *'Experience teaches fools':* A translation of the Latin tag: experientia docet stultos.

p. 205   *retrenchment became the universal shout:* A curious anticipation of the current competition between the Conservative and Labour parties to represent themselves as parties of low taxation and low public expenditure.

p. 206   *Spagnoletti:* The Spanish painter, Jusepe de Ribera (1591–1652), spent most of his life in Italy where he was known as Lo Spagnoletto (the little Spaniard). He painted several starkly realistic pictures of the martyrdom of emaciated saints.

p. 207   *De Coverleys and Westerns of other years:* Eighteenth-century squires as described by Joseph Addison in the character of Sir Roger de Coverley in the *Spectator* (1711–1714) and by Henry Fielding in his character, Squire Western, in *Tom Jones* (1749).

p. 209   *Sinking Fund:* A fund into which periodic payments are made to provide for the future repayment of debts.

p. 209   *Mr Thole:* Another instance of the use of a Scots word to provide the name of a character. (Thole means suffer or tolerate.)

p. 214   *Esculapian mummery:* The tools of the medical profession from Asclepius, the Greek god of medicine.

p. 216   *'Man wants but little'* etc.: Oliver Goldsmith (1728–1774), *Edwina and Angelica or the Hermit.*

p. 231   *Demosthenes proud on the Areopagus:* Demosthenes (383–322 BC) was the most celebrated orator of Ancient Greece. The Areopagus is a hill to the west of the Acropolis where public affairs were debated.

p. 233   *the Bruti:* According to tradition, Lucius Junius Brutus liberated Rome from the tyrannical rule of the Tarquins and put to death his two sons who attempted to restore them, so putting public duty before family feeling.

p. 234   *potwallopers:* Before the Reform Act of 1832, parliamentary franchise in England was regulated by local customs. In some places, such as Preston and Westminster, it was very wide and extended to all householders who had their own kitchens. They were called 'potwallopers' because they boiled their own pots.

p. 245   *John Galt's unfortunate tragedies:* Early in his writing career Galt wrote a number of tragedies; but, as he admits in this piece of self-mockery, they were unsuccessful.

p. 253   *Zion House:* Syon (as it is usually written) is a great house on the Thames, west of London. It contains a magnificent suite of rooms designed by Robert Adams for the Duke of Northumberland, and a huge greenhouse, designed by Charles Fowler.

p. 254   *Draco enactments:* Draco was an Athenian legislator who codified the laws in 621 BC with notorious severity. Hence 'Draconian,' the usual form of the adjective.

p. 255   *Ridgway:* The obvious implication is that Ridgway recorded the names in red ink of the M.P.s who voted for Reform; but I have not been able to trace any other reference to him.

p. 257   *spilled in the very act:* the first Reform Bill was carried in the Commons on 23 March 1831 by a majority of one, but an opposition amendment was also carried and Parliament was dissolved. The bill did not finally become law until after it was passed by the Lords on 4 June 1832 after months of debate.

Glossary

airt, direction.

anent, concerning.

arcana (Latin), secrets.

art or part (Scots Law), accessory.

a-trip (of an anchor), raised and ready to be 'weighed'.

auld farrent, 'old fashioned', experienced and wise.

bodie, person.

bum, hum, buzz.

by common, uncommon.

by times, betimes, in good time.

canny, artful, snug.

carle, old man.

carmagnol (French), revolutionary soldier.

cess, tax.

charming, 'chirming', chirping (of birds).

clanjamfrey, low worthless people; (hence) nonsense.

cleek, clutch.

clok on, sit on (eggs), brood on.

cloots, hooves; (hence) feet.

condescension. See The Member note p. 24.

corbies, crows.

corruption, anger.

couthy, kindly.

daunering, strolling.

desjasket, dejected.

dungeon of wit, phr., profound intellect.

enfeoffment (Scots Law), possession.

enfeofft (Scots Law), possessed.

erysipelas, inflammation.

ettarcap, spider, irascible person.

evendown, direct, blunt.

farm-steading, plot of farm land; (also) farm-building.

fash, sb. and *v.,* trouble.

fashed, troubled.

Findhorn haddock, 'finnan haddock', smoke-cured haddock.

fozy, fat, stupid.

frank, privilege of free postage of letters by means of signature; a 'cover' so signed. *See The Member note* p. 45.

freeholder, elector deriving parliamentary franchise from freehold property. *See The Member note* p. 112.

friend, close relative (e.g. wife, husband, nephew. *See The Member note* p. 5.

gaffer, elderly man.

gash, sharp, witty, shrewd.

gathering, savings, capital.

gruing, shivering.

gude son, son-in-law.

haffit, temple; 'thin haffits' – receding hair on the temples.

handling, dealing.

hithers and yons, 'to-ing and froing', preliminary conversation not related to the real topic.

hobbletehoy, clumsy boy.

hogmanae, New Year's Eve.

inns, inn.

hur, sb., stir.

invidia (Latin), envy.

jalouse, suspect.

laborous, adj., labouring.

laddie, boy.

Little-good, the Devil.

loch, lake.

logive, extravagant.